HE'S A CHARMER
SPECIAL EDITION

STACY TRAVIS

HE'S A CHARMER

STACY TRAVIS

Cover Design: Hang Le

Copyediting: Castle Walls Editing

Publicity: Valentine PR

PROLOGUE

LINNIE

"I'm confused, love. Are you breaking up with me?" His voice has that scratchy post-sex rasp, a sound that used to send a river of chills snaking down my spine. I've known him for all of two hours, and had we not been the last two customers at the aptly named Love Shack pub in Chester, I wouldn't be in his flat at all.

Lying here naked makes me antsy. He needs to move his leg, which feels like a bear trap.

"I'm just going back to my flat." Like I do every time I hook up with a bloke.

"So you're breaking up with me."

He loosens the vise grip on my legs enough so that I can squirm out of his grasp. After rolling to the side of his bed, I stand and begin putting my clothes on. I'm moving quickly— shirt and jacket in one go, pants pulled over my hips with a small grunt, bra stuffed in my back pocket.

"We aren't dating. I can't break up with you if we're not dating, Sean." He looks like a Sean, an Irish ginger.

"But we *could* be dating."

I exhale a frustrated breath. Dating was never going to be

part of the equation when I returned his flirtatious wink and allowed him to buy me a pint. It's never part of my equation. Stranger plus snogging equals fun—it's math anyone can understand.

Sean was nice enough this evening and solicitous of my body's needs, and rollicking sex is always a brilliant end to a night at the pub. Except, meh. Lately, all meh.

"Come on, Sean. Do you really want to be dating?" I sound like a schoolmarm, but he needs some sense knocked into him.

Taming my wavy blond mane into submission with a hair band, I pull my horn-rimmed glasses from the pocket of my jacket and put them on so I can get a better look at Sean. Rumpled reddish-blond hair curling around his ears, rakish smile that tells me he's used to getting his way, light-brown eyes that tell me absolutely nothing.

He shrugs. "I want you back in my bed, love."

He's not terrible. We had a bit of fun. Normally that would be enough for me to slide back between his arms and lose myself in carnal oblivion for a while. Because, why not?

Normally I don't try to answer that question.

But nothing's normal anymore, so it's time to leave.

I lean over and kiss him on the forehead because I feel like he needs the affirmation. Some form of closure. Then I fumble through his dark flat until I reach the front door, let myself out, and skip down the front steps to where I parked my car.

Giving the car a pat on the hood, I notice that the engine is still warm. "Hi, girl," I whisper when I slide behind the wheel of my faithful ride. The only warm body who's been in my life for more years than I can count. "Let's go home."

Sean is the last one, I decide. I'm done with hookups.

So very, very done.

The next morning I book a ticket to visit my brother, who plays football in California. I suppose I'll have to call it soccer

when I get there, but it's been years since I've seen him play, and I've never been to San Francisco. Never left England, actually.

All the more reason to go. It's time to make some changes in my life.

CHAPTER 1
LINNIE

Three Months Later—San Francisco

"I'm so chuffed to be here, you have no idea!" I feel like I drank four cups of coffee on the plane, when actually I've had only . . . four cups. Well, there you go.

The scenery whizzes by and I have no idea what I'm seeing, but it doesn't matter. Even if it's just cars on the freeway headed north from San Francisco Airport, it's California. I imagine beaches and Hollywood celebrities and glamour.

I can't stop bouncing in the back seat of my brother's car. "Why do you drive this tiny car?" I ask, measuring a two-inch space between my head and the roof of the MINI Cooper.

He looks at me like it's obvious. "I'm a Brit."

"Yeah. And this company has been owned by BMW for nearly two decades." Catching sight of myself in his rearview mirror, I notice my braids have gone lopsided on the ten-hour plane flight, so I try in vain to straighten them and eventually undo the plaits into wild waves. I feel like I have a spring under my bum and the energy of a hundred busy squirrels. "Did I tell you how excited I am?"

"I think I have some idea," Tim grumbles, unapologetic

about being his best grouchy self. "You're not especially subtle, Lin."

"Why are you in a mood?" I ask, swatting his shoulder and searching his profile for answers. He was kind initially, loading my luggage into the boot of the car while I settled in and reapplied my lipstick, but things have taken a turn.

"Because I'm not your bloody Uber driver. And because it's eleven at night, and I'm going on a sixteen-hour day—half of it on the soccer pitch doing drills. And because it's giving me a headache to watch you bounce." He tips the mirror away.

"Uber driver'd be friendlier," I mutter.

"Happy to find you one if you'd prefer."

I scoot forward and wrap my arms around my brother's neck. "No! I want you, Tim Cheltenham. Is it tea time yet?"

My brain hurts from trying to calculate the eight-hour time difference from home, and after sleeping for a few hours on the plane, I'm all turned around.

"When did you ever drink tea?"

"Half past never. Not when there's a pint of beer as an option." I haven't told him I'm attempting a life change. The fewer people who know about it the better, in case I fail.

Tim allows a small smile, and I know we're okay. The bickering comes from a place of love.

"Glad you're here, Lin."

"Yes, me too! What do you have planned for me this week?"

He bends his neck around to crack it and stays focused on the road. "Few dinners, day in Golden Gate Park, a walk on the bridge, maybe drinks with some of my mates. You need to meet Weston, he's a charmer. You'll like him. All the ladies do."

"Oh, I'm not looking for that kind of good time."

"And I'm not suggesting it with my best mate. Just saying he's a good guy."

I'm surprised at how many cars are on the freeway at this hour, but Tim is always talking about the Silicon Valley diehards, who basically live at their ergonomic desks. He moved to the States years ago to play professional ball, so he's practically a native now.

"Think we can get Mary and Dad on a plane?" he asks, referring to our father and youngest sister. They won't come for very different reasons. Dad's health isn't good enough to travel, and Mary is too devoted to her boyfriend and her job.

"Eh, just be glad you got me. Those two won't stray from the motherland, even for a free vacation." I protested initially when Tim offered to pay for my plane ticket, but then I gave in. I *need* to get out of my comfort zone, see more of the world, be the empowered woman I'm desperate to be, now that I've decided it.

But flights are expensive, and I've been working hard to save money the past few months for business school classes. I wouldn't have come if he hadn't insisted on paying and letting me stay with him and his fiancée, Jordan, who I've been dying to meet.

"Where's Jordan?" I ask, leaning so far forward it stretches the seat belt to an uncomfortable degree. I hold it forward so I can breathe and hover over Tim's right shoulder.

"Probably asleep. She wanted to come get you herself, told me to go to bed—"

"Of course she did. Because you're crabby."

"I am not crabby."

He's pretty crabby. I know he needs his sleep, but a little energy after I've flown ten hours doesn't seem like too much to ask.

"I am so not tired. Are there pubs near your place where I can go hang out if you insist on going to bed like a ninety-year-old man?"

Tim chuckles despite himself and shakes his head. "Still a handful."

"I am hardly that."

"You're shouting, and we're the only two people in the car."

We zip up the peninsula from San Francisco Airport, Tim pointing out landmarks like the Transamerica spire and other downtown high-rises. "I love all the lights. Are we going over the bridge?"

Raindrops start spattering on the windshield, and I groan. I didn't fly all this way to be in the same kind of gray weather we've had for weeks in England.

"Not unless you want to be in Oakland."

"Tomorrow. I want to go over that bridge." I point at where the lights rain down from the bridge's spires.

My face is about six inches from my brother's, sandwiched between the front seats, and he intentionally conks his against mine. "You know, you could've just sat in front if you wanted to be this close to me."

"Nope. I like having a proper driver. Especially since you're a famous footballer and you never drove me anywhere when we were younger."

That finally gets a smile from him "What seventeen-year-old bloke wants to drive his fourteen-year-old sister and her friends all over the county?" Maybe the same goes for a thirty-one-year-old brother now.

"Especially when she's a better driver than you," I quip, knowing exactly how to get his goat.

"Hardly," he grumbles, apparently still not over his speeding tickets. I drove faster and got none.

Not only that, but I had an instinct for cars and how to fix them, so my dad trusted me more than my siblings to use the cars he worked on at our family's garage. I didn't need Tim driving me at all.

He continues pointing things out as we enter San Francisco. "That's SoMa, big tech hub, some good restaurants." He points vaguely to the left. "You might want to walk around the Mission. There's a place with hot chocolate you'd probably like."

The streets are slick with rain and dense with buildings. I'm not committing any of his information to memory.

Tim navigates around a bedraggled man pushing a shopping cart filled to the brim with cardboard boxes getting soaked in the rain. He's crossing the street against the light, and all the cars have come to a halt so he can pass. I'm about to ask about him when a siren blares to life, red and blue lights bouncing off the sides of buildings as the police car screams past.

Tim stops again while a streetcar goes by, attached by wires to a grid that runs overhead. While I'm busy staring up at it, I notice all the skyscrapers, one taller than the next. My pulse quickens with every car that flies past, every brightly lit storefront, restaurant, and club. I've wanted to come here for so long. I've craved things I couldn't even name, but I've always felt sure they're here, in a buzzing city like San Francisco.

"What's with this rain? I thought I was coming to sunny California. I want to do *everything*."

He laughs. "I know, Linnie." The windshield wipers slap back and forth against the glass as the smattering of drops turns into a steady downpour. "It's sunny a lot, but you've caught us in the middle of winter." Tim's voice takes on the brotherly tone of know-it-all, and I fight the urge to slug him. Because I'm an adult. An adult who no longer hooks up with blokes in pubs or makes decisions about my life to spite other people. I want to do better. I can do better.

Just keep telling yourself that, and it will become true.

The city lights squint through the droplets, blurring in reds and yellows. Tim presses his lips together, his telltale sign he's holding in a secret. Like he thinks he can physically keep it in his mouth if he tries hard enough, but he'll inevitably blurt it anyway. So I wait, my smile spreading so wide my cheeks begin to hurt.

He looks in the rearview and startles. "Why do you look like a serial killer?"

The implication dims my smile only a bit. "You're keeping a secret. What is it?" I know I'm bouncing on the seat again and Tim is about four seconds from slugging me, but I don't care.

"Actually, we're taking you to Lake Tahoe. We bought a mountain place there, and the contractors have been renovating it for months. With this storm, some fresh snow, it'll be stunning. You'll love it."

It might be stunning, but it doesn't sound like pulsing city life. "Well, that sounds . . . nice." I flop back into my seat and unwrap the fuzzy blue scarf from around my neck. I mess up my hair even more, but I don't care.

"I sense a 'but' in that sentiment."

"I was keen to have fun in the city."

Tim nods slowly, his face turning a little frowny. "Of course you were. Jordan thought it might be fun, but I forgot who I was talking to, my super-social sister who wants to shag ten blokes while you're here."

He doesn't have that exactly right. Coming here has less to do with aimless fun than it does with getting away from our small town and proving to myself that I can survive in the real world and exceed my father's low expectations of me.

So . . . maybe it's not such a good idea to run around to bars for a week. I've done very well sticking to my no-hookup rule at home, but that's partly because I've already been with anyone halfway interesting. Here . . . it could test my resolve. I hadn't thought of that.

"I'm not saying I don't want to see your fancy mountain house."

"When did I say it was fancy?"

I wave a hand. "You're a soccer star. I feel confident it's fancy." His shrug only confirms that I'm right.

"It was only a thought. We'll stay in the city. Better for me anyway because I have training during the week and I'd have to drive back and forth."

I make eye contact with him in the rearview mirror, but I can't tell if he's disappointed, so I lean forward again and talk next to his ear. "I feel as if I've offended you."

Unclicking my seat belt, I awkwardly climb into the front passenger seat. That's when I see a very phallic-looking building to our right. "What is *that*?"

"Coit Tower. It was built as a monument to firefighters who died fighting here. Resembles a fire hose, no?"

"Um, sure, if that's what you want to call it." It does not resemble a fire hose.

I see Tim's phone sitting in his cup holder, so I grab it. "How about some tunes? Look this way." He does, and the face recognition unlocks the phone.

"We're almost there, Lin. We have time for maybe half a track."

Instead of music, I focus on a worrisome string of texts. "Tim, do you know you have a bazillion texts from someone named June? Stuff about a water main bursting?"

"Wait, who?"

I read a few of the texts before nodding and summarizing. "Your neighbor at your fancy mountain house. She says a pipe burst. There's water coming onto her property from your house."

"What? Nooo." Tim pulls up to a closed garage door and

slumps over the steering wheel. "I'm gonna need to drive there now and deal with it. And I'm gassed."

"Can't June handle it?"

"June is ninety."

An idea strikes me with such force that I start waving my hands. This is exactly the kind of adventure I've come here for—a midnight drive, a broken pipe, an elderly neighbor in need of rescue. Tim reaches over and stills me. "Stop. You're giving me motion sickness."

"I'll go! Let me deal with the disaster. You know I'm handy, and it's daytime in England. I'm wide awake, and I drank loads of coffee. Plus, I've always wanted to drive in America."

"Linnie, no. You just got off a plane. It's a three-hour drive and it's raining."

"But I want to do it! Please, Timmy. I swear I'll drive sensibly. And then I'll get to spend a night in your fancy house and still have time for fun in the city. Please?"

"Hell, no. It's the middle of the damn night. Not to mention we drive on the right side of the road here."

"I'm aware. I can do that."

"No."

Stubborn. And foolhardy. He's too crabby and tired to be of much use in the mountains. When he gets out and goes over to a keypad next to the garage and starts punching numbers, I make a decision.

Sliding carefully over the gearshift, I land in the driver's seat and adjust it so I can reach the pedals. I throw the car in reverse and have begun rolling backward by the time the garage door starts rising and Tim turns back to the car. The goggle-eyed look on his face would be comical, except that I'll pay for it later when Tim disowns me.

"What the fuck? Linnie . . ." I hear him through the closed

window, and then I hear nothing because he's soon in my rearview.

His voice resumes screaming all around me because he's figured out how to ring my phone through his car speakers. "Turn. Around."

"You're being overprotective. This is a perfect solution," I tell him, driving carefully and signaling at the light where we sat a moment earlier. I paid attention enough to reverse course and go back toward the freeway, but I'm going to need some assistance.

"Linnie, this isn't a fucking joke. Come back." His exasperated breathing sounds like Darth Vader coming through the car speakers. I search for the volume control.

"Please let me do this for you. I really want to. Please." As much as he seems annoyed, I know he's not shocked I took his car. I used to pull this kind of stuff all the time when we were teens.

"You don't know where you're going."

"GPS is a magical thing, Timmy. Just give me the address, and I'll take care of everything. It's the least I can do to thank you for flying me out." It seems like a good idea, even if it's a terrible one.

"Jordan is going to murder me for letting you do this."

I feel a glimmer of hope. He's coming around. Exhaustion strains his voice. And maybe exasperation, but he's always been a grumpy bugger.

"Tell Jordan I love you and she mustn't murder you."

He knows me well enough to understand I'm not turning around. It's not just me being impulsive. I'm showing my gratitude, but more than that, I'm taking responsibility for making shit happen in life, rather than letting shit happen to me. Tim may not understand how important that is to me, but I'll explain it when I get back from rescuing his neighbor.

Tim's worry is completely unnecessary. It's just a little driving. What could possibly go wrong?

~

"Look at me, driving on the right side of the road like a badass," I declare to anyone within earshot. Which is no one.

It takes me less than an hour to realize that my impulsive decision might be flawed. Yeah, driving on the wrong side of the road in a tiny car with shoddy wipers seems foolhardy in retrospect, but I'm not a quitter.

At least, not yet.

I know my way around the dashboard of a MINI Cooper, so I punch the Bluetooth pairing dial and try to get my UPBEAT ROAD TRIP SONGS playlist going on the speakers. It's a great list, mostly American bands.

I know, I know—I'm a traitor to the British Invasion, but I've always followed American pop culture, so these songs are my jam. Besides, I don't take many road trips in the beat-up Land Rover that barely makes it between my work and home, so the playlist is aching for a listen.

Problem is it's not working. "You've got a wonky dial, Tim Cheltenham." My grumble is followed by a series of beeps and some annoyed throat clearing.

"Would it have killed you to listen to me for once in your life?" Tim's voice booms through the stereo speakers after the fancy thing autodials him.

I ignore his question, as has been my habit for most of our lives. Stubborn, party of one.

"Your car rang you without my permission."

Silence on the other end of the line makes me wonder if the call got dropped. I start fiddling with buttons on the dashboard

and hear the sunroof slide open. Then the wipers swish across the glass at a much faster clip.

"Shit, shit."

"What? What happened?" The panic in Tim's voice heartens me. He's still on the line.

"Your car has a sunroof. What the heck, Tim? Why do you need that?" The rain has tapered a bit, so I'm not getting drenched while I figure out how to close it.

He exhales a long breath, and I can imagine him rubbing a hand over his creased forehead. I can see him shaking his head, a muscle ticking in his cheek as he comes up with ways to hide my body after he has me murdered. "Lin . . ."

"Yes?" I ask sweetly while successfully closing the sunroof. Now I just need to deal with the wipers, which scrape across the windshield as though they're as annoyed as my brother. He probably programmed his fancy-ass car to sense his moods, even when he's not in it.

"This isn't a joke. Sugar Springs is way up a dark road, and that's assuming you make it over the pass in one piece. Take the next exit and turn around. Come back to the city."

"I'm having fun. Just keep me company while I drive."

"Lin, abort mission. Turn around." Gruff, annoyed, and so overprotective.

"Why?"

"Because—"

"What?"

Some hash of garbled words stutters through the speakers, and I'm about to ask him to repeat himself when his voice is replaced by a dial tone. Apparently, the call has dropped.

Oh well. Back to my playlist. "Life Is a Highway" sets me back on track and I'm content.

As the words blast through the dark car, I picture Lightning McQueen zooming across a hand-painted landscape that bears no resemblance to the black nothingness ahead of me. Then I tell Tim's fancy car to redial him with a voice command.

The music is replaced by the beeps that indicate dialing, but the call goes straight to voice mail. "Redial," I instruct, enjoying that the car's Bluetooth obeys my command. No one else in my life does, so I'll take the win where I can get it.

But I don't hear any telltale beeps indicating my call went through. "Ugh, come on." Before I try three or four more times, I already anticipate the outcome. But I try three or four more times.

Nothing. I'm on my own.

Even without knowing the lay of the land, I can tell from the way my ears are popping that I'm gaining elevation. Maybe I'm out of range of the nearest cell phone tower. I take it as a sign I should ferry onward, my stubborn streak validated by technology.

I silence the music and enjoy the peaceful solitude of tracing curves of the mountainside. The fast-moving clouds part, yielding a brief display of stars that I rarely see in England, where the clouds often blot out the night sky.

Thinking back, I do remember Tim telling me something about a mountain cabin, but that was months ago. Now I recall he said Sugar Springs is tiny, smaller than Saltney, where I live in England. Some of the houses are on septic systems. I can't remember whether Tim said his was one of them. Oh well, I probably won't be there long enough to find out.

A few new splats hit my windshield. Wet gobs of snow.

My GPS told me to look out for a turn just past a ski resort named Sugar Bowl. I'm picturing light wisps of sugar white swirling around in a giant snow globe—who wouldn't want to visit that?

Every time a car's headlights appear in the distance, I freeze a little, gripping the steering wheel because I half expect the driver to veer into my lane.

This isn't the first time I've driven under challenging conditions—our family owns an auto garage, for heaven's sake. If I didn't know how to handle all different types of cars and situations, I wouldn't be a Cheltenham. Before I was thirteen, I learned to drive a manual transmission car on backcountry roads. Before that, sitting atop two dictionaries and a pile of blankets, I drove a hand-operated tractor on our neighbor's farm.

And when my dad needed a break from work, I helped out at the garage, which meant sometimes taking the train to pick up spare parts in France. For a short while, I dated a guy who lived in the Loire Valley, so I taught myself to drive on the other side of the road.

It was my only long-term relationship, lasting exactly three months. That's how long it took before I realized Yves saw me exactly how my father did—as an aimless party girl who'd best find a husband to support her before she accidentally got knocked up. No hope of a career, no danger of wanting more from life.

He saw my limitations rather than my potential and hid insults in compliments. "You're too pretty to hide under the chassis of a car. You should be a cocktail waitress. No skill required, just a push-up bra and some heels," Yves recommended helpfully.

This after I told him I intended to be a mechanic and had a plan for my future. He scoffed at my supposed plan, so I said *au revoir* to Yves. All was not lost, however. *Always leave a relationship with a marketable skill*, that's my philosophy. And thanks to Frenchie, I'll always have the ability to drive on roads around the world, left side or right.

I turn my music back on to keep me company and sing along with a few choruses of "It's Raining Men."

Splat, splat.

The pelting globs of snow are getting fluffier the higher up the mountain I go. So far the roads are dry enough for me not to worry about snow tires or chains, assuming Tim has those somewhere.

According to the glowing green digits on the dashboard, I've already been driving for nearly three hours. When I see a sign for Sugar Bowl, I slow the car on the off-ramp and turn onto a quiet mountain lane. A gust of wind sends the snow flying diagonally across the windshield, making it harder to see.

"A bit early for all this snow," I gripe to unresponsive skies. If anything, it picks up the pace, falling steadily and starting to pile up between swipes of the wiper blades.

I don't know much about California at all, other than its position on a map. It's not like I've spent my life pining to leave my town. I love me some adventure, but it's home—with a few footnotes and caveats that make this time away feel necessary.

I've been working extra shifts at the pub lately to save money for my business school classes, and I don't live lavishly —a few nights out at local spots with friends, a few quality groceries to cook yummy dinners with other friends, a few impulse purchases of cute jeans, warm sweaters, and boots with heels high enough to boost my barely five-foot frame.

I normally don't take handouts from my stupidly rich brother, who can afford to fly me to the States and back every week in first class if he wanted. But this time, I accepted the ticket because it would be rude to turn down a belated birthday gift. He probably knew it was the only way he could get me to accept his generosity. It's also why I want to repay him by rescuing his neighbor from a midnight flood. The least I can do.

Cracking the window, I feel a rush of mountain air that's

chillier than I expect. I breathe in the crisp smell of fir trees as snow flurries dance into the car like toddlers unleashed into a petting zoo.

The headlights illuminate a stand of pine trees flanking the road, white snowflakes glistening amid pine needles. I've slowed down to a crawl, partly because I have no idea where I am and partly because it's really dark.

The quiet swirl of snowflakes makes me feel at home, even though we don't get more than a handful of snowy days in Saltney. I've always loved the chilliest days when, as kids, we'd sit fireside and put together jigsaw puzzles and drink hot cocoa.

Rolling up the window, I focus on the road, which is barely wide enough for a car to pass going in the other direction. Everything feels desolate and a little spooky.

Stay calm. It's just the mountains.

Growing up in the countryside, I never felt afraid driving alone at night. But here it's different. Unfamiliar, sure. But also . . . foresty. As I look to the left, the trees are so dense it's impossible to see beyond the ones closest to the road, which twists and turns as the car hugs the lane. Surely bears and wolves are just beyond the trees, and with no one else here, I'd be a plump, tasty treat.

What other animals live in the mountains?

I feel like a third-form student taking an exam I didn't study for—*animals?* Blinking like I used to do in school when I wanted to stall, I think about wild beasts lurking in the dark. Surely not mountain lions.

Surely not?

I squint through the glass, willing a house to appear. I know there's a ski lift out there somewhere and imagine chairlifts crisscrossing the mountains, metal chairs swaying jauntily in the wind. Over the heads of mountain lions.

The road narrows further, and I take the next right turn.

Now there's no way for two cars to pass each other without one pulling to the shoulder. Up, up I climb until I see the small descending driveway Tim told me to expect.

Phew. Made it without a mishap.

A surge of adrenaline pumps through my veins at my success. I'm mentally high-fiving myself when a flash of fur darts in front of the car. I can't identify it through the insistent snow flurries, but I'm certain I see it bare its menacing teeth. Its yellow eyes taunt me—prey. Like it knows I hate all cardio and have a full, round bum to prove it—a juicy midnight snack.

The massive animal moves past as if in slow motion. A giant lion or a mule deer or a moose. Stampeding toward the car like it's daring me to fold first.

"Shit!" *I fold, I fold!*

I swerve to avoid the giant thing, and the tires skid on the snowy, icy pavement. Jamming the steering wheel hard into the skid, I lurch harder to the left before righting the car and skidding the other way.

The tires hit a pothole full of water, making the car bottom out hard on the pavement and list to the right. As I'm pumping the brakes to pull out of the skid, I feel the car speed up.

"Shit, shit!" Those weren't the brakes. My foot's on the gas, then the brake. Then it goes rogue and hits the gas again, and before I correct the problem, the largest pine tree known to man corrects it for me. I clip the front end of the car hard on the tree.

Wham!

The jolt of metal on wood throws my head forward and back against the headrest, but then my foot connects with the brake and everything goes still.

Amid the falling snow, a cloud of steam surges from underneath the hood of Tim's car. Probably cracked the radiator or broke the oil pan when I hit that pothole.

Since I've only just nicked the tree, the airbag doesn't acti-

vate. I have the presence of mind to know that's a good thing when it comes to car repair, so I say a silent prayer for that, not to mention a big fat one for the fact that I've gotten off easy—I could have taken the whole car over a cliff.

But I'm no longer moving, thank heavens. Looking in the rearview mirror, I expect to see the moose's open jaw ready to devour the small car in one bite, but it's not there.

Taking a deep breath, I try to still my thudding heart.

It doesn't obey. My breaths come hard and fast.

Don't panic. This is fine. I'm fine. That's all that matters. Everything else is fixable.

My eyes fall closed for a moment as I collect my wits.

Call Tim, find his water leak, fix his car.

I can do all these things. Letting out a long exhale, I start to feel a modicum of calm wash over me.

Okay.

Feeling slightly better, I look through the glass.

Which is when I see two large moose eyes staring back at me.

And I scream.

CHAPTER 2
WESTON

Not gonna lie, my day could have been going better.

I could have been mugged for every dollar I had in my wallet, overcharged for watered-down coffee in a cup with a leaky lid, and laughed at by a passel of skate punks for having toilet paper hanging out of my pants.

Yup, that would have been a better day than the one I'm currently having.

Not that I'm in the mood to rehash it. Not when I spent four-plus hours in traffic, driving up a mountain to bail out my best friend—literally.

And to be fair, I'm half owner of this disaster of a mountain house, so I had a fifty-fifty chance of being the one to deal with the water leak. But Tim Cheltenham had my back today, which made those odds more like ninety–ten. If I'm being generous.

As my teammate on the San Francisco Strikers and my best friend for nearly a decade, Tim has been there for me in every type of imaginable crisis. He's the guy who talks me down every time I beat myself up for a misstep during a soccer match. I know it's part of the game. We all make mistakes. But I still hate myself when I'm the one letting the team down, and Tim doesn't allow me to wallow for more than a day.

And he's been there this week, which we've dubbed the "anniversary of the shitstorm," even though I told him only the barest details of what happened way back when. He just knows that every year this week hits me between the eyes like a hundred-ton sandbag, and I take it out on anyone within ten feet. Fortunately, most of them are wearing cleats and shin guards, so they can handle it.

Today, however, my mood got a bit out of hand, resulting in a near fistfight at practice and unnecessary slide tackles that could have led to serious injury. I'm not proud of it, but it is what it is. Tim had my back, even though our coach wanted my head on a platter.

"Cool your jets. Go to the Roaming Goat, get yourself some pussy and an attitude adjustment," Tim advised. Like everyone, Tim assumes I never get into serious relationships because I like playing the field. He nods along, listens to my stories, and feigns interest in each new temporary girlfriend, even when he knows every relationship is doomed.

He doesn't need to know the real reason.

Only for a friend like Tim would I be ankle deep in sludge and snow, hunched over a busted pipe on what's turning out to be the worst day of my life.

Coach kept me at the field for two extra hours of punishing drills after ranting at me for upward of forty minutes. "I don't care if your other coaches put up with this bullshit. On my team, you leave your baggage at the door and don't jeopardize your health or those of your teammates. You don't like my rules, find a new team." Then he told me to take a couple days off to figure out whether I really want to be on the team, which might very well mean he's already looking for a new starting center midfielder.

With his threat ringing in my ears, a tweaked hip and bruised shin from a reckless slide tackle, and a shitty fast-food taco platter wreaking havoc on my stomach, I got the SOS call from June, our neighbor down the hill from the cabin we bought six months ago. She'd tried to reach Tim a half-dozen times, but he didn't pick up. I knew his sister was arriving tonight from England, so I took one for the team and came to see what's wrong with our irrigation pipes.

The place has good bones and lots of potential, but it needs work.

We hired an architect to draw up plans to renovate, and our contractor has been updating us on the progress. "Kitchen's done, bedrooms are framed, everything should be finished by spring."

Well, spring is in a month, and I arrived to find only a small percentage of the work actually finished. The kitchen is mostly complete, save for the fact that the ancient stove hasn't been replaced and there's no fridge. But the cabinetry looks nice, for what that's worth. I'll add "yelling at the contractor" to the list of tasks for tomorrow.

He can be the next beneficiary of my mood.

Eventually, with a few new bedrooms and a giant deck to take advantage of the view, the place will be amazing. Tim and I plan to use it on alternating weekends during the off-season.

For now, while we're about to start league season, all I can do is dream of the finished product. The place is tiny, with a living room and one small bedroom. What sold me was the land around the house. We own two acres at the top of a mountain, and there are hiking trails straight out our front door. We're five minutes from the nearest ski area.

Neither one of us needs to own it outright, so sharing the mortgage and the responsibilities makes sense.

And here I am, enjoying our first responsibility.

The house is surrounded by pine trees and manzanita that gets its water from rain and snowmelt. It's not like we rigged up a watering system for a vegetable garden. I have no idea what pipes we have, how they turn on, or how much damage they can do.

Problem is I have no idea how to fix plumbing. If something doesn't involve cooking or a ball and cleats, I don't have much use for it. It was news to me that we even had irrigation pipes.

Cue the first issue with having two guys with no experience and fix-it dreams deciding to buy a hundred-year-old cabin. If I'm honest, part of my interest in the place is my *dream* of being handy with fixing things. Judging from my success at finding the leak, I have a long road ahead.

I barely arrived before the snow started and June trekked up the hill in rubber boots and a fur-lined coat to explain that she'd looked for a shutoff valve and couldn't find it.

"I'll get to the bottom of it," I assured her, having no real plan for getting to the bottom of anything except maybe a glass of whiskey when I'm done.

It's goddamn dark up here in the mountains, I'll say that. First thing I'm going to do once I get this water situation under control is hire an electrician to install some outdoor lighting. Big floodlights with motion sensors. No more fumbling through overgrown brush and sapling pines.

I've been on hold with the water and power company for so long I'm pretty sure I've set a record for obscenities yelled at an automated system. "Fuck you," I mutter, hanging up the call.

I notice a few missed calls and a string of texts from Tim.

TIM: *Hey, pick up your phone.*

TIM: *Fine don't. Just letting you know the water situation's handled. My sister's driving up.*

Squinting at the screen, I try to make sense of it. Driving up from where? England? I thought she was flying in. Didn't know they made roads across the Atlantic.

Reading the next text, I feel my blood pressure rise. I blink in disbelief because I can't be reading this right.

TIM: *June said she called you too. Sorry. I know you've had a shit day.*

Wait, I'm still stuck on the sister-driving-up part. *She's coming . . . here?*

Quickly, I stab at my phone and wait for Tim to pick up.

"Hey, why didn't you answer?" He sounds groggy, which makes me want to throat punch him through the phone.

"I'm at the cabin dealing with the water," I say through gritted teeth.

I hear movement and the rustle of sheets; then Tim clears his throat, speaking normally. "Wait, you're there? Shit." The English lilt of his voice somehow makes his swearing sound polite.

"Yeah, I'm here. Why'd you send your sister out in the middle of a storm, asshole?" Maybe it's because I've spent the last hour freezing my nuts off out here, but I'm not following this conversation, even though I'm part of it. Maybe my brain is frozen too.

"She stole my car."

I can't have heard that right. "Come again?"

"If you knew Linnie, you'd understand. There's no stopping her when she gets an idea. She likes to fix shit. Stubborn, that one."

"Yeah, I have no idea what that's like," I deadpan.

"So she hasn't made it there, then?"

"No, she hasn't. Why don't you call her, make sure she's still alive?"

"You think I haven't tried about seven billion times? She

must have her phone off. Or her music on. Or she's been eaten by a bear and I'll hold you entirely responsible."

"I didn't let her drive here in a snowstorm."

"Wait, it's snowing? When did that happen?"

"When water coming from the sky hit the freezing-ass air I'm standing in trying to fix the goddamn pipe. It's called weather."

"You're snarky when you're cold. Just . . . when she gets there, have her call me. And please, no matter what she says, don't let her drive back down the mountain tonight."

"Course not. I'll tuck her right in next to me. I remember what you said earlier about getting some pussy."

I can hear the smoke billow from his ears over the phone line, and it's the first time I've felt a tiny bit happy all fucking day. "No," he says tersely. "I most definitely do *not* want that."

"Oh. Thanks for clarifying. I was confused."

"Asshole."

"I'll find a hotel. She can stay. All good."

"Thank you. You're a good mate." His voice drips with sarcasm, and I know he'll find some way to make me suffer at practice.

"This has been lovely, but the longer I talk to you, the more water ends up in June's kitchen. You paid up the insurance policy, right?"

"Wait, are you serious? Is it that bad?"

"It's—wait, oh no . . . I'm washing awaaayy . . ." I let my voice fade out and hang up. Not like it matters if I give him the exact water flow rate when he's not the one trudging through mud in the dark.

Fortunately it's more of a low, steady stream than a flood, but I can't leave June with water threatening to seep under her kitchen door.

This is why I've been searching around the house for the

past hour, using only the flashlight on my phone to attempt to find a shutoff for the water. It's also why I'm outside when Tim's small dumb car comes careening down the driveway and sideswipes a tree before stopping three feet short of a steep cliff.

I take off at a run, or as much of a run as I can manage up the muddy hill, struggling among scratchy plants that look like giant clovers on spiked legs.

Now, peering through the driver's-side window with my phone flashlight, I'm greeted by his terrified-looking sister, who promptly screams in my face.

The force of her lungs produces an ear-piercing shriek, and the glass between us is no match for the volume. I'm surprised it doesn't shatter. Maybe that's just a movie thing.

Regardless, her fright makes me take a step backward, and I teeter perilously close to the edge of the cliff. Reaching back for the car to steady myself, I see her react to my incoming hand. I wouldn't have thought her eyes could open any wider, but they do.

Gorgeous eyes. A greenish-gray so unusual and striking that I can't help but stare at them, and I don't do things like stare at eyes for no reason.

She fumbles at the switches on the door until the window rolls down a few inches. "Are you okay?" I ask.

"Geez. I thought you were a moose."

I can't stop myself. I laugh. "Gotta say, that's a first."

She doesn't seem amused. In a split second, her eyes shift from wide and fearful to a squinty glare, and I realize I'm probably blinding her with the light. I lower it, but not before taking a final peek at the bottomless sea green—if an ocean that color exists, I have no doubt that unwitting sailors have been lured to their death chasing its jewel tone.

"It might still be there, you know. Might want to watch your ass instead of laughing." She lets out a long exhale and slumps against the seat, eyes darting behind me.

"What might still be there?" I cross my arms over my chest and fight the urge to look behind me, because there's nothing there. I'd know if there was.

I may live in San Francisco now, but I grew up in Colorado. Mountains at night are just like mountains during the day— really dark but safer than the city and full of animals that are more frightened of me than I am of them.

"The moose. That's why I hit the tree. A moose ran in front of my car."

Her chest heaves behind the steering wheel, and I can see her pulse flitting under the pale skin of her neck. Under the car's interior light, her skin takes on an ethereal quality, so milky and smooth that I have to fight my urge to reach out and touch it to see if it's real.

Stop.

I shouldn't be fixating on her skin or her eyes or anything else. She's my best friend's sister. And then there's the small matter of the fact that she's nutty. Or maybe she hit her head when the car nicked the tree.

"A moose did not run in front of your car."

She juts her chin out and exhales as though she doesn't have the time in her busy schedule to educate me in the ways of moose, of which she's some kind of expert. "It did."

"Honey, there isn't a moose within five hundred miles of here."

She scoffs. Rolls her eyes and shakes her head, smiling into her hand. Then the car door swings open and she gets out. One tight jean-clad leg at a time. She comes up to the top of my shoulder, but her sass towers eight feet above the pines.

"My name's Linnie. Not 'Honey.'"

"I know who you are. Tim told me you were driving up. I'm Weston. We play together." The lady-charmer Tim mentioned. Great, just great.

"Brilliant. Like, you share a sandbox and go on the monkey bars at recess?"

"No, like we play for the Strikers." Her smirk halfway through lets me know I'm telling her what she already knows.

"Weston, huh? It's like your parents were trying to make sure you'd grow up a cowboy. Did it work?"

"It's my last name." No way I'm answering the other part. Talking about my family is off limits. It's actually written into my contract that no reporters will ask me questions about my upbringing. Not that she has any way of knowing that.

Linnie stands a little taller, throwing her shoulders back like a gladiator and matching my stance. It does not make her look one bit menacing.

"Nice of him to let you know. Would've been even nicer if he'd have warned me about enormous animals on his property."

She raises her arms in the air and spreads her fingers like claws. I wait for her to explain, but she says nothing, a determined look on her face.

"What are you doing?"

"Making myself look bigger." Her clipped accent makes it sound like the reason is even more obvious than it is. Which is . . . not obvious at all.

"And . . . why, exactly? You're not fooling me, if that's what you're thinking. I can still see how small you are."

"I'm not small."

"Fine. You're a giant."

Shaking her head, she lowers her arms slightly, fake claws still pointed straight at me. "It's for bears. You're meant to look big so they'll leave you alone."

I point to my chest with both thumbs. "Do I look like a bear to you?"

She huffs out a laugh like I'm the dumbest man in the world. Even in the dim light I see the corners of her lips edge up into a smile that says she knows she's right. Maybe I *am* a bear.

"Not you, the *actual* bears. We're in the woods." She slowly gives me the side-eye like I'm the one who's deranged, and her defensive claws inch higher.

That's the exact moment when I understand that a broken pipe is the least of my troubles. I have her to contend with until we get the thing fixed.

"Seems like a dangerous place for Tim to buy a house, if you ask me."

"We both bought it." No idea why I feel the need to let her know I'm an equal owner. Brutal adherence to the truth? Or stubborn pride?

"Pardon?"

"Never mind. There are no animals on the property, and no moose in California at all. I can guarantee you that."

"Well, you shouldn't be so quick to offer that kind of assurance, because one just darted in front of my car."

"Okay, first off, a moose wouldn't do that."

"Why, is *not darting* in the Moose Code of Conduct? Friends with a lot of moose, then?" Her accent is a bit stronger than Tim's—and even more charming. The British lilt of her words makes her questions sound more curious and ironic than she probably means them. Nevertheless, her scowl lets me know exactly how she feels about the conversation. And me.

"Not a lot. Some."

Another eye roll. "Well, next time you see your friends, ask them why one of their mates tried to run me off the road."

I nod, unwilling to engage in nonsense with this delusional woman, sister of my friend or not. Instead, I walk a few paces up the driveway in the direction Linnie pointed accusingly. Holding up my phone flashlight again, I shine it around the area, intentionally flicking the beam up toward the trees to demonstrate that nothing lurks just out of sight. But after that, I focus on where the driveway curves.

"Um, Linnie, you want to come up here?" I cast the light back in her direction, careful to keep the beam on the ground so she can see where she's going without me blinding her.

Not uncrossing her arms, she walks slowly up the drive, glancing from side to side as though a pack of moose might be hiding and ready to run her down.

"The coast is clear. I promise. No moose."

"You shouldn't do that."

"What?"

"Promise something you can't deliver. You have no idea what's here in the mountains."

"Actually, I do. I grew up in the mountains."

"These right here?"

So skeptical, this one.

"No, but I know mountains." I walk back down the driveway to meet her halfway and extend my hand toward her. Her eyes flit down to my hand and back up at me. Tentatively, she reaches out and I grasp her fingers. The skin on her hands feels surprisingly soft, so much so that I want to ask questions —does she follow a specific skin-care routine, use a special hand lotion?

Idiocy.

I appreciate the warmth of her hand after I've been out here with my freezing hands stuffed in my pockets for so long.

Leading her a few paces up the drive, I escort her to the spot I want her to see, then shine my flashlight over the wet soil to make my point clear.

"What am I looking at?"

"Honey, those are rabbit tracks."

Still gripping my hand, she takes a step back so she can level me with a stare, her hip jutting out, sassy.

For the first time since I started mucking around in the wet dirt tonight, I'm actually glad that the soil flanking the driveway has the swampy texture of pudding, because it makes clear why Tim's sister crashed into a tree.

"You swerved to avoid a bunny," I tell her, watching her expression morph from disbelief to stubborn defiance. She drops my hand, and I feel the deadweight of it slap my thigh. Like a punch in the gut. Rejection.

"It was a moose," she insists.

"These tracks say different." Sure enough, just past where the tracks cross to the opposite side of the driveway, there's more evidence of burned rubber from where Linnie slammed on the brakes. The skid of her tires gives way right before the tree she clipped with the car's front quarter panel.

She follows my finger and the light I'm shining along the path while I lay out my theory about how and why she hit the tree. "Humph," she says finally. "I really don't think it was a rabbit. It was brown, for one thing."

"Rabbits aren't all fuzzy and white." Surely she must know this.

"Yes, but . . ." She looks upward, and my gaze follows to where the dark, stormy sky is visible amid tree branches. "The snowflakes are so big here. Pretty."

I have no idea if the change of subject is her way of admitting I'm right, but I decide not to push the issue.

I'm right, though.

Confirming her observation, large, wet snowflakes pelt us through the pine needles and remind me for the first time since

Linnie screamed down the drive that it's snowing the kind of heavy snow that skiers call California concrete. Colorado snow is dry and light, but this stuff comes down hard and piles up fast.

And we're out here standing in it like fools.

My shoes are already soaked through from hunting around in vain for the water main, but the rest of me is mostly dry under a heavy, waterproof parka I found on a hook inside the front door. Not mine. Maybe one of the construction guys left it.

Whelp, they're not here and I am, so it's mine for now.

"You want to argue about this, or do you want to come in and get out of the snow?" She's not dressed for inclement weather. Shining the flashlight beam, I notice that her skintight jeans show off the curve of her hips and ass. Things I shouldn't be noticing.

"If I say I want to come in, it doesn't mean I agree with you about the moose."

I can't hold back a laugh. I respect how fiercely she holds on to her convictions. Even when she's wrong.

I can also anticipate that if I spend any length of time with her, that respect could quickly turn into frustration. "Fine. Done." I extend my hand in tacit acknowledgment of a truce on the subject.

We shake and she follows me back down the driveway.

"Hold on," she says. I turn to see her rooted to a spot on the pavement, her arms open wide. "I'm here to turn off the water main. Let me do that first." She points to where the glistening trail of water seeps through fresh snow, headed downhill.

"Um, yeah, I've been working on that for about the last hour."

She comes up, stands about three inches away, and fixes her gaze on me. "So why haven't you turned it off yet?"

This woman is unbelievable. "Because I have no idea where the shutoff valve is."

"Oh, come on." She waves a hand like she's closing down the conversation and sweeps past me, walking toward the front of the house. "It can't be hidden. The whole point is to be in plain sight so you can find it."

"Really? You don't say." My sarcasm lashes at her wake.

She marches toward the front of the house, whipping out her own phone and shining the flashlight on the ground around the front planters—two terra-cotta rectangular pots that flank the front door and contain the remnants of the summer daisies the real estate broker planted to pretty up the house when Tim and I came to see it.

Clearly the broker didn't know her audience. Tim and I cared not one whit about daisies, but we peppered her with questions about ski passes and construction permits for the addition we began planning before we'd even signed the escrow papers. The place has everything we were looking for—tons of potential for weekend projects, but it's not so much of a disaster that we can't use it now.

By the time I reach the front door, Linnie has begun tracing the perimeter of the house, just as I did when I got here. The snow abruptly starts pelting harder, almost like it's saying to me, "Hey, asshole, do not leave your friend's sister out in the snow, no matter how stubborn she is."

"Linnie." She stops and looks back at me. This time I see less defiant insistence and more questioning. It's already dawning on her that her search may be futile.

"Yeah?"

"Are you okay?"

"You mean, am I impulsive and unpredictable? Yeah, I'm that girl." She looks slightly apologetic.

"No, did you hit your head back there?" I point to where

Tim's car is kissing the tree. "Does anything hurt? Your neck or your back?"

In the light of our phone beams, I watch her blink up at me like she's not sure what I'm saying. No, it's not that. It's more like disbelief. "You . . . you mean when I crashed the car?"

I nod. "Yeah."

"Oh." She places a hand on her chest and blinks some more, almost like she's touched. It's like no one has asked about her well-being before.

"I, um . . . I think I'm okay. Yeah. Thanks."

Now it's my turn to nod. "Why don't we go inside? I've been here for over an hour already, and there's no sign of the valve." Spreading my arms wide, I gesture to the piles of fallen pine needles around us. "Not saying you're looking in the wrong place, but it could be under a foot of foliage. The chances of finding it would be much better in daylight."

She stammers. "But . . . what about the water? You want to leave it on *all night*?" Her voice pitches up an octave. "That's liters and liters of water you're wasting. We have to find the shutoff. Or figure out the source so we can dam it."

Now it's my turn for an incredulous look. "You want to hold your finger against the leak all night?"

"I would." She tips her chin up defiantly, a fierceness in her eyes that I can imagine in all sorts of other circumstances. I know nothing about Tim's sister, but I can imagine her taming wild horses or . . . my cock.

Jesus Christ, where did that come from?

I can't help that a rogue part of me wants to rile her up even more to see just how feisty she gets. A smarter part wants to get her to back down.

"I wouldn't let you."

"It's not your choice. Besides, I'm sure we can do better."

Her eyes stay fixed on me, but she's not angry, just insistent that we finish the job she drove up here prepared to do.

Well, fine.

I can see that there isn't going to be a thing I can say to wrest the stubborn from this woman, so I rake a hand through my hair, which is getting frosty as we stand here in the snow.

"There's a toolbox in the house with a bunch of junk in it. If we can figure out where the leak is, maybe we can use something in there to stop it."

For the first time, she laughs. The sound is so startling after all her sass that I look to make sure she's not choking or something. No, her full lips are quirked into a smile, and the carefree sound emanating from them is, in fact, laughter. "Spoken like a guy who isn't the owner of the toolbox. Or maybe has never seen one before?"

"I've *seen* a toolbox." I do not own one. "Hey, fixing things isn't required on the soccer field. We all have our strengths."

"Okay, show me this toolbox. Hopefully there's a stronger flashlight in there or at least a blowtorch or something useful."

"Yeah, I'm going to let you use a blowtorch," I say.

"Great." Her perky tone tells me she either doesn't get sarcasm or she's really that stubborn. Either way, it's trouble.

I lead her to the front door, which is painted marine blue, something I plan to change when we get around to painting the house.

"I love this color blue," Linnie says. Of course she does. I have a feeling that whenever I zig, she'll zag, so the sooner we find the problem with the pipe, the sooner I'll get her out of my snow-covered hair and out of my life.

～

THE TOOLBOX IS "BLOODY BRILLIANT," according to Linnie. Not that I ignored its potential usefulness earlier. I just figured I'd locate the shutoff valve and would figure out what tools I needed at that point. Then I couldn't find the shutoff valve . . .

Now, with Linnie who "likes to fix shit" rifling through the tools, half of which look deadly, I can't stop a growl from escaping. I don't want to make a career of this, and Linnie feels the need to examine each tool and comment on its usefulness.

"Oh, a socket wrench. Could help if there's a loose bolt . . . oooh, a proper caulking gun. Now that's great for a crack," she says, prattling on like she's opening a new Lego set on Christmas. I don't know what half of the tools are for, which is probably why I was still stomping around in snowy mud when she arrived. My handyman dreams were supposed to begin *after* purchasing a cabin in the woods, and probably not for several years.

I stand with my arms crossed, regarding the red metal toolbox like it has the jaws of a piranha, liable to snap at me if I put my hand inside. Linnie's bewildered eyes flick over me.

"Just want to make sure there isn't anything sharp in there. Box cutter or a saw," I explain.

Without hesitation, she shuffles a hammer and box of nails aside, picks up a large flashlight, and grabs a wrench. Unhelpfully, I pick up a handsaw. I know she's watching me, but I don't dare look up.

"What's that for?" She's fighting a smile. And losing.

I put down the saw and grab a hammer. "If we don't know what's broken, we can't know what tools we need to fix it."

"I can assure you we're not fixing a leak with a hammer."

I glance at Linnie, fairly certain she's forcing back laughter at my ineptitude, but she waits patiently while I assess the useless-looking tools.

"Do I want to know why you're so knowledgeable about tools?"

"I do a lot of dismembering at work. Tools make it quicker."

I take a step back, unsure if she's kidding. *"What?"*

Her eyebrows bounce; then she cracks a smile. "Kidding. My family owns an auto garage. When other kids were playing with Barbie, I was using tools to give Ken a lobotomy." She watches my reaction, which is somewhere between relief and a new round of horror. "Again, kidding."

"Fun." I rake a hand through my hair again in awe of this never-ending disaster of a day, made slightly less awful in the presence of Tim's wacky sister. She has a certain brightness and levity that's cutting through the worst of my mood.

In the light of the kitchen, I'm stuck on her eyes again. I want to name their color, but none of the hues I recall from the jumbo box of Crayola crayons do it justice. They're like a deep-water cove in the Caribbean where sunlight cuts the water and illuminates a rainbow of fish.

Stop staring at her eyes.

So I look at the rest of her face—berry-stained full lips, round cheeks, and scattered freckles across the bridge of her nose add up to the kind of natural beauty that's normally my type—and then I immediately stop looking because this is Tim's sister, and he'd crush my head in a vise if he saw the way I was gaping at her.

Instead, I crane my head toward the living room, which is a hodgepodge of the previous owner's ski memorabilia, board games stacked three feet high, and mismatched furniture we haven't yet replaced. Tim and Jordan came up for a weekend right after we bought the place, so at least they've stocked it with toilet paper and bare essentials.

"This is an impressive wrench." She's weighing it in her

hand and wrapping her fingers around it and all I can think of are a hundred inappropriate jokes. I close my eyes and breathe.

"Just. Pick. Something."

She gives me a side-eye and continues examining each damn item in the box before making a choice. Normally I'd appreciate a person's thoroughness. But it's nearly three in the morning.

"Look, the sooner we get this fixed, the sooner I can find you a cute hotel to stay in. Tim told me not to let you drive back in the dark."

"Tim isn't the boss of me."

"Shocking," I mutter before my brain has time to edit.

"Sorry?"

I backpedal, if only to keep her focused. "You seem like your own boss. That's all."

"Oh." She puts down a screwdriver and stops to think about it. She bites her bottom lip before nodding. "Well, isn't every-one? The boss of their choices?"

I notice the color rise on her cheeks, and she blinks a few times. Maybe I offended her, but there's no time to ask. Not with the laws of gravity pulling water downhill toward a ninety-year-old's kitchen.

I'm about to wave the white flag of surrender when her hand covers mine and maneuvers it to a wide elastic band in the corner of the box. The gentleness of her touch contrasts with her take-charge nature.

"Put this on," she says calmly. Removing her hand, she leaves me clutching the elastic item, which I pull from the box and examine. It's a two-inch striped headband with a light on it. Linnie gestures to me with a nod, so I slip the thing over my forehead. She reaches up and taps the front of it until a steady beam shines directly into her eyes. Squinting at the brightness, she adjusts the beam so it's pointing slightly downward and hands me a roll of duct tape from the box.

"So you really looked carefully for the shutoff?" she asks, jogging out the front door and down the porch steps.

I make a circling motion with my finger. "Walked the perimeter, looked near the hose and the sprinkler valves. Nothing." I point toward where the mountain road intersects with the driveway. "Checked near the street, but there's no evidence of a box, not like what I have in the city, anyhow."

"Ohhh," she says, nodding slowly, as though I've just explained everything. "You're a city boy. No wonder."

"San Francisco being the city. People in the Bay Area call it *The City*. And no, I'm no more a city boy than your brother. I grew up in the mountains, remember?"

I've barely finished talking before she's heading away from the house, carefully making her way down the hill and stopping when she gets to the muddier area. "Thanks for the geography lesson." Poking through the underbrush with the wrench, she shines her flashlight on the ground, which is quickly getting buried under a blanket of white. "Leak has to be coming from this area. Here's where it starts getting wetter."

"Yeah, that was pretty much my conclusion before you got here."

She raises an eyebrow. "Hmph."

"What?"

"It's just . . . you seemed kind of outside your comfort zone with the tools, so I . . . never mind."

"You figured I'm just some inept city slicker who doesn't know how to use a flashlight to find mud?"

Her cheeks pink up again, but she meets my gaze, challenging. "Didn't say that."

Nope, but she thought it. The competitive asshole in me needs to prove her wrong. Just because I'm not on a soccer field right now doesn't mean I don't feel an intense need to win. That urge runs deep.

Snatching the hand that doesn't contain the wrench, I pull her over a few paces to the spot I'd identified earlier as seeming the likely source of the leak. Under a new layer of snow, water puddles on a flat area before descending along an eroded pathway to June's house.

Linnie is gone in a swirl of blond streaks whipping behind her as she scoots back up the hill, returning a minute later with a hand shovel. She holds it up, victorious. "Let's dig."

I don't even bother asking how she knew where to find a shovel. I vaguely remember seeing a handle sticking out of one of the planters near the front door, and apparently she noticed it too.

"Here, let me." I put my hand out for the shovel. I don't care how capable she is; I'm not about to let a woman who just flew ten hours and then drove three more bend down and dig in the muck at night. Not to mention she crashed the car, and even if she's in denial, her body is probably a little bit jacked up from the jolt.

Linnie holds the shovel to her chest protectively. "Can I? I'm excited about finding what's going on under there," she squeaks, her face turned up to mine and glowing in my head-lamp beam. Her glee almost makes me forget it's the middle of the fucking night. Almost.

"We can tag team it. You start. I'll jump in if you get tired of digging. Wet dirt's heavy."

"Deal." She starts digging, the mud giving way in soft clumps that splat on one side of what's starting to become a small hole. I watch, hands on my hips, as the hole gets bigger and just as quickly fills with snow and water from the pipe.

"Seems like this is the right spot." Linnie glances back at me, satisfaction in her smile. She jams the shovel once more in the soil and gives it a hard shove with her foot. I'm about to warn her to ease up since we don't know what lies underground. But before the words leave my mouth, she starts muttering, "No, no. Oh no. Oh NOOO!"

Just as a giant spray shoots up into her face.

She backs into me. I lose my balance and fall on my ass. Linnie lands on top of me in a splat of mud just as the clouds choose that moment to decide this is, in fact, a fucking blizzard.

CHAPTER 3

LINNIE

I never listen to reason. It's a problem, I know, and I'm working on it. Not really. But I should be.

By all accounts, I should have let Weston do the digging. He's the athlete, and it's his house. Plus he offered.

Yeah, but I'm stubborn. I can do hard things. I can take care of myself. Hence, here I am, flat on my back with Weston spread-eagled beneath me.

Snow splats into my eyes, and I squint against the offending fat flakes. I hear Weston groan and roll myself to the side. In the beam of my large flashlight, I see Weston grimacing and gritting his teeth.

"Oh shit. Are you okay?" I try to scramble to my feet, but with the spray of water and the heavier snow, it's slippery, so I make it only halfway to standing before sliding and falling again, this time facedown on top of him.

My cheek hits the wet Gore-Tex shell of Weston's jacket, leaving me staring into his eyes. They're softer than I noticed earlier, almost vulnerable. Maybe it's his position. Vulnerable, indeed. Our faces are inches apart, too personal for someone I just met—and even for someone I know well. And yet . . . for a few more seconds I stay here and look at him because I can.

Dark storm cloud eyes, strong jaw, a day's worth of stubble, lips that look butter soft.

Okay, that's enough looking.

As I try to push myself up, my hand slips and I compensate by throwing down a knee to land on. He lets out a yelp as my bony knee connects with his flesh. "Did I just . . . oh Jesus."

If I've maimed him or destroyed his future chances of having children, I'll never hear the end of it from Tim. Plus the guilt. If I've deprived the world of little future soccer stars, I'll feel horrible about it, even if it's not my fault.

"No, just my inner thigh. And I tweaked my hip . . . which I already injured yesterday at practice," he chokes out. "Probably why it hurts so much."

Gingerly, I manage to get my feet underneath myself and flush with the ground, so somehow I don't fall forward again onto Weston. When I succeed in crouching next to him, I look him over from head to toe. "You're crooked."

"Sorry?"

"The way you're lying here. Your hip is fixed one way and your torso is going the other." I start pointing at his various body parts, using the nonsense I'm spouting to distract myself from his face, which I want to look at again. Instead, I jut my own hip out to the side, demonstrating. "You're hurt."

Hefting himself up so he's leaning on his elbows in the snowy mud, he straightens out a bit. "I'm fine."

"Are you sure? You want a hand up?"

He hesitates before grasping my extended hand. "Careful. I weigh twice what you do." He pushes himself to sitting using the other hand, and we're caught frozen in place, eyes locked and holding on to each other. Again, a bit too close for near strangers.

I jerk my hand back, suddenly self-conscious. More self-conscious than when I almost kneed him in the groin, which was already mortifying. His eyebrows arch upward at my sudden movement. "Sorry," I say.

"What?" The bewildered crinkle of his eyes looks playful, and I fortify my jumbled nerves and get my wayward brain back on track.

"Nothing. All good." I extend my hand again bravely, but he's mostly righted himself by now, and he uses my hand only to steady himself as he gets to his feet. Nodding, I take a step backward and slip on the fresh snow. Reaching for purchase, I flail, but he brings both his hands just above my hips and steadies me.

"Careful," he says.

"Right." I'm intensely aware of his hands—and of how no man has touched me in three months.

"Good?"

"Sure. You?"

"Yeah."

After reaching up, I turn his headlamp around so it's pointing away from my eyes. I should keep my hands to myself. I know this from a decade of making the same kinds of mistakes with men—feeling too free to touch them, be with them, sleep with them—and then discovering I was just another cow giving them milk for free. Just like my dad warned me not to be.

I shudder at the memory of that. Then I conjure a smile. "Okay. Back in action."

He studies my face, eyes roaming from mine to my cheeks, darting to my lips for a moment before returning to my eyes. His expression is hardened and resolute.

For good measure—and because old habits die hard—I reach a hand for his chest to make sure I'm good on my feet.

Yup, his chest is as solid under that jacket as I suspected. Check.

"Okay, steady now," I tell him, though I'm not feeling particularly steady, and I'm afraid it has nothing to do with the fact that we're standing on a hill in slippery mud. But he's no longer looking at me. Instead he's poking at something a few feet away. I follow his gaze to where water has begun burbling up through the mud. It's the same location where I stupidly pounded in the shovel. "What's up?"

He points. "That's the leak. See, the bolt's loose."

"Unless I made a new leak with the bloody shovel." Frustration at myself lodges in my throat, straining my voice.

Shaking his head, he picks up the shovel, crouches down, and starts sloshing the water out of the hole, which only fills up faster as he works. He barely gets a clear view of dirt before the hole fills up again. And yet he's hovering over the ground in a delicate squat.

I start to laugh and he looks up at me. Futilely wipes snow from his brow. "What now?"

"Just . . . you know you're covered with mud, yes?"

He looks down, and his headlamp confirms that there's more brown than gray in his sweats. "Your point?"

Shaking my head, I force myself to stop laughing. "You seem like you're—I don't know—trying to stay clean or whatnot, squatting down like that. Don't be afraid of a little mud."

"I'm not afraid. I can squat for an hour. Soccer, remember?" He points to himself with a thumb, which succeeds only in putting a new stripe of mud on his jacket. "You could join me, if you're so at one with the mud."

"Hang on," I say, grabbing the big flashlight and beginning to wobble my way up the hill to the house.

"Careful. It's snowy and wet," Weston yells after me.

"You don't say!" I call back, slogging my way to the driveway and back up to the house, where I retrieve the cordless soldering iron I saw in the toolbox.

In the kitchen, out from under Weston's watchful eye, I take a quick look around. A collection of ceramic roosters in varying sizes sits in a box on the floor near the old metal stove. On the wall hangs a circular clock without numbers and THE TIME IS NOW in block letters on a white background.

An empty wall with unfinished plumbing seems to be the location for a future refrigerator. The room is a quaint mixture of timeworn touches like red gingham curtains still framing the windows and a more modern design direction of distressed wood cabinetry with poured concrete counters.

I need a moment without Weston's intense stare bearing down on me. He looks at me like I don't make sense, which is not particularly unusual, I suppose. I'm used to men staring at me and wondering why a pretty barmaid knows how to fix an engine. A lot of them say it outright.

Being viewed as an oxymoron has never bothered me, not really. I'd much prefer to surprise a person with my ability to get out of a pickle than confirm the assumption that I'm just nice to look at with no underlying skills or grit.

I pick up the soldering iron and walk outside again.

Carefully I make my way back over to where Weston is still bailing water like a champ, and I hunker down beside him until my feet slip out from under me and I land flat on my ass. "I meant to do that," I say after I catch a smirk.

With one more large scoop of mud, Weston gets enough water out of the hole and enough mud pushed aside that we can see a rusted pipe with a crack in it. Water seeps out and trails down the mountain.

"Eureka!" Weston exclaims.

"Pardon?"

"It's what the oil barons say when they strike it rich."

"You're an oil baron? Or friends with some?"

"I'm friends with exactly zero oil barons."

"Perfect. Shall we get to work repairing it so we can get out of the snow? Look what I found." I hold up the cordless soldering iron.

Weston's wary gaze tells me he doesn't seem to share my enthusiasm. "What the hell's that?"

"A soldering iron. To weld the crack in the pipe."

He snatches it from my hand as though it's a raptor about to take a bite from my arm. He holds it behind his back like I'll forget it's there. "You can't use that around water. You'll electrocute us both."

"I checked the thermocouple. It's not near the tip, so we should be okay."

"Um, not willing to risk my life on a machine part I've never heard of because you think it 'should be' okay."

"Live on the edge, Weston. It's fine. Just stay back a bit. It'll heat to four hundred degrees, melt the snow off your hair."

He continues to hide the soldering iron behind his back as though somehow that will stop me. It's kind of charming, if ridiculous. "Only as a last resort. Let's try duct-taping it first."

I look away to hide the skepticism splashed across my face. "Okay, sure. Let's try that." We're just wasting time, but I don't feel like battling City Boy's ego, and he seems legitimately freaked out by the soldering iron. "Just FYI, you're holding that thing awfully close to your bum with you finger on the *On* switch."

He flinches and moves it to the side while he tips the miner's headlamp to shine it more directly around us. "I put the duct tape somewhere here." He spies it over where I fell on top of him and goes to retrieve it. In the meantime, I put my finger against the crack in the pipe to gauge the strength of the water flow. "Got it."

Weston holds up the roll of tape.

"I don't think that'll work," I say, aware of sounding too bossy. His expression turns cloudy.

"Why not?"

"The water's coming out with some force. And it's wet. Obviously. Tape might not stick."

The storm clouds that shroud Weston's eyes outdo the ones overhead. "It has to. We'll tighten the bolt first, hopefully reduce the water flow, then get the tape to stick." He seems certain and desperate at the same time.

I hand him the wrench, and he throws his weight into tightening the bolt. After a few hard turns, the water visibly tapers off.

"Nice," I tell him.

It seems like a fool's errand to try to tape a pipe with water still running from it, while a light wind has sent the falling snow sideways into our eyes, but I do my best to hold my tongue.

For exactly three seconds. Not even long enough for Weston to get a piece of tape unfurled from the roll. "Wait."

"What?" I sense his frustration level rising, but if we're doing this, we're doing it right.

"We need to dry it off if the tape is going to stick."

"It's snowing."

"I know."

"So . . ." He pushes a hand through his wet hair, which slicks it back and somehow draws my attention to the hard line of his jaw, where I can see a muscle jump. I can tell he's frustrated with me—and the snow and the situation—but he's doing his best not to blow his stack.

"Are there towels in the house?" I ask, imagining some fancy monogrammed towel set my fancy brother purchased.

He lets out an exasperated sigh. "I doubt it, seeing as I haven't bought any. No one lives here."

I raise a finger and disagree. "Tim invited me to spend the week here, so I have to imagine he's bought some towels. I turned it down, just so you know. I'm staying with him in the city."

"Thanks for the itinerary. But if you haven't noticed, it's pitch black out, it's snowing, and we're standing outside arguing about towels."

"I wasn't arguing. I was just asking."

"Still. Arguing," Weston says, tension in his voice. "Fine." He stomps off, waving the soldering iron in the air to make a point that he's not leaving me behind with it. After a few paces, he disappears behind the curtain of falling snow.

"Wow, trust much?" While he's gone, I bail out more water. Weston has dug enough of the mud away that the hole is three inches below the pipe, so as long as we keep the water away, we *may* be able to dry the pipe and wrap it in tape.

My scarf isn't exactly snow-proof, but I pull it off and use it as a makeshift tent to keep falling snow off the pipe.

Weston returns a couple of minutes later with a fluffy yellow towel. "Towel." He hands it to me like a surgical tech. I dry the pipe as well as possible, save for the area underneath that's leaking water.

"Tape," I say, extending my hand. He tears off a long piece and sticks it to my palm. I stick the tape to the dry part of the pipe and look at Weston. "Okay, it's go time. When I give the signal, you wipe the pipe dry underneath, and I'll start wrapping. You ready?"

He nods.

I nod back.

He quickly dries the metal, and I start winding the duct tape around the pipe, making tight loops that do nothing to hold back the water. Snow pelts us while Weston sops up the moisture that forms and scoops away mud with the shovel. I loop the tape up and down the pipe, putting it into a silver duct tape cast. Eventually I stop, and Weston admires our handiwork.

Then we look downhill at where the rivulet was running in a steady stream toward the neighbor's house. Other than snow pelting the ground, there's no more river.

Weston observes the situation a bit longer before turning slowly toward me, a questioning look on his face. "Yeah?"

I nod, surprised it worked and impressed that Weston stuck to his guns and didn't let me boss him around. I never realized how much I like that in a man. Maybe because I've never seen that in a man.

"I think we're good. At least until morning. Nice work."

We amble up the hill toward the driveway and back to the house, both of us surprised to find someone standing on the doorstep.

"June, you okay?" Weston asks. He introduces me to his neighbor, who's my height but bulky under what looks like ten jackets and a fur hat. She's standing in the dark with a Maglite and a can of bear spray.

Maybe that's what ran in front of my car. A bear. On rabbit paws.

I don't get a chance to ask about bears or bear spray because June starts talking a mile a minute. "Forget about me. You two are icy and soaked to the bone. It's snowing like the dickens out here, and I look out my window and see either a couple of bears or a couple of humans, and I'm not sure what's worse. Then I figured out you were still working on the leak out here. My word. You're going to catch pneumonia."

"We're okay," Weston says. There's an ample overhang that protects the porch, but we're so muddy and snowy that it doesn't matter. "Are you?"

"I'm fine, dear. I just wanted to check on you and make sure you have what you need at the cabin for a couple days."

He dismisses her concern with a wave of his hand. "Thanks, June. We're good. We'll be heading down in the morning," Weston assures her.

"Oh, but dear, you can't head down. They've shut the pass. This is looking to be a record storm."

"Wait, what?" Weston says.

"I just drove up that road. It was fine," I contribute, certain she must be talking about a different road. We can still use it to drive back to San Francisco. Separately. In the morning, if not right now.

Can't we?

"Well, now it's closed. No one's leaving here anytime soon. Do you two have food in the fridge?"

I look at Weston.

He looks at me.

"About the fridge . . . ," he says.

CHAPTER 4

WESTON

"You two get some sleep, then come down to my house when it's light out. I'll bag you up some groceries and give you an ice chest to keep things cold. I store lots of canned goods in the basement. Always wise to keep a two-week supply of food. You just never know up here."

Linnie steals a glance my way, and I quirk an eyebrow, still trying to fathom how we got into this mess.

June prattles on, unaware. "Come by anytime, day or night. I'm a night owl. Knock loudly, though, in case I'm upstairs." She goes on about needing to get a doorbell, and Linnie offers to install it for her. Using the soldering iron, no doubt.

When we finally get inside, Linnie does not look happy to be stuck here until morning, even though it's technically already morning. The satisfied smile she wore moments before has been replaced with a scowl. Long blond tendrils hang soaked down her back, and shorter ones are plastered to her wet cheeks, pink from the cold.

"Is this normal?" she asks, dumbfounded. I'm not even sure what she's referring to, but it doesn't matter.

"No, I can't even count the number of things right now that

are *not* normal, starting with a blizzard. The weather report showed a light dusting of snow tonight, not an ice storm."

I duck into the bathroom where I found the yellow towel earlier. Plucking the second one off the bar, I silently thank whoever put it there and hand it to Linnie so she can wipe the water and dirt from her face.

She pats her cheeks dry and uses the towel to squeeze the water from her hair. Her eyes dart to mine. "You know this? Like, you know it for actual fact?"

So skeptical of me, even after I proved to be pretty handy wiping away water while she wound the duct tape. "Yes, for actual fact. I did research before we bought the place. The road has a historically high probability of *always* being open."

She snort laughs. "I can't tell if you're being sarcastic."

Ruffling the towel through her hair has the effect of sending flyaway strands every which way. I don't dare react, even though a few minutes more of it and she'll look like she stuck her hand in an electrical socket.

We're both soaked and muddy, and the best thing I can think of is to ransack my workout bag for dry sweats so our clothes can go into the washing machine. Instead, Linnie pulls my Strikers hoodie over her damp shirt and crosses her arms. It's down to her knees and she has to roll the sleeves three times, but I feel better knowing she isn't freezing to death.

Leaning over my bag, I yank the shirt over my head and find a training tee that may or may not be clean.

"Do we believe her?" she asks, watching me pull on the shirt.

"Believe her?" I parrot, confused.

"June. Do you think she's telling the truth about the road being closed?"

Well, that thought never crossed my mind. "Why would she lie?"

Linnie folds the towel into a neat square and offers it to me. I run it over my hair and toss it aside. My pants are too dirty to bother with.

Linnie shrugs. "Maybe it's a plot. To keep us here so she can murder us in the night."

I laugh at the image of a ninety-year-old mountain hermit coming for us while we sleep. "Did you see her? She weighs a hundred pounds max. She's tiny."

Linnie stands up straighter. "Maybe she's scrappy. Wiry. Small but mighty."

"Are we talking about her or you?"

"Her, of course. Maybe she made up the closure so we'll stay here and keep her company during the snowstorm. Who knows? She has her reasons."

The way she says it makes her logic sound completely normal. For a loony person.

I don't know her well enough to determine whether she's working with a full deck, and Tim never said much about either of his sisters, other than them living in the small English town where he grew up.

"Yeah, I don't know June well, but she doesn't strike me as the murderous type. After she called to tell me about the water leak, she mentioned she was baking bread and I should come help myself to fresh sourdough."

Linnie's eyes sparkle, and once again I try not to stare. I wonder how many men have lost their fucking minds looking into those eyes and obeying Linnie's every command. Poor bastards probably never saw it coming.

"Sourdough? You think she still has some?"

"So, a minute ago, you were convinced she was luring us to our death with a fabricated road closure, and now you want to hit her up for bread? How do you know she isn't the granny from a Grimm brothers fairy tale, waiting to throw you into her oven?"

She shrugs. "The bread won me over. I like her now. Am I abhorrent?"

"Hardly." I'm still figuring out what she is, but abhorrent isn't it.

Linnie looks beyond me and takes in the cabin for the first time. She wanders into the kitchen, where the toolbox still sits open on the small butcher-block island, and I watch her eyes dart around.

"So this place is under construction, I see. Tim didn't mention that when he suggested I spend my vacation here. Guess it's good I said no."

"We were led to believe it was basically finished. Obviously that was an exaggeration." As I'm saying the words, the wheels turn in my head. This place has one minimally furnished bedroom. "We bought the place furnished, and Tim and Jordan came up here a couple times before we started construction. But we're in season now, so neither of us has used the place. Guess the contractor was banking on us staying away a while longer."

Linnie looks beyond me to where we stood in the entryway earlier. "Because . . . ?"

"It needs work and it's a bit . . . small."

She nods, catching my drift. "How small?" she calls, sweeping past me and walking to the living room. For a woman with short legs, she moves very quickly. She's already moved past the couch and table and has turned into the one bedroom.

"So this is it?" she asks, spreading her arms wide in the bedroom, which is barely large enough to fit both of us and the furniture. "I mean, it's quite charming, don't get me wrong."

"I was all set to find you a nearby hotel."

"Is there anything we can still get to, maybe in the opposite direction of all the road closures?" Her voice pitches up, and I can see her chest rise and fall more rapidly. The color pinks her cheeks, and she starts fanning herself. "Dunno why it feels hot in here. Are you hot?" she asks.

"I'm regular."

Signaling for her to follow me, I lead her away from the bedroom, which is doing nothing to soothe her jangled nerves. On a small desk in the living room, I spot a yellow notepad and a pen. "Here, let me show you."

I draw a large hump of a mountain and start sketching a winding road. "Ooh, I didn't know you were an artist." She looks on with more enthusiasm and interest than anyone should.

"I'm no artist, but I can draw stick figures and a road." I demonstrate by sketching the barest bones of a square house with a triangular roof, which, ironically, is pretty much what our cabin looks like. Then I draw another set of squiggly lines showing how the roads intersect. I make an X at the intersection June mentioned when she was telling us about the road closure. "So this is the only road in either direction. I don't know where June got her information, but she's lived up here for two decades, so I trust her sources."

"So that means . . ."

"Both of us here. One bedroom," I confirm, before adding in case it isn't obvious, "One bed."

"Well, then, I might just have to sleep in the car."

In the snow. When the temperatures are set to drop below zero. Not happening.

Even if having her this close to me is going to test my very last strand of personal restraint. Even then.

"You can have the bed. It's no big deal." I walk her back toward the bedroom, and she takes a step inside, seeming to consider the bed for a millisecond. It does look comfortable. So comfortable.

She spins around and crosses her arms. "Hell no. This is your house. I'm not taking your bed."

"We'll see about that." I cross my arms as well and stand in the doorway, prepared to hold my ground until she agrees.

I can be stubborn too.

CHAPTER 5
LINNIE

I end up sleeping in the bed.

It wasn't that much of a hardship to agree to Weston's terms: he'd take the couch, and if we end up needing to stay another night, we'll swap. Apparently I was too tired to argue, because now it's morning and I'm still in bed under a half-dozen cozy plaid blankets of different colors.

Weston must have put them there, because I'm pretty sure they weren't there last night when I fell asleep on top of the covers. Tapping around on the blankets as though proving I'm really here, my hands fall on a set of Strikers sweatpants and a long-sleeved tee neatly folded on a corner of the bed. He left me a change of clothes? In my entire life, I can't think of a man I know who'd do that for me.

I feel like I'm emerging from a sensory-deprivation tank, first becoming aware of my arms and legs, which are lazily coming to life under the covers.

Next it's my eyes, grainy because I slept in my contact lenses, so while I can see clearly, it hurts to keep my eyes open. The heavy burgundy curtains are drawn, so I have no idea if it's light out or not, but I do smell coffee, which gets my heart pumping even before the first sip.

Glad Weston is a coffee person.

And then there are sounds. At first I figure it must be the TV, but I don't remember seeing one in the living room. Besides, what I'm hearing sounds more like grunting and less like a conversation.

Maybe Weston is being attacked by the moose or some animal that actually does live in the California mountains. Either way, I decide to investigate.

Still wearing my jeans and Weston's hoodie from yesterday, I feel a bit ripe. Really ought to shower before I put on his clean clothes. Or roll around in the snow and apply deodorant. I'm not fussy.

A peek through the curtains tells me what June alluded to last night—the blizzard hasn't stopped. Ice coats the outside of the window while the sky dumps snow. I can't see much of the landscape even though it's light out, and now that I've left the bed, I feel how cold it is in the cabin. I wrap two of the blankets around me and pad out of the room.

In the living area, I find the source of the sounds—Weston on the floor doing push-ups, his elbows pumping like pistons, the muscles in his back flexing and working under a thin gray tee. He's focused, counting his reps to himself. "Ninety-five, ninety-six . . ."

Holy cow.

I should go back to the bedroom. I shouldn't stand here and gawk at him like he's my own personal Magic Mike.

But then I do . . .

Oblivious to me, he finishes his set of push-ups and flips over onto his back and begins a set of crunches. Under the wrinkles of his shirt, I see ab muscles that actually have their own muscles. His legs pump in and out as he pulls his head to his knees. Over and over again.

I feel a little bit torn, wanting to follow the siren song of the coffee aroma but feeling that my feet have suddenly become too heavy to lift. I'm fused to this spot, mouth agape, watching as crunches turn into a set of burpees, squats, lunges, jump squats, and more crunches.

I don't know about him, but I'm absolutely sweating.

This is exactly the kind of temptation I do not need. It's like dangling an ice-cold beer in front of a teetotaler on a blisteringly hot summer day. So I dart into the kitchen before I accidentally dart on top of him.

I find a french press filled with coffee and pour myself a cup. Then, now that it's a reasonable hour, I text Tim to let him know about the storm.

Linnie: *Morning. Still at the cabin. There's a snowstorm.*

I don't hear back right away, which is normal for Tim when he's training. And since I don't want to worry him, I decide not to tell him about his car.

Linnie: *I'll ping you later. Love you.*

If it's morning here, my dad will be having dinner right about now, so I ring his cell phone. He carries it in a Bandolier mini-purse strapped across his hefty middle and doesn't feel the least bit emasculated. Mainly that's because I told him it was a "men's phone cozy" when I gifted it to him last year. The goal was to get him to carry and answer his phone once his health started declining. My siblings and I couldn't do with the extra worrying when we couldn't reach him.

"Allo," he answers on the first ring. Even though I programmed my name and picture into his phone, I know he stabbed at the thing without looking to see who's calling.

"Hi, Dad, it's me."

"Me who?" He's not kidding. He can never tell my sister

Mary and me apart by voice alone, but he's the only one on the planet who can't make the distinction. So in my not-subtle way, I'm trying to encourage him to pay better attention. Been doing it my whole life to no avail, and there's no sense in stopping now.

"Your daughter."

"Which daughter?"

"Linnie."

"I knew that." He didn't.

"Of course you did." Same banter as we've engaged in for years, light and familiar, masking how we really feel about each other—that I'm the disappointing middle child who'll never keep a man long enough to wrestle a proposal from him, and he's the father who's incapable of showing approval for anything I've ever done.

Our impressions of each other are so firmly rooted that I sometimes think we both work harder to prove them correct than we do to prove them wrong.

"Just letting you know I made it to California. Flight was fine."

"Pointless trip," he grumbles.

"I'm visiting Tim. Celebrating my birthday. Hardly pointless." What's pointless is trying to defend myself when I'm talking to a brick wall in the shape of an old man in the last years of his life. We all know his health is failing, but he refuses to see a doctor. The most he's allowed is a friend who dropped out of nursing school to come take his temperature and look him over.

Small wonder, she couldn't say what was wrong with him, just that he looked pale, shaky, and thinner than he has in years.

"Everyone's been nagging at me to go on a health regime for years, and now that I've dropped a few stone, you all harp on me that I'm sick. Let me live my life in peace until my time's up," he barked. So we agreed to let him.

More or less.

"A week without wages . . . seems pointless to me."

It was always about the money. Even though Tim bought the land where the family auto garage sits and paid off all debts on the place, our dad never eases up on his "make an honest living" ethos. I respect it, even if I don't understand why a man in poor health drags himself to work every day when it clearly costs him something.

"Anyhow, just checking in. Wanted to see how you're doing today."

"Same as every day. Not getting any better, but I'm not feeling worse, so it's something."

"Good to hear. Call me anytime, okay, Dad?"

He grudgingly agrees, though I know from experience he won't do it. It's fine. I'll just call him again tomorrow, same as always.

Eventually the grunting stops, and Weston appears in the kitchen doorway. "Good, you found the coffee."

"I did. Thanks. I think I drank half the pot."

He lingers and I try not to stare, but it's hard to avoid seeing the outline of every muscle through the sweat-stained shirt. I sneak a look, figuring if I commit his rounded biceps and broad shoulders to memory, I won't need a refresher. When my eyes finish wandering upward from his abs to his chest to his angular face, I find it marked with a smirk.

Well, as long as I'm looking and he's smirking, I take in his face, which I saw mainly in the dark last night. Rumpled wavy hair that looks better each time he runs a hand through it. Dark eyes that seem calmly assessing but also a little playful. Strong jaw dusted with scruff—my own personal kryptonite.

Sure, he's got that gorgeous athlete look, but I can appreciate his handsome face and chiseled body and not feel the need to climb him like a tree. I am an adult.

"Anyhow, I'll probably shower, then do some yoga. You know, to stay fit," I say, cringing as the words come out—not because I think he'll take one look at my curvy figure and know I'm not exactly a gym rat. But because now I'll actually have to do yoga.

I've barely done anything resembling yoga other than the occasional stretching class, which is more like a lazy prelude to a nap. But after what I just witnessed, I ought not to be too much of a slacker. And despite myself, I care what he thinks.

I want to be the kind of woman who says no to hookups *and* jumbo bags of Maltesers. I want to be the kind who has a career she's proud of, and even though I have a long way to go on all those fronts, somehow I guess the road begins with a round of fake yoga in this cabin.

Weston nods slowly as though he can read my thoughts. "Yoga sounds like a great way to spend the afternoon."

"Afternoon? I was thinking about starting this morning."

He laughs. "Too late for that, honey. It's already two." He refills my cup of coffee, adds the right amount of cream to make it the same color as what was left in the cup, and hands it to me. As he does, our fingers brush, and I feel a spark of electricity that heats the back of my neck.

Blinking a few times as though it will help me calm my body's response to him, I process what he's just said. I've just slept through half the day?

My cell phone confirms it. I didn't even notice the time when I called my dad, and I probably woke him up. No wonder he was grouchy.

I stand up a little straighter and take my cup to the sink. "Well, then, I really ought to get started."

WESTON DOESN'T EVEN PRETEND he has better things to do than hang out at the table in the one room big enough for me to do yoga in—while wearing Weston's large, rolled-up sweatpants and T-shirt no less.

"Thank you for the outfit," I say, upside down in downward dog.

"No problem. Sorry I don't have anything smaller." Still watching me. And I feel the effect of his stare like a heat signature on my ass.

He grabs a deck of cards and starts dealing out a game of solitaire while I set myself up on a towel on the wood floor. Every so often, I hear the harsh flip of cards as he shuffles them, and it jars me out of my meditative state.

Who are you kidding? You're as wound up as a coiled spring.

Who wouldn't be with a professional footballer checking out her bum while she tries to breathe in downward dog without being suffocated by her boobs?

The only good news is that my fake yoga has me sweating enough that I'm no longer cold. Silver linings.

After about five minutes of contorting my body into poses that wouldn't pass muster with any official yogi, I remember why I don't like yoga at all. It's hard and boring at the same time.

But rather than admit defeat, I persist, stretching tall, bending over, breathing deeply, and eventually sitting on the floor and doing some twists. Every time I look up at Weston, his eyes meet mine with such total calm I start to wonder if yoga is more in the eye of the beholder. He seems very relaxed, and I'm all wound up.

Finally, I tip my hat to the Savasana gods and lie on the floor for a few minutes, trying to come up with other ways to fill the time in a tiny cabin while the blizzard wears on in a race to see how fast it can fill the planet with snow.

The rest of the day ticks by in dog years, with each of us looking for ways to pass the time.

We try playing Scrabble, but he objects to my English colloquialisms. "Cripes is too a word," I insist, really wanting the high-scoring word.

As we're each picking up new letters, our hands brush, and I feel it again—proof that if he touched more of me, I'd feel turned on in a lot more places. Pulling my hand back, I wait for him to finish picking up his tiles before I select the rest of mine. Safer that way.

"Fine." He carefully surveys the board, taking in every possible empty square and rearranging tiles for what seems like a half hour.

"Do we need to set a time limit on turns?" I shouldn't be so impatient. We have nowhere to go.

He huffs a laugh. "I don't know. *Do* we?" That smile. It's criminal.

Candy Land lasts about ten minutes. We play six hands of gin rummy.

Weston bundles up and goes outside, returning a half hour later with a bag full of winter clothes he borrowed from June for me to wear.

"I figured you'd want to check on the pipe, and you'll freeze in what you're wearing."

My mouth drops open at the gesture—and how well he knows me already. "That's . . . so nice."

I throw on a parka, Sorel boots, and a hat, then pull Weston behind me through the snow, which he's still navigating in his soggy shoes. But he insisted on coming with me. It's like we're creeping in to check on a new baby, making sure he's sleeping. We high-five each other when the duct tape seems to be holding. In the five minutes we're out there, it snows so hard that we both come inside covered in white.

"What now?" I ask, afraid to look at my phone and discover we still have eleven hours to go until bedtime.

"I dunno. Chess?" he says, gesturing at an old set between boxes of board games.

"You play chess?" My eyes light up. "I love chess. You really play? Or did you just watch *The Queen's Gambit* on TV?"

He huffs an annoyed breath, though he looks amused. "I *play*. Do you?"

I nod and tip my head from side to side. "I watched *The Queen's Gambit* on TV . . . but I also play. Okay, Weston, let's go."

Turns out Weston is really good at chess. He's a careful, smart player. We play for hours, leaving us both quiet, contemplating our moves.

Except that all I'm doing is contemplating Weston. And wondering what else he's hiding behind that chiseled athlete exterior.

CHAPTER 6
WESTON

We play chess for so long that day turns to night and we're finishing our fifth game. "You have no way out," I tell her.

"Wait. Let me think." She moves her last pawn but doesn't take her hand away so she can still switch it back. "No, hang on."

There are only two possible moves, and either way I'll take her queen. But I don't tell her this. She knows. Just hates to lose.

"Okay, I'm going with this." She sacrifices her rook.

I move my bishop, hemming her in. "Check."

She sits back, acknowledging her defeat. "I know. And checkmate. Can we play once more?"

I hold up a hand. "After we eat. Can you handle not being victorious for one hour?"

"Maybe a half hour." Linnie is wearing a half-wet hoodie that goes down to her knees because she thought it looked "comfy."

As the day turned to night, the cabin dropped a few degrees colder, if that's even possible.

Chess can wait until I have a fire burning in the fireplace

and food cooking on the stove—though I have no idea what's in the bag of canned goods June had me lug from her basement earlier. For all I know, June is a survivalist vegan who eats only canned mushrooms.

Linnie shivers, her whole body racked with chills, but she tries to play it off like she's shimmying to music only she can hear.

"You're freezing. You should take a hot shower, and I swear I must have something that won't fit you like a dress." I lean against a wall, letting my hand trace the contour of the interior wall—rounds of wood stacked like Lincoln Logs. Every wall of the house looks like this—the interior side of rough-stacked logs—even though I know there's cement and rebar somewhere. The rustic charm is part of what I liked about the place.

Linnie perches on a corner of the table. "Oh, I have my luggage from the airport. I didn't unload the car before I headed up." And yet I've been loaning her clothing all day because I thought she only had the clothes on her back.

Shaking my head, I mutter, "Craziness."

"Pardon?"

"I still can't believe you got off a transatlantic flight and drove three hours in the rain. And snow."

"Didn't know about the snow," she mutters.

"Would it have dissuaded you? Please say yes so I know you're not an insane person."

Pressing her cherry lips together, she shrugs, which tells me everything I need to know about this woman—headstrong, determined, and unlikely to listen to advice. Ironically, she sounds a bit like me and every other athlete I know. Traits that are the building blocks of greatness on a soccer field. Just not what I expected when she came barreling down the hill, mistaking rabbits for moose.

"More than that, I can't believe Tim isn't freaking out about the car," I say.

"Oh, that." She bites down on her bottom lip, and it takes me a beat to realize I'm staring. My eyes dart up and I focus on the matter at hand.

"Linnie . . ."

"I didn't want to worry him."

"So what did you tell him?"

"I haven't talked to him. I sent a text saying there's a storm."

I run a hand over my face and look at her, still digging her teeth into that lip. I have an urge to set it free. Instead, I put a hand on her arm as if to steady her. "You need to call him."

"I know. He's just weird about that dumb little car. I fear his wrath."

Tim is grumpy, but it's hard to imagine anyone being too mad at Linnie. Even so, they're siblings and I wouldn't know anything about that. What I do know is that somehow being around her has lightened my mood, and yesterday I didn't think that was possible. "I know how to handle him. It'll be okay."

Linnie nods and calls her brother. It turns out she doesn't need my help. She calmly explains the situation, doesn't get flustered, and assures Tim she'll have the car repaired, though I have no idea how she plans to make that happen in a snowstorm.

After she hangs up, she seems more settled, but her gaze is fixed downward, new strains of concentration visible on her face.

"Everything okay?"

"Your leg. You said you hurt yourself at practice. Then I hurt it more when I fell on you yesterday. Have you been icing it?"

"Have I . . . ?"

"Been icing it? Plenty of snow out there to make into a little ice pack." She demonstrates how she'd pack it, her hands moving like she's forming a snowball. "I don't know how you treat your injuries, but when my neck and shoulders get tight, I alternate with ice and heat and keep the swelling down with ibuprofen. Maybe you have something stronger from the chemist."

"The chemist?" I feel my lips curl into a smile. I never miss an opportunity to give Tim shit when he pulls out an English word or phrase that no one uses in America, but when she speaks, the lilt of her words charms me. "Here we call it a pharmacy."

"Is that really the point, then?" Rolling her eyes, she reminds me of the point—she cares. A lump forms in my throat, and I force it down. "We're talking about your injuries. Now that we've fixed the water leak, let's fix you."

Her concern feels like a downy overcoat when I had no idea I was freezing to death. No one worries about me. Other than this one week a year when things always get to me, I keep up a consistent, cheerful facade. I work hard at it, and people don't ask about anything they can't see. I like it that way.

"You're . . . worried about my hip?"

"Seeing as how I may have made it worse, of course. How did you injure it? What was the scenario?"

She drops into the high-backed chair next to the table and fixes me with a gaze I can't escape. I wander a circle around the room, feeling my way through my leg's current condition. After a few paces, I feel the heaviness that set in after I took the hit at practice. My hip aches, and I bend down to see if the golf ball–sized lump on my shin has dissipated. Not really. She's right. I should deal with it.

Leaning against the wall again, I take the weight off that leg and give it a shake. "Typical defensive slide tackle. Nothing I haven't experienced a hundred times before, but this one caught me at a bad angle, and I fell hard on my hip, probably a deep bone bruise."

"Ouch. Dangerous sport."

What I don't tell her is that I had it coming. I'd been edgy all day, amping up my intensity at practice as a way of dealing with my shit mood, pressing my teammates with aggressive moves until one of them pushed back with a dirty slide tackle.

I shrug off her concern. "It happens."

She shudders. "Lucky, I guess. Could've torn something."

I imagine she's thinking of her brother, who played half of last season with a pretty severe injury and kept it from all of us. "Always lucky when I get to play another day," I say, bucking up. As much as it's sweet that she cares, I'm not particularly comfortable with people fussing over me. Besides, I'm fine.

Liar.

She shakes her head like she doesn't believe me. The way her eyes trace over every inch of my leg, finally rising up along my torso to meet my gaze, makes me feel like she knows intimate things about me, even if that's impossible.

And she doesn't need to know me.

"Brr," she says at the end of another shudder. "I think I'll take you up on that shower."

"Go for it." Taking a peek out the window confirms that it's still snowing hard. I start to worry that the road closure might not be the biggest of our problems.

With the number of large, ancient trees on the property, limbs heavy with snow tumble down. To say nothing about the snow that will need to be cleared from the roads.

"Wow, it's really picked up," Linnie says, peering through the window, where a chunk of snow falls off the porch overhang, sending a cloud of snowflakes into the air.

"Give me your keys."

"What? Why? I'm not aiming to drive anywhere in this, don't worry."

"I'm going to get your bag from the car. You're cold enough."

She shakes her head. "You don't need to do that. I'm a big girl." This time it doesn't come off as stubbornness. It feels almost like desperate insistence. Like she needs to prove something, and I wonder why.

She flings open the door and all I see is a curtain of white outside, but she doesn't look at all deterred.

After popping the hood over her hair, she pulls up the hem of the hoodie so she can stuff her hands into her pockets. As she turns and steps out onto the porch, I can't help but notice how cute and round her ass looks under the billowing sweatshirt fabric. I curse myself for noticing.

Then I take one more look, and fuck me if that isn't the moment she casts a glance behind her, sees me doing it, and winks. Before I can make up some lame excuse she'll never believe, she's walking out into the snow.

If it were a scene in a movie, this is where I'd run out after her and insist on helping her. She'd put her hands on my chest to push me away, but I'd draw her in close. With the snow drifting around us, we'd be oblivious to everything outside our tiny bubble. We'd kiss in the lightly falling snow; then I'd carry her back into the cabin and over to a pile of blankets in front of the fireplace. And then . . .

But as I'm letting this fantasy play out in my head, Linnie is running back through the relentless snowfall and rushing past me into the house.

Because life isn't a movie. And I'm just a guy in a cabin with no heat.

So I get to work building us a fire.

CHAPTER 7
LINNIE

Yes, I saw Weston checking out my bum, and no, I'm not flattering myself. I've been around enough men over the years to know when one is looking at me like a piece of meat—the way most men look at me.

Up until now, I never minded. Little affairs with different men every weekend was fun, and I felt more or less empowered by my choices.

More or less.

Okay, the excitement of catching a bloke's eye began to fade when I decided I'm worth more than a night of fun, but men haven't necessarily gotten the memo. Even in a larger town like Chester, where I work, a girl's reputation spreads fast.

Doesn't hurt that it also annoys my father. He and I haven't seen eye to eye in years, so my escapades with men are a way to get back at him. He wants me married off? I'll have only hookups. He won't let me take over the family business? I'll work in a job with no future potential.

My dad squashed my dream of owning our auto garage by saying he'd never let me take over, so I squashed his dream of a married daughter with grandkids.

Did I do it to spite myself?

Of course not.

It just worked out that way.

Now that I'm approaching thirty, I've committed to making changes. I am my own boss, as Weston said yesterday. He's right, even if he fancies my bum.

So what? I fancy his. Doesn't mean either one of us will do anything about it.

I may have spent a little extra time in the shower dreaming it was Weston soaping up my breasts, but that's only because it's smart to let one's fantasies play out in the imagination to prevent them from happening in real life. I swear I read a study about that. Or I made it up.

For now it's taken the edge off the budding prickles of lust I feel every time I notice Weston's pecs and abs through his shirt. Which is all the time. My temporary inner peace might get me through dinner, at least.

Looking in the mirror, however, I have a new problem. When I packed my suitcase, I didn't plan on having anyone see my sleepwear.

Why would I?

If Tim and I cross paths in the kitchen, he'll ignore me like he's done for most of our lives. We shared a bathroom during our childhood years, and with two preteen sisters, he learned to steer clear of us in the mornings. I think he brushed his teeth at the kitchen sink and combed his hair on the way to school.

But I don't know if it's proper to wear my normal pajamas around Weston, given that my normal pajamas consist of a pink threadbare—that is, worn thin but butter soft and comfy— flannel top and matching shorts.

Find something—anything—to sleep in that's not half-invisible.

Rifling through my bag, I realize I don't have anything else. I've packed cute outfits for going out in San Francisco, not frumpy sleepwear appropriate for Tim's hot friend. I don't find any alternatives to the shorts.

Sleeping in jeans would be weird. The best I can do is a pair of tight pleather leggings, and I think it might be stranger to walk around in front of Weston wearing those. I don't have any options other than Weston's sweatpants, but I've just gotten them wet dashing into the snow.

So I'll keep what I have on, and the first chance I get, I'll wrap my lower self in a blanket.

For good measure, and possibly as a last-ditch distraction, I search my bag for the longest pair of socks I can find. There's exactly one pair that meets the requirement, red knee-high wool socks rimmed in white fur to resemble a Santa hat. An impulse purchase over the holidays.

The socks match nothing, but I can't be concerned with that now. The point is that they're covering part of my legs that the shorts do not. After tying my damp hair in a knot on top of my head, I look like a deranged elf.

Using a towel rack for balance, I stand on the rim of the claw-foot tub and survey my reflection in the mirror above the sink. My outfit is nearly sheer and even tighter than I'd realized. I may have gained a few kilos in the past year. Probably because I may have added a case of Cadbury Flake once or twice to an Amazon Fresh order to meet the forty-pound delivery minimum.

It's ironic because I intentionally did not pack any cheeky lace knickers. Packing them would have been an acknowledgment that I intended for someone else to see them. Even accidentally on purpose.

Packing a set of bland flesh-colored knickers would all but guarantee that I keep my pants where they belong—on my person. Only now I wish I had something in my bag resembling a Christmas pajama set, emblazoned with reindeer or candy canes, to match my socks.

With no good options, I put June's parka on over the pajama top and zip it up to my neck.

"I think this tiny cabin has the best shower in the entire world," I tell Weston, who's busy at the kitchen sink. Two brown paper grocery bags sit on the island, but when I stand on tiptoe to peek inside, I find them already empty.

For now, I position myself behind them so only my head appears over the top and Weston can't see what I'm wearing. So far, so good.

"Best in the world? That's high praise." When he turns around, I notice he's removed the Strikers jacket he was wearing earlier and now has on an unbuttoned flannel over a very tight black tee.

Inner resolve. In. Jeopardy.

I don't spend much time looking at my brother's physique, but I watch plenty of footie, and I know what a player's build looks like—lean but muscular, killer quads, rock-hard abdominals, no body part wasted by merely existing. Every bit of a footballer is strong, sculpted, and beautiful.

Especially what I keep glimpsing of Weston.

His biceps stretch the fabric of the flannel, and his T-shirt hugs his chest and accentuates his abs, stacked up neatly so I can count them. I swallow the tiny gasp that emanates unbidden from my throat and hope he doesn't notice. Bloody hell, the man is chiseled like Michelangelo took a pass at him and gave up because he's already too perfect.

Evidently I'm gawking, because he follows my eyes and looks himself up and down. "I know, I'm still grimy and awful. I'll clean up, don't worry."

"Oh, you're perfect . . . I mean, you look good." *Jesus, stop already.* But I can't.

"I just mean you must be cold too. You should have jumped

in the shower." Blinking back mortification at the words, I feel my cheeks redden as I stammer and backpedal. "I mean, after me, of course. Not *with me*. You could have showered before worrying about dinner, is all."

Daring a glance at Weston, I see his expression bouncing between concern and a smirk.

I mentally manifest a mudslide that will sweep me out of this kitchen and back down to San Francisco, where I can just be an airhead tourist in a bar with people who don't have distracting abs.

This . . . sharing a small cabin with a hot, muscled footballer is not something I feel equipped to handle.

I feel myself overheating under the parka. Did it suddenly get super warm in here? As beads of sweat gather on my brow, I realize I can't keep this thing on in the house, so I unzip it and start fanning myself with my hands.

"You must be starving. Here. Eat."

He points to a different countertop, where he's assembled some snacks on a cheese board along with a couple of bottles of cold beer. Grabbing the paper bags in front of me, he begins folding them and clears more space on the countertop.

Then his eyes fall to my chest, where the fabric is very thin, and even if it weren't, the top button of the pajama top hits right at my breasts, leaving a healthy amount of cleavage on display.

What is *a healthy amount, really? A bare hint?*

Yeah, this is more than that. It's like an oil spill, only with breasts.

I'm tempted to grab the bags back from him and return them to the counter—or, better yet, put one over my head.

I'd zip up the parka, but I'm really sweating now. If anything, I want to throw it on the ground and throw myself into the snow.

But instead I twist my lips into a half-crazed grin like this is what normal people wear to bed and exhale, daring him to say a single word about what I'm wearing.

He doesn't. Or, at least, he can't. Not while his mouth is still hanging open. And he hasn't even seen the shorts, which feel a bit snugger than the last time I wore them. They're definitely hugging every curve. Like if my bum needed oxygen, it would die from suffocation.

It was ten below zero in this house all day. And now suddenly it's warm? The thought stirs up childhood memories of one belt-tightening winter when my mum was still alive and set upon getting us to wear anoraks in the house all the time.

She made it into a game, challenging us to see how many layers of clothing we could each fit under a heavy coat, offering bragging rights as the only prize. Nevertheless we bought in, piling on thin shirts and thicker sweaters until we could barely fit our arms through the sleeves of our coats.

My mum could make anything fun, even freezing your tits off in a house with no heat.

Speaking of which, my nipples are standing at attention and saluting Weston like he's their hired commander. Under the thin fabric of my top, there's no hiding their allegiance.

Some throat clearing occurs, and Weston briefly looks like he might be having an aneurysm, but he mostly succeeds at composing himself and picks up a beer. He slugs back a long drink, his eyes never leaving my body, then puts it down and wipes his forehead with the back of his hand. I think he's sweating.

He hands me the half-finished beer, then seems to realize it's the wrong one. His ears grow a bit pink before he hands me the other one and takes his back.

"Thanks."

"Sure."

I squat down behind the butcher block and pretend to be busy adjusting the height of my knee socks. They really ought to be the same exact height.

With the visual break from my cleavage spill, Weston seems to regain some control over his vocal cords.

"So, you should eat. Not sure if you like any of this, but it was the best I could do with what June had. Anyhow, enjoy. I'll go shower, and you can have the kitchen to yourself. I made some coleslaw for June—she said it's her favorite. I'm just going to drop it off to her." He's talking awfully fast.

Eye level with the counter, I stare at the spread before me. June's fresh sourdough, sliced and topped with cold, sliced chicken breasts and grainy mustard; tiny pickles in a bowl; pistachio nuts; sliced green apples; a chunk of hard salami; scattered saltine crackers; dried apricots; and a bowl of . . . canned corn.

It's pantry crap turned into something amazing.

"No," I urge, just as he starts to turn to leave the room. I stand up, walk out from behind the butcher block, and cross my arms over my chest, hoping to disguise the breast brigade. Unfortunately it has the effect of pushing my cleavage up to my chin.

"No?" He squints, using every available muscle in his face to force his eyes upward.

"This looks absolutely incredible. Truly. But I'm not eating this alone. I'll wait until after you shower. Would you mind if we turn down the heat just a bit?" I ask.

"Yeah, about that . . ."

He looks sheepish. This is where he tells me that he left it at subzero levels as a form of torture and now I'm his prisoner.

"I think it might be broken. It was turned up all the way all day, and you probably noticed how cold it was. So I built a fire."

He points toward the living room, where I now hear the crackle of burning logs.

"You built a fire?" I sputter, needing Weston to stop doing sweet things like laying out dry clothes for me and making food and building fires. He's cranking my libido to a thousand with each gesture, and I continue fanning myself, needing to dial down the heat.

That's when I happen to look up and notice that Weston has rigged up a tan wicker bread basket so that it covers the bare bulb hanging from the ceiling. That's why the light looks different in here, golden beams creeping between the woven slats, casting a warm glow over the kitchen.

I mean, are you fucking kidding me?

It's like he knows crafting is my love language, and now he's just messing with me. Nothing gets my attention like something beautiful made from something ordinary. And the basket light is beautiful.

Breast spillage temporarily forgotten, I point to the light. "This is absolutely charming. You could sell this on Etsy. You could sell this whole adorable fairy-tale cabin on Etsy. Are you for real?"

His sheepish smile does more to warm me than the ten-minute shower. "Glad you're not laughing at me for the bowl of corn."

"Well, you've got me there. I don't know what to make of the corn, but the rest . . ." I make a chef's kiss gesture. "I take back everything I said about you not being handy with tools."

"You didn't say anything about me not being handy with tools."

Oops, must have just thought it.

"No matter. This is what having a cabin in the woods is all about. Division of labor. You creating magic with canned goods and me handling your rogue pipe."

He presses his lips together as a smirk creeps across them. And again I feel my cheeks heat crimson.

Why does every damn thing out of my mouth sound like a sexual proposal? And a bad one at that. I exhale a long breath and look up at the ceiling. I pray he's not still looking at me when I meet his gaze, but he is. And the smirk looks only more permanent. And even hotter. "Go on, let's get you into the shower."

Still smirking. Still looking hot while doing so. Still taking a moment every few seconds to check out my legs.

"Just to be clear, am I showering alone?" he asks, his cocky, sexy smile settling in for a long winter season. Like a shadowless groundhog.

"Alone," I grind out, willing the thermostat on my face to turn down a few hundred degrees. "I'm still getting used to the way you Americans speak, is all."

"We speak English."

Smirk. Still. Alive. And. Well.

"And the jet lag."

"You slept for half the day, and you said you drank half a pot of coffee."

"You have an annoyingly good memory. What, do you have a bloody recording of everything I've said? That's illegal, you know."

"What's illegal? Remembering things?"

"Recording people without their permission."

"I haven't done that, so I think we're good."

I'm doing my best to glare, but his smirk has morphed into a full grin, and I'm defenseless. "I'm about to rescind my offer to wait to eat."

"You won't do that. You'll wait." He laughs, a low chuckle that I feel everywhere in my body, ending between my legs. Which I should ignore. Which I will ignore.

New Year's resolution. Must keep.

"I'll take a quick shower. Then we'll eat. Meantime, make yourself at home." He turns to go, and this time I'm the one checking out his ass.

Which I shouldn't do.

Which I do anyway.

This is how it begins with me and men. This is how it always begins.

CHAPTER 8
WESTON

As soon as I'm out of the kitchen and out of Linnie's line of sight, I slump against the wall. I'm sweating, salty rivulets running down my temple like it's halftime of a soccer match. In the desert. In August.

And that's with minimal heat in the place. One look at her tits and my body warmed up enough to power the furnace, if only physics worked that way.

She has got to be kidding me with that fucking outfit.

Maybe she meant it as a joke and she's in there wondering why I didn't get it. Maybe she thinks I lack a sense of humor *and* I'm incapable of using tools.

I pause in the living room and realize for the first time how goddamn tired I am. I barely slept last night after the longest day in the history of the world, beginning with the aggressive slide tackle, continuing with the chewing out by my coach, and ending with a three-hour errand into the wilderness. Now my defenses are low, and those pajamas aren't helping.

"Are you okay?" I hear the soft clip of Linnie's voice, and I'm overcome with the scent of lavender and what smells like freshly baked cookies. Same thing happened when she walked into the kitchen, but before I could process the confluence of senses, I got an eyeful of her barely there top, and all conversation ground to a halt.

But here it is again—the smell of sugar cookies. How is that possible?

For as good a job as Tim and Jordan did stocking the place with linens, they did not leave any candles, bodywash, or soap in the bathroom. I checked.

"Did you bake something while you were in the shower?" I ask before I realize how ridiculous it sounds. And accusing. Right after she asked if I'm okay.

"Did I—" She squints in confusion, and I realize that the non sequitur must be jarring.

"Sorry. Yes, I'm okay, except that I may have a brain tumor because I smell dessert."

She laughs. "No, it's my conditioner. I know, it smells like biscuits, doesn't it?"

"It smells like sugar cookies."

"Exactly. Do you hate it, then?"

"No. Not at all. I was just confused."

"Because you thought I was baking biscuits in the shower."

She's smirking at me. I deserve it.

"And because I called them biscuits, not cookies." She draws the word out with a decent attempt at an American accent.

I can't get a bead on her—stubborn, self-effacing, and funny. She's nothing like her brother, who's a beast on the soccer field and doesn't lighten up that often. The difference between them is throwing me off.

"Sorry. To me, a biscuit is a puck-shaped bun you dip in gravy."

"Sounds like something I'd like. Nothing bad about gravy," she says, her smile slipping across her face like the sunrise. "But I still prefer my version. It's sweeter."

"Okay for you, Biscuit," I say.

"Oh, now I'm the biscuit? Does that mean you want to eat me?"

She doesn't even get the words out of her mouth before her face is turning a new shade of crimson. The look of horror in her already-large eyes makes her look like a frightened cartoon. She throws her hands into her hair and grabs her temples between her palms. "No, I did not just say that. Please forget I said that."

"Forgotten," I promise. *So not forgotten.*

"I have a habit of letting ideas wander from my mouth before I've thought them through. Sorry."

"It's fine. You're Chelty's sister. Think of me like a brother. Family says stupid shit all the time to family, and no one worries about it."

I'm trying to convince myself as much as I'm convincing her, and from the way she's still pink cheeked, I don't think it's working.

Nodding, she backs away toward the kitchen before turning around and jogging out of sight. The last thing I see is her pert round ass and those damn knee socks. An image I won't forget anytime soon.

If ever.

When I get to the bathroom, I close the door and call Tim. If anything will kill the wood in my pants, it's talking to Linnie's brother. He answers on the first ring.

"Hey, everything okay, mate?"

"Just peachy." I'm not about to tell him his sister has me half-hard, but there is the matter of the deadbeat contractors and my chewing out by Coach Jaynes to discuss. Tim doesn't seem that upset about the contractors.

"It's always over budget and late. Haven't you heard that about construction?" he asks. I can picture him back in the city, having dinner with Jordan, who works for the Strikers as medical director. They fell hard and fast for each other last season and will probably be planning a wedding soon.

"Yeah, I've heard, but I didn't expect to come and find basically nothing done. I called to give him hell, and he blamed supply chain issues. Whatever."

"Yeah. Sorry. So it's going okay with my sister? She driving you nuts?"

"It's fine. She's fine. She's pretty funny, actually. And don't worry about the car. It doesn't look too bad."

"Wait, what's wrong with the car?"

"She didn't tell you? It's nothing. Minor fender bender in the driveway because of the ice on the road."

"Ugh, okay. I'll call her."

"Don't yell at her. It wasn't her fault. It's blizzarding, man. And she's not hurt."

"Glad you see it that way. Take care of her, okay? She's one of the good ones."

"Of course. Your family is my family." She's my best friend's sister, and he trusts me.

Hard-on officially gone.

CHAPTER 9

LINNIE

Well, that was fun. Nothing like a chewing out from my brother. "You weren't there. It was a moose," I said. My excuses did nothing to appease him. He insisted on scolding me for a full minute before saying he's glad I'm not hurt and he trusts me to get the car running if there's damage.

At least one person in the family thinks I know my way around an engine.

After I promise to "alert him to anymore mishaps," he says he's sorry about the blizzard and wishes me well.

That allows the tension in my stomach to unwind.

As if.

Weston-induced tension sends my heart rate rocketing into my throat before I down half my beer in an attempt at washing it away.

No use. I have got to get a grip on my runaway mouth. It's never been a problem before, mostly because I didn't mind if a suggestive comment here or there led a bloke to fancy me a bit more. But this cannot happen.

I've never had to work this hard to ignore temptation. The

first time is always the hardest—right? He's just a bloke. I'm making way too big a deal out of this.

Then I call my sister, who I know will answer the phone only because she'll think it's an emergency. It's nine at night here, so at five in the morning, I know exactly where she'll be— reading in bed. She's always been the early riser to my night owl.

It rings twice and she answers. "Morning."

"Am I waking you?" I'm not. I just want her to say it.

I hear her rustle around, pushing the laptop away and hunkering down in the sheets. I've seen her do it so many times I feel like I'm right there with her.

"No, been up for a bit already. You know how I am."

"I do." We were roommates until she moved in with her boyfriend, Harry, a year ago. They'll get married. They've been together for half a decade, so even when she and I were room- mates, I really lived with both of them.

I'm happy for them, even though it forced me to move back in with my dad. "If you were more like your siblings, you'd have some money saved," he tsked when I asked if I could sleep in the spare room by the kitchen. It wasn't my childhood room, but it was downstairs, while the rest of the bedrooms were up. I figured it would give me a little extra space and once in a while my father would forget I was there.

He never forgets.

"Don't know why you're so bad with money. Well, guess some people just aren't born with that kind of sense," he's fond of saying.

The truth is that while I've lived with him, I've been saving money so I can take business classes and work toward a degree. Part two of my self-improvement plan. The degree will lead to better career opportunities, which will allow me to get out from under the weight of the low expectations that have followed me for years.

My dad will always think of me as a disappointment, and I've come to accept that. It's just the way he is—never satisfied but somewhat loving nonetheless. Our mum died when we were little, and I barely remember her. I know my father did the best he could.

I hear Mary take a sip of her coffee and set it on the pink wooden chair she uses as a bedside table. It has a rabbit's face on the backrest and ears sticking up at the top. One of the childhood treasures she convinced Dad to buy for her—of the three sibs, Mary's the only one he could never say no to.

"How's California? How are Tim and Jordan? Did you send them my love?"

"Of course I did. And they're fine, I think."

I don't think twice about our conversation waking Harry, who could sleep through a cavalcade of horses passing by the bed. I fill her in on the water leak, my decision to drive to the cabin, and the unexpected presence of Weston. "I still swear it was a moose."

"It wasn't a moose." Mary draws her conclusions the way other people order food—she assesses the options on the menu and chooses the one she feels like, ready to be satisfied.

"You weren't there."

"Neither was the moose."

"The front end of Tim's car begs to differ."

She laughs. "Is he freaking out? I'm surprised he didn't drive up there to make sure you're not bumped and bruised. Protective, that one."

"I didn't tell him about the crash. And apparently he trusts his best friend to take care of me. Though not in the ways I would very much like."

"Ohhhhh." There are a thousand unspoken conversations

between sisters in that one, long syllable. She's had a front-row seat to all my escapades with men, and because she's been in a solid relationship for so long, she takes a special vicarious interest. She also knows most of my hookups were a way to get back at Dad, and she doesn't judge.

Even though she's two years younger than me, Mary has always been the sage sister, the better student, the one most likely to succeed. She runs the pub Harry owns, and no one has any illusions about who's really in charge. Mary barks out orders to the line cooks and the bartenders while balancing the books and ordering provisions. I've never quite understood what Harry does for the business, other than owning the place, but I never ask.

"Right. He's so my type."

"They're all your type, love. But you wanted to make a change, and you have important reasons for doing it. More important than Tim's hot friend."

Mary has been the biggest supporter of my resolution. "It's like being on a diet—ten days no men, eleven days no men—before you know it, you'll have a streak going and you'll have broken all your bad habits," she says. "You owe this to yourself. You've been living under the shadow of Dad's incorrect perception for too long."

"I know. You're right." In the next room, I hear the shower turn off. "I should go. Just wanted to share my struggle so you can picture me here, resolute." Joking aside, it will take more than a nudge from my sister or a proper set of abs to sway me in one direction or another. I will stay resolute because it's important to me.

"Okay, call me later. I'll be at the pub at noon and for the rest of the night."

"Harry works you too hard." I'm tempted to ask if he'll even be awake by noon, but I figure I'm not pointing out anything she doesn't already know.

While I wait for Weston, I pull up a playlist I listen to during the morning shift at the pub—upbeat music without a lot of distracting words, i.e., jazz.

As the saxophone belts from the tiny phone speaker, I open the cabinet and ice chest to survey the haul Weston acquired from June. I find a plethora of canned goods—more corn kernels, green beans, tuna, and several shapes of pasta. Popping corn and a box of pancake mix round out the selection.

The ice chest yields a slightly brighter supply of fresh foods —oranges to go with the apples, a red round of some type of cheese encased in wax, and a quart of cream I saw earlier with the coffee. I grab the cheese and examine it for an indication of its type, but there's no label, nothing etched into the red wax.

"She stocked us up for a week," Weston's voice rumbles behind me. I turn to find him in a different shirt, just as tight as the other one, only this one is long sleeved and gray. At least his forearms are hidden away for now. That helps.

"Does she know something we don't? Are we trapped here for the week?" I ask.

"Better not be. If they don't start clearing the road tomor-row, I'll go down there and shovel it myself. I need to be back for practice."

"Coach wouldn't understand acts of Mother Nature?"

"He doesn't even know I drove up here. He'd have my head if he heard I left town in the middle of the season." He mutters something that sounds like, "If I even still have a job."

Not sure I heard him correctly, I ask him to clarify. "Did you just say you might not have a job?"

He shrugs and scrubs a hand through his hair, something I'm coming to understand he does instead of using words.

"Why would you not have a job?"

"It's probably fine. He and I got into it the other day, and he made some threats." Weston grimaces, recalling it. "And considering soccer's the only thing I'm good at, it would really suck if I can't play."

I can't tell if he's overreacting to the situation. "I'm sure you're good at other things."

He huffs a laugh. "Not really. Soccer's it. And normally I don't let attitude problems get in the way."

"Does this have anything to do with why someone slide tackled you?"

He startles, and I watch his shoulders rise and his jaw tighten. Then he relaxes. "Something like that."

"I'm sure you had your reasons."

His eyes search my face, roaming from my eyes to my mouth and back again. "Why would you assume that?"

I shake my head. "You made coleslaw to take to your ninety-year-old neighbor in a blizzard. I don't think you get into battles without a reason. I don't need to know the reason. Just saying I'm sure you had one."

He stands motionless, like a deer caught in the sights of a crossbow. His dark eyes glint, and he nods ever so slightly. Then he swallows hard.

"We should eat in there." Weston picks up the platter and tips his head toward the living room. It's then I realize I'm still clutching the round of cheese to my chest like a prize.

Gesturing to the platter, I explain, "Thought I might add some cheese to your lovely selection. Not that it's lacking."

He nods. "Good idea. Make it more of a charcuterie plate."

I extend my palm. "In that case, I need to grab your sausage, slice it up." Good god. Again. I turn away so I don't have to look at his pretty face while I crumble from mortification.

"Why don't I take care of that. You work on the cheese."

We slice our respective snacks silently, and I contemplate stapling my lips shut.

When the platter is overflowing with meat and cheese, Weston grabs a saltine cracker, tops it with a dab of mustard, a slice of cheese, salami, and a pickle. He hands it to me and prepares a second one for himself.

I hold mine up. "I feel like we should toast—to surviving one more night here?"

"To surviving."

We "clink" crackers, and I crunch through half of mine, savoring the mix of pickle juice with the sharpness of the cheese. Weston downs his in one bite and waits for me to finish. I nod and swallow. "That's better than half the food we serve at the pub."

"I'll take that as high praise from a Brit." Weston picks up his half-finished beer from earlier and hands me mine. After the salty appetizer, the suds go down easily, bitter and still cold.

Weston carries the platter to the living room, where he puts it on the coffee table and goes over to poke the logs in the fireplace with a stick.

I snuggle down in front of the fire and wrap a blanket around my ridiculous pajamas. Not so I can ogle every taut muscle in his back.

But also that.

CHAPTER 10

WESTON

As the fire starts to wane, Linnie looks around the room top to bottom, side to side, and nods. "I can sleep out here on the couch." She points to the tan leather thing in the middle of the room. It's too big, shiny with leather that's been sat on a thousand too many times, and it gives off a vague scent of cowhide—not the good kind like a new suede jacket. The other kind, like the cow might not be fully dead.

Tim doesn't hate it as much as I do, but I'm wagering that Linnie will see eye to eye with me in a matter of minutes.

"I tried it last night, ended up on the floor," I tell her. "It's slippery, not really a fair fight."

I walk over and demonstrate. Coach puts us through brutal core-strength drills daily, yet it still takes an uncomfortable amount of ab and quad clenching to remain upright and keep myself from rocketing down the slick leather to the floor. Then I give in and demonstrate the slope, landing on my ass.

My knees hit the coffee table, and I find myself wedged between it and the couch.

"So where'd you sleep last night?" she asks, skipping over to the couch like it's an amusement park ride, sitting and promptly sliding down to the floor next to me. A bark of laughter peals out when her ass hits the ground.

"Slept right here." I shake my head. "Had to see for yourself. Didn't you believe me?"

"It's the way I'm built, I'm afraid. Didn't Tim warn you?"

She looks at me, but because we're next to each other, I can see only part of her face. A dimple in her cheek pops when she smiles.

"In my family, stubbornness isn't a personality trait—it's a survival skill."

"Why's that?" I ask.

Her eyes dart to mine, and I watch the color shift in hypnotic irises, the green deepening, blazing to life. She opens her mouth, then closes it again. I watch her blink as though she can push back whatever she's thinking.

Then she shrugs and says only, "You know how families can be."

I feel like I've failed a test. For a moment she seemed ready to tell me something, or at least dole out a tiny morsel. Now I'm getting a pat response.

"Not sure I do, honestly." It's the truth, not one I planned to tell her, but if she tells me something, maybe I'll return the favor.

"Sounds like you got one of the good ones, then."

Now it's my turn to shrug. If she only knew. My so-called family is barely a tangible memory.

"Anyway..."

We're both silent, the air thick with tension. I hate it, because Linnie is a talker and I feel like I've stifled it somehow. I don't know her well enough to understand what topics are off limits, but I want to know.

I put a hand on her shoulder, reassuringly. My body reacts to the warmth of her skin beneath my palm. The thin fabric of her pajama top does nothing to blunt the sensation of electricity tingling across my hand and up my arm.

She turns to face me more directly and exhales a deep sigh. "Weston, we're not going to hook up."

My hand is off her shoulder and back in my lap with the speed of a jackrabbit. "What? No, I wasn't making a move."

Her eyes go wide with embarrassment and shock. "Oh, of course not. I didn't mean to assume."

"I just felt bad about what I said, the family stuff." I move over about a foot to prove I'm not trying to mount her.

She puts her head in her hands and continues talking, her voice muffled by her cleavage. "I'm sorry. Ugh, this is mortifying. It's just . . . hookups haven't ended well for me in the past, so I've vowed not to do that anymore. I guess I had it on my mind and projected it onto you."

I so badly want to reach for her and tell her it's okay. But I know now what I'll feel when I touch her, and I can't do it again. I *want* to do it again.

We sit in silence, and I pile up a couple of blankets between us, building a wall of sorts. "Okay, look, if I'm honest, hooking up was not the furthest thing from my mind, so you're not completely wrong."

Taking her hands from her face, she looks at me with one eye only. "Really? You were thinking that?" She appears relieved, then horrified. "But we can't. I can't."

"Fine. No, we won't."

"Okay, great. I mean, not exactly great because it would be a nice way to pass the time, but it can't happen. I'm serious about getting my life together."

"I think that's great. And for what it's worth, you seem very together."

"Thank you."

She looks at me, but when I try to meet her gaze, she turns away.

"Linnie."

"Yes?"

I gesture to how she has her arms wrapped around herself protectively. "Relax. I'm not going to jump you. I actually can control myself."

"It's not you I worry about. It's a pattern with me, and I've been perfect all year, and now I'm stuck in this cabin and . . . ugh!"

Realizing I might live to regret it, I shove the blankets aside, venture my hand toward her, and rest it gently on her arm. She flinches but then relaxes and slowly brings her eyes to mine.

"Want to talk about it?" I ask. "I've got all night . . ."

Her petrified expression cracks, earning me a fractional smile. "Congratulations, Weston, on the cheesiest pickup line I've ever heard."

"Pretty good, right?" I can't avoid grinning at her.

She nods. After a silent beat, she exhales and begins telling me about her dad, his low expectations of her, and, hence, her low expectations of herself.

"I s'pose I went about with men to spite him, embarrass him if he heard stories. Prove he didn't control me. But I ended up losing respect for myself and losing track of my goals. And now . . . I want that back."

Mostly I just listen, watching the stress leave her body as she unburdens herself, and I wonder what it would feel like to do that. I've never tried. My secrets stay locked firmly inside.

"Wow," I tell her when she finishes. "I'm impressed, Linnie. Good on you for taking charge of what you want."

"You don't have to try to make me feel better about it all. Really."

"I'm not."

Her brows rise, and a tiny fire ignites in her eyes. "Really? So you're not thinking you're here with some slutty, mule-headed, directionless basket case?"

"Um, no. Hardly. But you're going to need to unpack that now that you threw all those adjectives my way. What gives?"

She sinks a little lower. "Nothing. It's an expression. Is that not a thing in America?"

"Nice try." Chuckling, I give her my best big brother smile, gentle and helpful—at least that's how I hope it looks.

Sitting side by side on the worn gray area rug, our knees are almost touching. I should move away, give her some space, but I don't. I catch her looking down at the small space between us, noticing the proximity. She doesn't move away either.

Progress.

She takes a small sip of her beer, which makes me realize she's really nursing the thing. "That has to taste like piss water at this point. Here," I say, extending my hand for the warm beer. "I'll grab you a fresh one."

She smiles as she hands it to me, but the smile doesn't reach her eyes. She seems distracted. Kneeling in front of her, I peer down. "You okay?"

Shaking herself out of her reverie, she stretches her legs in front of her and toes the blanket away from her feet. Once she's free of the material, her knees come to her chest, and she encircles them protectively with her arms. She won't look at me.

The happy, relaxed expression I saw earlier is replaced by something more complicated, something I can't decipher. Knowing she has a dimple makes me want to do or say something to get it back. I also want to know what caused her to shut down.

"Yes. Good. Great."

Her smile is fake, her body stiff like a cord of wood.

Something about the fact that she tries so hard to be tough

and self-sufficient makes me want to know what lies underneath the capable exterior. Is she as breakable as an overbaked
cookie?

Are you?

"Linnie?"

"Yes?"

"Why won't you look at me?"

"I-I don't think there's a reason. I just didn't want to freak
you out with eye contact."

She widens her eyes and looks at me obviously, removing
emotion and turning it into a staring contest. Now that the
vulnerability is gone, I lean back in defeat.

Bringing my thumb and finger to her chin, I gently turn her
face so I can see it. I'm aware of a slight tremble in her jaw.
Whether it's emotion or her reaction to my touch, I can't be
sure. But I'm dying to know.

I'm also aware that I've ruined any chance of her telling me
more by demanding it. So I shrug and pull my hand away.

She shudders slightly when I do.

"And if you have anything else you want to tell me . . ." I
point to my head and make a circle with my finger. "Cone of
silence. What's said in the mountains stays in the mountains."

She considers the proposal, and eventually her forehead
creases.

"Fine," she says. "If we're being honest, you might as well
know one more thing about me. I can't cook."

LINNIE

Weston is freaking me out with eye contact.

"What do you mean, you can't cook? You were quick with a knife slicing up cheese earlier. And you're from the countryside."

I wave a hand dismissively. "I serve meat pies and snacks at the pub, but I don't cook them. And the cheese—who doesn't know how to slice cheese?"

"You did it well."

"I love cheese. And I'm not an animal—hardly going to nibble from the block. It requires slicing."

"Fair enough." He looks me over as though I might still be lying about the cooking. I really ought to paint a better picture of the town where I grew up. He seems to picture a storybook place where the women are milkmaids who seduce cows into producing beautiful cream that we churn into perfect butter. Right before we run through the pastures in flowered dresses to pick the ripest ingredients from perfect rows of garden vegetables and have a new farm-to-table masterpiece ready by the time the men return from the factory.

Fairy tales.

"I grew up in a working-class town. Family business is auto repair, not farming. I can fix an engine, but if you ask me to do more than boil a potato, I'm afraid I can't help."

"Great." He looks downright jolly about my description of my lowly cooking talents, and I'm not sure he's heard me correctly.

"Great?"

"Yes. I love to cook."

"Where'd that come from? Did someone teach you?" I'm not trying to pry, but it's an opening if he feels like jumping in.

He shakes his head. "Nah, mostly self-taught, trial and error. I have a channel."

"What kind of channel?" I'm picturing a body of water.

"YouTube." He dials it up on his phone, and there he is, wearing a faded chambray apron, talking to the camera about mushrooms. His hair is slicked back, sleeves pushed up to reveal some top-notch forearm porn, and he's smiling more than I've seen since I got here.

"I can tell you a hundred stupid facts about mycelium, but I can't hang a picture straight to save my life," he quips, holding up a handful of weird-looking mushrooms and gesturing to an empty wall that is, in fact, devoid of art.

It would be adorable if it wasn't insanely hot. He stands there, pecs and forearms flexing as he chops onions, a close-up on his hands sprinkling parmesan cheese in a way that makes it feel like he's dusting it over my naked body. I sit there, holding his phone in my hands, fully aware that I'm salivating. And not over the food.

Then I notice the name of his series: *Balling Out in the Kitchen*.

"Okay, I'm speechless, Weston. This is awesome."

He tries to take the phone back, but I shove his hand away, aware that I'm touching the same hand I see in the video pinching a sprig of Italian parsley and popping it into his mouth. I've never felt jealous of parsley before, but that damn green sprig has something I want. "By the way, that's something."

"What?"

"Something you're good at besides soccer. You need to start seeing yourself better."

He slowly reaches for the phone, but I hold it behind my back. His expression is a mix of disbelief and wonderment.

"What?" I ask.

He studies me for a moment as though I confuse him. Then he shakes his head and lets me continue with the videos.

After watching him pit olives, grind pepper, and whip up a tapenade in a blender, I let out an audible sigh. I return his phone, secure in the knowledge that I will be watching these videos on my own for a very long time.

When I meet his gaze, he looks apprehensive. "What?"

I shake my head. Is he really that clueless about the effect these videos must have on the female population? "Do you have a big following?"

He shrugs. "Few million."

"Oh, just a few million," I deadpan. "How many are women?" I mumble to myself, but when I look up, the smirk is back.

"Anyhow, I cook. I'm into it. I'm such a nerd about it that I drop by a women's shelter once a week and make a big dinner for them just so I have the chance to use giant pots. So you don't need to worry. And our odd array of ingredients makes it more of a challenge. It's like *Chopped*, where the chefs are given random ingredients and they have to make a dish using everything."

I must be looking at him blankly, because he continues explaining, making knife motions with his hand as though it makes his story any clearer. "You haven't seen *Chopped*? They must have a version in England."

I'm still stuck on him cooking for a women's shelter so he can use big pots. Mind. Officially. Blown.

"I don't watch much TV. Other than *The Queen's Gambit*, but that was a one-off. Mostly I crochet animals and donate them to the children's hospital or I read." I know my quiet hobbies make me sound like I haven't joined the twenty-first century, but so be it.

Weston stares like I've grown a second or possibly third head. "Well, that's super cool."

"Cool that I'm culturally illiterate?"

"Cool that you donate your time and that you read. No wonder you're so smart."

The unintentional laugh that barks out is louder than expected. "I'm not smart. I just . . . read."

"Um, yeah. You're smart. Are you fishing for compliments?" He crosses his arms, watching me, and I get the impression from his stern expression that fishing for compliments is a no-no in his world.

"Hardly. Let's drop it, okay?"

His gaze stays fixed on me as though I have a magic trick up my sleeve and he doesn't want to miss it. When no rabbits or colored scarves appear, he nods slowly. "Okay."

So glad he agrees. It frees me to blurt out the exact thing I hadn't planned to tell him. "I'm not educated, just so you know," I admit, looking away. Oh well, he might as well know it about me. It's not like I can hide it for long. Once people start talking about universities, the conversation inevitably comes around to where I went to school, and I'm forced to be honest.

I don't know why.

I could lie—it's not like anyone in America is going to run a background check on me. Most people haven't heard of the unis in England, and even if they have, they don't understand the school system. It would be so easy to say I went to any number of small schools, and no one would be the wiser. I could even say I went to Cambridge or make up my own bloody university, and someone like Weston would nod and be suitably impressed.

But I can't pretend to be someone I'm not. Never could.

When I dare a glance back at Weston, he's studying me, head tilted to the side. "Why would you say that about yourself?"

"Just being honest."

"But it's not true."

He can't know this about me. He doesn't know me at all. I feel my frustration mount. He's not the first bloke to come along and tell me what he thinks I want to hear. Men will say anything, I've discovered. Especially if it leads to getting into my knickers. They'll flatter, they'll outright contort the truth.

Sweet talk is a balm to my ears, terms of endearment the butter to my bun.

It doesn't take a degree to understand I'm probably looking for affirmation and tenderness that I never got from my father. At least that's what Mary and I have concluded. Still, it doesn't mean I have to continue the trend.

"It is true. I never finished uni. Barely got through second year. Never got a degree."

"Okay," he says, studying me. I don't know what he's waiting for. There's no part two to this story. His eyes bear down, more curious than judgmental. He shakes his head slowly. Disappointed. Why wouldn't he be? He probably thought he'd be able to go toe to toe about dead philosophers or compound fractions or whatever the hell they teach at uni. I never bothered to ask Tim what he was learning there. There was no point in knowing what I was missing when my father said it wasn't worth his money for me to get a degree.

"Yeah, okay," I conclude, standing and pulling the blanket around me as though it might do me a solid and swallow me whole. He and I come from different worlds, obviously. He's American, and I know most of the players who come up through the soccer programs in the States play for important colleges before going pro. Tim explained it to me when he moved abroad. "So . . . I'll see you in the morning."

I move as far away as I can, but this cabin is so damn small. Crawling into the one armchair in the corner, I sweep a blue plaid blanket off the floor and cover myself with it, tucking my head underneath. I hear Weston's heavy feet coming closer, and he lifts the blanket off.

"What are you doing?" he asks.

"You said the couch won't work, so I'll sleep here." I reach for the blanket to pull it over myself, but he holds on to it. My cheeks are hot with embarrassment, and he doesn't need to see more of that.

But then . . . he drops the blanket, places his hands on my shoulders, and gently leans toward me. Warm hands. I feel them through the thin material of my top, and their searing heat radiates everywhere else in my body.

Of course it does.

His eyes are soft with concern, and I promptly look away. I don't need his concern. I don't want it. "What just happened?" he asks, his voice deep and calm, like an ocean wave.

"Nothing."

"Not nothing." His hands rest on my shoulders for another moment before he drops them by his sides. The skin under my shirt immediately goes so icy cold that I nearly grab his hands and put them back where they were.

"It's fine," I say.

"It's not."

"I figured we were done with the conversation." Might as well look him in the eye now, or he'll never decide that I'm okay and leave me alone.

He slides his hands down my arms until they reach my hands. Pulling me from the chair, he leads me back to the pile of blankets in front of the fireplace. "Come on. Let's start over."

I pull a blanket protectively around me and look at Weston from under my lashes, suspicious. None of this feels comfortable, and I wish he'd let me hide so I don't have to look at him.

For a while, neither of us says anything, which is fine with me. I feel like I've already overshared, and I don't want his hollow sympathy.

"Linnie." His voice is a deep rumble that both comforts me and sends a delicious chill down my spine. How does he make my name sound like pure sex?

"Yes."

"I don't know who got in your head, but it didn't take me more than an hour to see that you're incredibly smart. That's not up for debate. It's fact. So the rest of that garbage . . . get it out of your head."

His words vibrate within me, and something shakes loose— maybe it's a lifetime of feeling *less than*, or maybe it's a voice I've been desperate to drown out. But hearing him say the words somehow gives me the permission I never gave myself. And it's freeing.

He leans a little closer and I suck in a breath. His lips are inches from mine, and I feel my defenses crumble. If he kisses me, I won't be able to push him away.

"And let's get one other thing straight." He's practically whispering, which makes me lean in so I don't miss a word. My whole body thrums, and I feel every syllable shoot through me like a comet, ending between my thighs. "No way in hell I'm letting you sleep in this chair."

He backs slowly away, and I feel a small void in my chest, which grows bigger along with the space between us.

I nod, aware of the creep of feelings I don't want to have toward him. But I can't stop them either.

CHAPTER 12
LINNIE

I'd say I'm mad at Weston for having me sleep in the bed again, except that for the second evening in a row, I had an exceptional night of sleep. It makes me feel both guilty and grateful.

It also makes my eyes hurt, because this is the second night in a row I've slept in my contact lenses, and I have to get them out before I do some real damage. I'm supposed to take them out at night, but I've fallen asleep unintentionally.

Looking at myself in the bathroom mirror—or rather, looking at my blurry self once I take out my lenses—I try to get a grip on the situation.

The facts as I know them: I cannot get away from this cabin —or Weston—anytime soon, not if it continues to snow. I also can't let the runaway feelings that clouded my dreams last night make me conjure something between us that isn't there. I cannot mistake kindness for intimacy. I cannot sleep with Weston.

It would only prove that my father is right about me. Right in his early assessment that my value is tied to men—tied to their interest that might lead to a wedding proposal, so I'll no longer be a burden.

My dad wasn't always this way, at least I'm fairly certain. Before our mum passed, we were a family. My earliest childhood memories are of all of us bouncing along in the boot of my father's truck, going to pick up parts for the auto shop. I loved the smell of motor oil and grease because it felt familiar, and to me, it signified hard work.

I cherished the weekends, when we were off from school and I could go to the garage with my father and watch him work. He'd give me small jobs—twisting a wrench to tighten bolts, degreasing parts in an old metal tub, shining the chrome on his customer's cars.

"We're not in the business of car washing," he'd remind me with a wagging finger, "but I want any car that rolls out of Cheltenham Auto to be polished to a shine worthy of the Queen Mum."

I dreamed of the day I'd get more responsibilities, carefully cataloging how my father made repairs, what body parts could be pounded out and salvaged, and how to recognize something that wasn't worth the time or energy to fix. By age nine, I decided to follow in his footsteps and take over the family business.

When I told him, he smiled but didn't say anything. Didn't tell me he felt flattered. Didn't express excitement. Didn't tell me no, either, so my nine-year-old mind took it as a yes. I took his smile as encouragement.

He and my mum loved each other; there was never any question about that. They talked about leaving Saltney when the three of us were grown and traveling the country by car, staying wherever they could afford, handing off the family business to Tim or to one of our husbands.

Back then I never paid much attention to the sexist nature of his assumption. I didn't know any women who ran auto garages, but that wouldn't stop me. He was from an older generation, and maybe he assumed that Mary and I would want to be like our mum, that we'd want to marry, have kids of our own, and let our husbands take over the business.

When our mum passed away, something shifted in my father—something beyond grief and anxiety over raising three young kids by himself. He folded into himself and made the garage his main home instead of his second home.

He still talked about seeing the country someday, but he'd do it alone once the garage was in capable hands.

Of the three of us, I was still the natural choice, I reasoned. In fact, I felt unbelievably happy that neither of my siblings was putting a hand up for the job. I'd be a shoo-in.

Mary had no interest in cars, never did. Her business mind could handle that end of things, but she hated the smell of the grease, the grime that covered my father and me at the end of a shift, and the sound of a rattling engine or a whining belt.

And even though my father set his sights on Tim as his potential protégé, everyone could see that football would be his future. When he made the Manchester City academy team, the only one who didn't salute him in the street for his accomplishment was our own father. He viewed soccer as a game, not a sport. He thought Tim was throwing his life away to act like an overgrown lad.

For the first year or so after my mum passed, I still worked every weekend at the garage, same as usual. Eventually I noticed a few bottles of liquor in a cabinet behind one of the rolling tool chests. I'd also gotten a whopping smack on my bum when my father showed up and saw me taking stock of the bottles. "Mind your own business," he said.

But I couldn't. I worried about him. He seemed sad, and when he drank, he got sadder.

So I started sneaking peeks into the cabinet when my father was busy to monitor how much of the brown liquor was left the bottles. It helped me gauge how sad—and sometimes how mean—he'd be when he came home. Then I'd warn Mary and Tim.

Only I got caught. My father wasn't one for a warning or three strikes. He'd told me to mind my business, and I hadn't. I was never invited to work at the garage again.

Even then I still figured that when I was old enough and knew enough, I could relieve my father of bending over truck engines and sliding under car chassis. I could give him the future he'd dreamed of—he could travel and I'd run the business.

His words on the day I proposed it will stay with me for the rest of my life. "You'll bring the place down in ruin."

I remember standing in front of him, tears pricking the corners of my eyes, my brain trying to come up with variations on the meaning of his words.

"On the contrary, I want to keep it running."

"You get engaged? That what you're telling me?" For the first time, I saw a glimmer of hope in his drooping gray eyes. The folds of skin surrounding the creases pulled back enough for me to see a tiny shred of pride.

Not in me.

In my perceived ability to snag a man to take over the business.

"No. I'm not engaged."

I was twenty, halfway through uni and willing to quit straightaway so I could begin working. Mary had decided not to attend uni at all because her boyfriend wanted her to run his family's pub. Dad seemed proud of that. I couldn't understand why he wasn't equally proud of me for wanting to work.

But he wasn't.

That day he told me exactly how he saw me—useful only if I could use my feminine wiles to land a husband to properly take over the garage. Otherwise I was useless.

CHAPTER 13
LINNIE

I'm about to put on my glasses when I catch another glimpse of my blurry self. She appears relaxed, I think. A contented-looking face stares back at me, seeming as if it were washed over by a Photoshop filter.

Wouldn't it be nice if the whole world saw me this way, edges blunted by softness and curves, stubborn opinions made a little less jarring by blurring sounds with the background? Or maybe, more importantly, I could see myself this way, cut myself some slack, lend myself a bit of grace.

"No. Not until you've done something to deserve it," my father's voice echoes in the recesses of my mind.

I know he's right. And it's a reminder to stop letting every tiny brush of Weston's hand against mine set fire to my nerves and make me want something that shouldn't happen. Can't happen.

It would also be useful to ignore the very sight of him, the intensity in his eyes that seems to thaw a few degrees when he looks at me. Something tells me he needs that eye contact, needs someone to warm up the world as he sees it and make it more palatable.

There's hurt or betrayal or disillusionment beneath his detached exterior, and he probably thinks it sits protected behind his stoic shield. Hidden behind the chiseled, gorgeous exterior most people fixate on. Of course he encourages that shallow view—a sleight of hand that distracts from what's really happening in plain sight.

People don't pay attention to what they can't see.

I know this as fiercely as I know myself, but I can't do anything to help him. Not without giving myself over to him, filling in his gaps the only way I know how.

It would be so easy to seduce him. Wrap him up in sex and lust and distraction. One more night with one more man. Maple syrup on a stack of pancakes, dusted with powdered sugar. One more delicious treat before the diet.

But I can't do it.

I know I can't, and the blurry version of myself staring back agrees. At least I think she does. It's hard to tell much of anything when I'm this nearsighted. I have to lean in close to allow my features to come into focus, which results in nearly banging my head on the mirror.

I retreat to a safe distance and embrace the blur, which gives me an idea.

Maybe I won't find Weston so distracting if I can't see every damn ripple of his abs through his shirt. Maybe if he's blurry, I can engage him in idle conversation and get through another day of cabin fever without helping myself to a taste of his skin.

I twist the contact lens case closed and leave my glasses on the bathroom sink. And since I can barely see myself, I decide that I look okay with my hair twisted up in a bun on top of my head and no makeup. It feels like a relief not to scrutinize my appearance too carefully. Maybe I'll ditch my contact lenses permanently.

I find a pair of jeans in my suitcase and pull them on with a

T-shirt. Weston's hoodie is the closest warm thing I find, so I pop that on over my shirt, liking that it covers half of me like a blanket.

Then I trip over my shoes and stumble into the living room, striped with daylight edging between the slats of the window blinds as if the morning is insisting I notice. I tiptoe to the window and peek outside to find that everything is covered in white. I can see the large form of Tim's car up the hill, entirely blanketed in snow.

I can't even identify where the driveway is in relation to the snowbanks around it. Maybe it's because I don't have the benefit of good eyesight, but I fear that a night's worth of snowfall may cause a day's worth of new problems.

I'm still creeping around the room like a bandit under the assumption that Weston is still asleep. A pile of blankets sits on the floor, and I don't see him on the couch or anywhere around the cabin. Padding around and checking nooks and corners, I conclude that he's not here.

Maybe he's at June's house having a nice cuppa and coming up with a plan to get us down the mountain. Going with that bright, shiny thought, I turn my attention to the kitchen, where I'm drawn to the french press like a moth to the one incandescent bulb in a dark house.

Still hot, it's half-full of rich, dark coffee.

Bumping my way around the kitchen and gouging my hip on the butcher-block island, I search for a mug, bumping my nose on the cupboard handle. I settle for the first blurry ceramic-looking thing I find, which turns out to be a cereal bowl. Filling it to the brim with coffee, I take a life-giving sip and decide to repay Weston's kindness by cooking him breakfast.

I open the ice chest and muck around like Mr. Magoo trying to identify something I can prepare easily.

Beans on toast? Blood sausage? I don't see any of those things.

Bread and jam at a bare minimum would go nicely with the coffee, even if serving it isn't technically cooking. We still have June's sourdough, but there's nothing resembling jam in the cupboards.

Think, Linnie.

I find a carton of eggs. Americans like eggs for breakfast. And with new determination, I set about fixing us some eggs, making a point of pushing all thoughts from my mind about that one day at the pub . . . eggs on the floor, burned eggs that no one could scrape from the pan even with a wire-backed sponge.

That was one time.

When I bend into the ice chest to search for butter, I clock my forehead on one of the drawer handles. Weston isn't even here, so I consider putting in my contact lenses, but for now I persist, gathering supplies—the carton of eggs, a stick of butter, the same cream that went into my coffee. I grab a cast-iron skillet and put that on one of the stove burners.

I've watched the cook at the pub make soft-boiled eggs many times. I wonder if Weston would like those. Scrambling them seems slightly more difficult because I need to get the temperature just right and manage not to burn the butter, but at twenty-eight years old, I think I can manage.

Selecting another bowl like the one that contains my coffee, I crack the eggs carefully into it, bending close to inspect that I haven't dropped any bit of eggshell.

I add the cream, beat the eggs, and turn on the stove.

Nothing happens. No flame, no indication the stove and I are on the same page about breakfast.

Growing up, we had a stove that was probably even older than this one. Sometimes, on a windy day, the pilot would go out, and I remember my dad relighting it. He kept long matches in a kitchen drawer just for that purpose.

Maybe last night's storm knocked out the pilot. Logic would imply that I should turn the gas on and light the burner. Easy enough. I turn the knob and light a match. But a sudden draft in the kitchen extinguishes the flame before I can get close to the stove. I light a second one, but it goes out as well.

Determined to get the job done, I don't stop to wonder why it's suddenly so drafty. I don't focus on noises in the next room. I just light another match, cupping the flame. Then Weston's panicked voice rings out from behind me.

"Linnie!"

Even without my contact lenses, his eyes are big enough to see from across the room.

CHAPTER 14
WESTON

My eyes sting from the icy crystals that have pelted me for an hour as I jogged through ankle-deep snow in wet running shoes, but the unmistakable smell hits me the moment I open the door to the cabin—gas.

Barely able to focus through melting ice, I see Linnie standing in the kitchen with a lit match, and all I can think of is how she's a millisecond from blowing the place up.

Turning toward my voice, Linnie freezes, a tiny fire burning in her fingers.

"Blow it out!" I command one second before she feels the heat singe her skin. She waves the matchstick, and the flame turns to an upward trail of smoke.

"Way to frighten a person." She says it with her usual sass, like I'm the trespasser here and she isn't standing in a room filled with a flammable substance. Her eyes trace over my frame, and I ready myself for a comment, given that I'm wearing most of the clothing I found in my workout bag, none of which matches.

Instead she lashes me with nothing but an adorable grin and nods. "Ooh. It worked."

"What worked?"

"Sorry?"

"You said it worked. What worked?"

"Oh, nothing. Never mind." Her dismissal does nothing to diminish the exuberance in her jack-o'-lantern smile. I glance around the kitchen for evidence of a liquor bottle, wondering if she's taken a morning nip.

But no. Just her brandishing a matchbox in a kitchen that reeks of gas. Must be why she keeps blinking every time she looks at me.

"What are you doing?"

"Making you breakfast."

"Making—" The words combust in my throat because there are too many, all of them at war with each other. Very sweet, a little silly . . . "But it's two—" I fumble as though the early afternoon hour is important. "Don't you smell—" As though the health of her nasal passages is the chief issue here. "Linnie," I say, finally. "It smells like gas. And you were holding a match."

"Yes," she says.

"Yes?"

She nods. "I needed to light the stove. The pilot's out."

Shaking my head, I move closer and snatch the matchbox from her hand. Then I go to the stove, turn off the unlit burner, and wedge open the kitchen window. An icy breeze bites my cheeks just as they were starting to warm. "There's too much gas in the room. It would have blown your hand off with that tiny match."

"Oh." She stares in my general direction, and I try to snag her eyes to confirm that she's okay. But she looks around the room, seeming to get her bearings with me in her space. "Gosh, I'm sorry. Where did you go?"

I'd assume it's obvious from my workout clothes, hot cheeks, and snow frosting my hair, but I answer anyhow. "Out for a run." I gesture to my clothing as though it will explain something, but of the two of us, she looks more like a member of the Strikers in my oversize hoodie. In my mismatched collection of gear, and with socks on my hands, I look more like a homeless snowman.

"Linnie."

"Yes?"

"What were you planning to cook?" I look around at the smattering of ingredients she has on the counter and guess she was making eggs.

Her face falls. "Oh, well, I can't really cook, remember?" Her look of defeat untethers a piece of my heart. "You'd best consider yourself lucky that you caught me when you did. Before I poisoned you with burned eggs."

"Hardly sounds lethal."

She shakes her head and looks at the ceiling, letting out a long sigh. "You'd be surprised. I tried once at the pub. We were down a cook, and I offered to step in for the day. I've been around kitchens for years, and I've observed."

"That's how you learn."

"Not me, it seems. I started out okay, putting butter in the sauté pans . . ." She trails off as if recalling her days in a war. "But then the pub got busy at lunch, and everyone was yelling orders. I burned the food to the pans, caused a grease fire, and dropped a whole tray of sausage rolls on the floor."

She blinks back the memory along with tears she refuses to unleash.

"It's a lot to expect someone who's never cooked before to handle a lunch rush, don't you think?"

I watch the lines disappear from her forehead like a warm wind clearing the last storm clouds from the sky. "I do think." Her lips quirk into a small smile, which feels like a fucking gold medal. "I tend to set high standards for myself."

"Yeah, I'd say."

She nods. "Some people are better at cooking. Some better at eating. I'm the latter." On her way to the area where she left the beaten eggs, she extends a hand out against the counter, almost like she's using it for balance.

"Linnie?"

"Yeah?" She turns around, but she's facing the table, and I'm just to the right of it. Something's off. I just can't tell what it is. My eyes still hurt from being blasted with snowflakes for an hour. I should have worn a hat or waited for the storm to lighten, but I woke up antsy and distracted by thoughts of how close I came to kissing Linnie last night—how much I wanted her, despite all her rules, which I'm trying to respect.

An hour of running barely took the edge off.

Maybe we're both out of sorts. Getting stranded in the mountains would test the patience of anyone.

"You feeling okay?" I ask, peeling off the outer layer of the several I'm wearing. The Gore-Tex is dry, despite getting pelted with fat snowflakes.

"Yes. Still a bit knackered, I guess, from the travel." She's still not looking directly at me.

Once we've aired out the kitchen, I find a box of long matches and attempt to light the stove. The burner catches, and I step out of her way.

Linnie gives her bowl of eggs a stir with a knife, then cuts a square chunk of mozzarella cheese. She flips it into the pan, and I watch it melt and eventually congeal to the cast-iron surface. Maybe that's how they make eggs in England.

She tries to give the piece of cheese a stir with the knife, and when it doesn't budge, she pokes it harder, her expression clouding. "Is this butter frozen or something?" she mutters.

"That's cheese."

"Sorry?" She continues poking, and the cheese continues cementing itself to the pan with an insistent sizzle.

I point to the pan. "It's not butter. It's mozzarella cheese."

She face-palms her hand. "Oh, drat." Without skipping a beat, she takes the pan off the heat and begins digging at the cheese with the knife. "You see, this is why I warned you against my cooking. Cheese instead of butter." She rolls her eyes, then leans down to inspect the lump of cheese stubbornly resisting her attempts to remove it.

"Linnie." My attempt at calm only inflames her frustration. She wheels around to face me, blinking rapidly, her lips set in a line.

"It's okay," I urge her to believe.

Her features soften at my words, but she doesn't answer. Leaving the knife on the counter, she walks from the room, giving me a few minutes to scrub the cheese off the pan.

When she comes back, she's wearing a pair of horn-rimmed glasses that make her look like a sexy-as-fuck librarian.

I'm busy trying to fight off a hard-on when she takes the clean pan from me, her fingers grazing mine. Dissolving my focus into filaments.

"Thank you for doing that. Start over, then?" I meet her gaze, looking for some reassurance that mistaking cheese for butter hasn't upset her.

The familiar fire has returned to her eyes, every bit as dangerous as I remembered. Having her gaze on me warms me so thoroughly that I tear off my three layers of outerwear, down to my long-sleeved tee.

"Sure. Need a sous chef?"

"I need you to make the eggs. And I need to watch."

Taking her phone from her pocket, she sets about queuing up some blues music and leans on the island opposite the stove. Decision made. She's not cooking.

I don't argue with her. Eggs are easy, and it takes only a few extra minutes to add sautéed mushrooms and onions.

I toss a dollop of butter in the pan, whisk in the eggs, and liberally salt and pepper them. When I suggest she slice up the mozzarella, she gives me a side-eye. "Slicing cheese isn't cooking, I'm told." I refuse to let her cooking mistake become a pivotal crossroads in her life—Before Cheese and After Cheese. No life-changing takeaways.

"Fine," she says, brandishing the knife in a way that makes me want to protect myself. Her slices are deliberate, as though she's being graded. Every few slices she looks over her shoulder, lashes brushing the tops of her cheeks like she doesn't want to meet criticism head-on.

"I get the feeling someone has made you feel inadequate in the kitchen."

The laugh escapes her before she covers it with a cough. "Families can be tough. Like we said." I watch and wait to see if she'll say more, but her lips stay pressed together like she doesn't trust them not to spill secrets.

We lay a few pieces of cheese on the bread before grilling it in the egg pan. "It took a fair bit of resistance on my part to not just eat the cheese," she admits.

"The sous chef is always allowed to snack on the ingredients, at least in my kitchen."

The smile I get this time is genuine, and I tuck it away. A carnival prize won after a thousand errant beanbag tosses.

Five minutes later we have ourselves an egg breakfast. Simple, buttery, good. Linnie digs in with gusto, slicing a piece of toast and loading a forkful of eggs on top. "This is amazing," she says through a bite, and I feel a twinge of pride even though it's just eggs.

"It's the little things, right?"

She nods. "It's everything."

Watching her delight in eating a simple plate of scrambled eggs, I have to agree. It's everything.

And I am so very fucked.

An hour later we've cleaned up the kitchen and come to terms with having to spend another night at the cabin. "June thinks they'll start clearing the roads as soon as the storm abates, and the weather service is predicting a letup by tomorrow." I yell to Linnie in the bedroom, even though the entire cabin is within normal talking distance.

"So we could be out then?" she yells back.

"Possibly," I grunt from the floor, where I'm in the middle of a set of crunches, followed by a set of push-ups. It may seem like overkill, but even missing a day of training is crucial during the season, so I need to keep active.

My abs are already on fire before I flip over and begin counting down push-ups from a hundred.

"You are absolutely mad," Linnie says from about two feet from my head. "Do you never sit still?"

"Not during the season," I huff out, trying not to lose count.

"Well, thank you for not trying to get my wobbly bits down on the ground doing fitness activities." I see her feet move from in front of me to the side. That's when I notice she's wearing her shoes.

"I'd never subject a kind human like you to this."

"My wobbly bits thank you."

By now I've lost count, and I hear her rustling around in the toolbox on the table, so I flip over and gratefully give my body a break, wrapping my arms around my knees and wiping the sweat off my brow.

Linnie picks up the entire toolbox and slings it under her arm, then heads for the door in my giant hoodie. Still no jacket.

"Where are you going?"

Without stopping, she answers over her shoulder. "If we're driving out of here tomorrow, I need to check Tim's car. Find out if it's running all right and fix it if it's not."

"Wait, you're going out in the snow to fix a car?"

"No." She turns and surveys me. I see her eyes catch on my arms, which admittedly are pumped from all the push-ups. Her cheeks pink up beneath the beanie she has pulled over her head, her long blond strands splayed over the shoulders of my hoodie, which I never want back. It looks too good on her.

Her gaze lingers a bit too long, and she sucks in a breath, realizing. I can't help but feel gratified that she's looking at me the way I've been looking at her since she arrived.

"No, you're not fixing the car?" I confirm.

"No, I'm not fixing it alone. *We're* fixing it."

A bark of laughter escapes me. "I'm not a mechanic."

She shrugs. "And I'm not a cook. But we made eggs, didn't we?"

I can't deny that logic. So I throw on some layers and follow her into the snow.

CHAPTER 15
LINNIE

I don't mean to laugh at Weston.

But he's so damn amusing out here pretending he knows where the oil pan is. I've been humoring him for the past half hour, when really the thing he keeps pointing at is the battery.

I feel like we're in a snow globe made for this moment—insistent, bloated snowflakes blocking out the world, two bundled-up misfits bent over an engine because we need a task, any task, to avoid our feelings.

Or at least that's how it's always been for me with fixing cars.

For all I know Weston isn't grappling with anything. His stoic expression could be focus, not introspection. But I can't stop thinking. Lately I'm always thinking, and that's new territory for me.

I've always been the fly-by-the-seat-of-my-pants friend who's keen to try a new pub three counties over or drive to the mountains in the middle of the night. I'm the messy one with no big life plan who shags men just because I can. I'm not the one who can't stop thinking about my choices.

Or about the man looking at an engine a few feet away.

The conviction I felt about staying away from men seems to be crumbling in Weston's presence, like he's setting tiny fires to each new decision I make not to notice him.

Flurries continue to swirl around us with no sign of stopping, but for the first time since I careened down the drive, I feel at home here. Always at home with my hands on a car engine.

"Fixing that pipe must've felt like child's play." Weston's gravelly voice fans the flames inside me every time he speaks. It contrasts with the quiet snow like the purr of a motor when all its parts are greased and working together. My own slice of heaven.

"It felt good, actually. I like to be useful," I admit.

"I get that. It's similar on the soccer field." I expect him to elaborate, but when I cast a glance his way, I find him focused on the last of four bolts I asked him to loosen so I can have a look under the motor without having to slide beneath the car. With a foot of snow on all sides, getting underneath is impossible anyway.

"That one stuck?" I ask.

"Like a dinosaur in a tar pit." He gives it a futile drag with the wrench and groans at its obstinance.

"Sorry, *what*?"

He stays focused on the bolt, as though it might escape if he lets it out of his sight. "Good and stuck. Like in a tar pit?"

"Nope, is that an American metaphor?"

He still doesn't look up. "Didn't think so. In Los Angeles, there's a museum and a pit of black tar that goes down to the center of the earth, or someplace where dinosaurs met their death."

Despite the grease on my hands, I reach for his shoulder and guide him out from under the hood. "Have you gone round the bend? Why are you talking about dinosaurs?"

"I was talking about tar, actually. And I have no idea why." His lips crook to the side in a sheepish almost smile. I'm grateful it stops there—I don't think I'd be able to take the devastating impact of an actual smile.

I also have to check myself for my initial leap to conclusions about him. At first blush, I saw a city-boy athlete who thought I was a ridiculous, moose-fearing country girl. Hence his suspicion of my take-charge attitude.

He's just quiet, not unfriendly. Busy observing rather than talking.

He takes a step back from the car, eyeing the bolt suspiciously. "Any suggestions on loosening this thing?"

I hand him a can of WD-40, and he gives the bolt a spritz. "Give it a couple minutes to lubricate the insertion point, and it might ease up." I blink hard when I hear him chuckle. The heat of my cheeks probably melts half the snow in Lake Tahoe.

Does everything out of my mouth always sound sexual or just when I'm with him?

He folds his arms over his chest and waits. Even though he's wearing several layers, I can't unsee the swell of his biceps when he was wearing just a T-shirt.

I give the bolt a whack with the end of the wrench.

"What's that for?" he asks.

"Just helping it along."

He laughs. "Impatient?"

"Thorough."

Pressing his lips together, he nods like he's just discovered a secret about me that only he understands. I hate that. Because what if whatever he's thinking is correct?

I match his stance, crossing my arms, maybe hugging myself a bit too protectively. "What?"

"I had no idea how sexy it was to watch a woman fix an engine, but I'm here to tell you . . . it's damn sexy." Weston's voice cuts through the chilly air, a motorcycle rumble on a quiet road. I feel a part of my resolve melt like butter in the sun. The real kind, not a square of cheese. "I may never recover."

That makes two of us.

He dials up the wattage on his smile, and I have to turn away so he doesn't see the blush creep over my cheeks. And with the cold weather, they were pink to start. "You can't say stuff like that to me."

He leans close, his voice low. "I can't not say it."

In an attempt to cool my overheated body, I take a long pull of cold air into my lungs. It's futile.

"Give that bolt another try." My voice croaks like it's been stuck in a musty drawer for a decade.

Weston leans under the hood and clamps the wrench onto the bolt with the confidence of a man who's already loosened the first three bolts. I feel a small surge of pride for him—my protégé of sorts. "Got it," he says, unwinding it with his fingers.

The motor immediately wobbles in its housing, and he grabs it with both hands. "Whoa. Don't want to lose the carburetor."

I stifle a laugh. He turns to me with a wry smile. "I know it's the motor. The carburetor's over here." He points to a knob very clearly marked WIPER FLUID, and I'm pretty sure he's kidding.

He slides the motor aside enough for me to check the oil pan. "Had a feeling," I conclude after I see a crack wide enough to see sunlight if the sky wasn't dumping snow. "But this is fixable. Remember the soldering iron?"

Weston rolls his eyes. "Why am I not surprised you'd find a way to use that?"

"Because it's the perfect tool for the job. I can repair the crack with that. Then it's just a matter of replacing the oil."

While Weston holds tight to the motor, I check around beneath it for signs anything else is broken or damaged.

Reaching into the headlight bay, I remove broken plastic and hold the pieces up to show him. "This is why the headlight is dangling like that."

The front end of the car is mostly undamaged save for the busted headlight, which hangs askew, and the front quarter panel, which took the brunt of my waltz with the tree.

"I still say you're extremely lucky. With the drive as slippery as it was and the clear-and-present moose danger, you could have slammed headfirst into the tree," Weston says.

"I resent your mocking tone about the moose, but thank you for your concern."

"I want only the best for you, Linnie." His deadpan delivery makes it sound like sarcasm, but I'm starting to realize the rough-sounding grumble is just the way he talks. "Which is why I'm not letting you loose in the woods with a soldering iron. Tim would kill me if you fused your hands together."

"Ha. First of all, that's impossible, and second, Tim ought to man up and learn to use some tools."

"That's a conversation you can have with him."

Glancing down the hill toward June's house, I wonder aloud, "How prepared do you think June is for doomsday? You think she's storing a few quarts of oil in her basement?"

Weston shrugs. "One way to find out." He extends his grease-covered hand to me. "Sorry about the dirt."

"I've never seen anything so beautiful." I try to ignore the tiny sparks I feel when I grasp his hand, but it's futile. His warm palm wraps around mine as we tromp through the snow to June's front door.

Thirty minutes later, we emerge victorious with two quarts of oil—"one for the road," according to Pioneer June—along with two frozen steaks, a bag of potatoes, an assortment of dried herbs, and a bottle of whiskey.

She loads it all into a large backpack, which Weston slips

onto his back.

"Clearly she knows something we don't about the road crew," he says, as we hike back up the hill, sinking in up to our knees every few feet. When I fall into a particularly deep hole, Weston has no trouble pulling me out, lifting my whole body with one hand.

"Thanks. Don't judge me for my utter lack of fitness," I manage to huff, surprised at how out of breath I am from trudging up a snow hill.

"It's the altitude. Mountain air's thinner. I get winded up here too . . . whoa!" One of his legs sinks down into the snow to his hip. His arms flail around like windmills, and I nearly double over laughing at the sight of this fit athlete about to drop on his bum in the snow.

"Here, grab on." I extend my hand, but I'm no match for his size. I pull hard on his hand and somehow end up half-buried in the snow instead of helping him burrow out. Now he's laughing, too, and I'm feeling snow edge up underneath my shirt, which I left untucked. "Oh, that's mighty cold."

I push down on the snow, hoping to lift myself out, but both hands sink in, leaving me facedown, sprawled on the snow with my limbs in deep. Weston manages to free his leg and creeps over to where I'm licking snow off my upper lip. His smile stretches the width of his face as he leans down, lifts me like a bundle of kindling, and carries me the rest of the way up the hill.

"You don't need to do that, you know. I can walk."

"All evidence to the contrary," he says with a smirk, rearranging me in his arms so my legs dangle and he's holding me against his chest. I still have snow up my shirt and down my pants, and melting ice crystals descend from my hair into my eyes, but I've never been more snug and warm.

Don't feel anything. Okay, feel it, but try to ignore it.

Fail and fail.

"I think I'm good to walk now," I say quietly as we near the driveway. The car still sits somberly, hood in the air.

Weston gently puts me down, and I press onward, shaking the excess snow off my shoes.

When I pick up the soldering iron, he frowns. "I still don't feel good about you using a tool that can melt metal. Have you used this before?" He looks frightened at the sight of it, and I realize he's just like me with the eggs.

I reach for his hand, which is unnecessary, but my body seems to be in charge. Carefully, he places his hand in mine, and I lead him to the engine, carrying the soldering iron under my other arm. "How about if you use it, then?"

His head whips to the side, a fair bit of excitement in his eyes. And also fear. I know fear—the first time my dad left me alone in the garage to work on a car, I felt it. And I felt even better when I did the repair correctly. I want to share that feeling with Weston.

"I don't know what I'm doing. And your brother would kill me if I set fire to his car."

"You won't." He stares into the engine like it's a foreign land, even though we've been here an hour.

"I might."

I shake my head and nudge the piece of equipment against his hand. He recoils like it's hot. "It's not even on. Just . . . hold on to it a sec."

Grudgingly, he grasps the handle. Using my body weight, I pitch the motor to the side so we can see the crack in the pan. It's how my dad trained me to work when I was a kid, knowing I was too small to lift the heaviest parts out of cars. "You just need to nudge them out of the way, is all," he told me. I've been nudging for the past fifteen years, and it's worked out completely fine.

"Okay, you see the crack, yes?"

"Yes. Because I have eyes."

"Brilliant, just making certain." Still nudging the motor away from the pan, I gesture with my head. "Okay, turn the switch on the gun and wait until it heats. You'll know because it will smoke a bit, especially here in the cold."

"And you feel comfortable with me handling a hot stick next to you." He presses his lips together, and I try to hold back my laughter, but I can't.

"I'm just so damn relieved that I'm not the only one making bad sex puns," I tell him.

He answers by turning on the machine. I manage to get the motor seated so I can stand up and watch Weston. He looks unsure, but after a moment, the soldering iron starts to smoke, and his eyes cast to mine. I nod.

"Tell me exactly where to insert the tip," he says. I press my lips together, doing my best to keep a straight face. Then he shakes his head, handing it off to me. "Forget it. I can't be responsible for what happens to Tim's car when you're laughing at me."

"I'm only laughing because you're holding a hot piece of equipment, and everything you say sounds like you're soliciting sex."

"Exactly. I can't do this."

I offer it back carefully, waiting until Weston takes it from my hands. "If you just relax, I'll tell you exactly where I want it, how hot, and for how long."

"Now you're just messing with me."

"Right there, love, that's where I want that hot rod of yours."

"Oh, fuck me." Weston leans over the engine and dips the hot end of the soldering iron over the crack in the oil pan. "Like this?"

"Exactly. Now give it some fire."

Weston does as told, and I watch the sparks fly as metal hits metal. He jerks back at the ignition, but after a moment he gets the hang of the soldering iron. "It looks like it's melting together."

"That's absolutely perfect. Get it good and sealed, no cracks."

He works a little longer than is probably necessary, but who am I to get between a man and his first go with a power tool? A minute later, Weston stands up and turns off the machine. His eyes dance and his lips twitch into a grin. I remember feeling proud like that when I impressed my dad by taking apart an entire engine and putting it back together in just one day. "You look like a kid who's gotten a jumbo bag of Maltesers after eating a plate of biscuits."

"That was fun," he admits.

I take over, refilling the oil and putting the cap on snugly. Weston helps slide the motor back in place and tightens the screws. I can't see anything else that looks damaged from the impact with the tree, so I'm hoping we've fixed the issue.

"Okay, can you hit the ignition and see if it starts up?" I ask, still standing over the engine with bated breath.

Weston hops into the car and looks at me before turning the switch. "I feel like Thomas Edison about to turn on the first light."

He's so damn cute it's killing me. I want to tell him that there are so many ways cars can break, and every time I find the issue and fix it, I feel a little bit like that. But I don't need to share everything. Even if I want to. Even if I want him.

Instead, I say quietly, "Give it a go."

The engine hiccups initially, but then it turns right over. The purr of all the parts working in unison will always be a balm to my soul.

The right headlight is smashed and won't light up, but everything else looks to be in working order. The tires are fine, despite skidding down the drive. I close the hood and come around to where Weston sits in the driver's seat with one foot on the brake and the other on the ground outside the car. He cuts the engine and gets out, towering over me as usual.

"Hey, City Boy. Turns out you're good at lots of things besides soccer." I hold up a hand to give him a high five, but he doesn't slap it. He reaches for my hand, intertwining his fingers with mine, and pulls me a step closer to him.

My footing slips on the snowy ground, so I crash rather indelicately against him. I expect him to say something about the snow or the mountain air or the altitude. But when I meet his eyes, I see none of the squinty intensity I've grown used to. There's still intensity, but it's different. Darker. His eyes look like they could swallow me whole.

Then they drop to my lips, and I have a split second to react, to tell him this is a bad idea. Instead, I say nothing, because maybe it's the perfect idea.

Weston's lips meet mine. My thoughts and words disappear.

The blooming of want low in my belly, that impulse I've done so well at denying—there's no stopping it now. A glimmer of heat ignites between my thighs.

So familiar because I've been here so many times before. But different. So very different.

I've been dreaming about these lips, this mouth, since I got here, and for a moment I let myself have them. I know the regret will come soon enough, but right now I want this.

Weston pulls our clasped hands between us and holds them against his chest. I wrap my free hand around his neck, letting my fingers roam in his hair. It's soft and a little wet from the snow, and my hand winds through the curls at the nape of his neck. A low rumble escapes his lips.

His other arm comes around my waist, and he tugs my hips against him while he licks my bottom lip and nips at it with his teeth. I part my lips for his tongue, which sweeps gently over mine. He tastes like coffee and mountain air, and I sink in a little deeper, the edges of my resolve colliding and melting against the heat of his body.

His hand moves from my waist and finds the hem of my shirt, pushing beneath it and sending waves of chills across my skin. Even in the cold air, his hands are impossibly warm. His lips impossibly soft as they torture me with just enough pressure to make every nerve ending come alive.

I want more, and I fuse our mouths together in an attempt to get it, tongues tangling against each other as though there could ever actually be enough.

Weston's hand drifts to my stomach, which I know is softer than his sculpted abs, but right now, I don't care. Not if he doesn't. The firestorm of feeling erupts anew when his hands glide higher and he pinches one nipple through my bra.

The sound I make is supposed to be a protest, but it comes out in a moan for more. I don't expect him to understand the nuance. Even through our layers and jackets, I can feel him hard against me. I love it, and at the same time, warning bells are sounding in my head.

In that instant I know exactly why I don't want to start anything with Weston. It's not for any of the reasons I've been telling myself since I got here—because I am devoted to making changes in my life, because I deserve better than one-night stands, because I am not the woman my dad thinks I am.

I know I don't want to start anything with Weston because I already sense that if I do, I won't want it to end.

And this has to end. And, really, it shouldn't have happened at all.

Which is why I pull back abruptly, awkwardly. "Weston, I can't."

As if a spell has been broken by the stroke of a midnight clock, Weston seems to shake himself out of the beautiful moment that almost feels like it happened in a dream. A decade ago. That's how much we're both instantly in the present and wiping away all traces of what we just did. "No, of course. Shit. I'm sorry."

"Don't be sorry." I'm not sorry, though I probably should be.

"I shouldn't have—"

"It's okay. But we shouldn't have. We agree on that, right?"

"Of course. Of course, we agree."

"Good. Okay, then." I take a step back, but our hands are still clasped, which feels so right but also impossible. So I let go. "I should call Tim and let him know his car is fine."

"Tim?!" He sounds hysterical, and worse, his eyes are wide like a rabid dog's. With the way he's running his hands through his hair, he looks a bit crazed.

"Yes, my brother. It's his car we just fixed."

"You call him. I'm not calling him." Weston shakes his head, and I have the urge to calm him down by any means necessary. Unfortunately the only thing that comes to mind is kissing him again. So I do.

It's more of an apology kiss, a soft, easy brush of lips. A softer landing than the abrupt uncoupling from a moment earlier. When I pull away this time, it feels like a more solid ending.

"I'll call Tim. You can get to work on the steaks."

Then I turn and do my level best to walk back into the house without bursting into flames. But with the way this man just set fire to every inch of my skin, it's like trying to stop an avalanche with a teaspoon.

CHAPTER 16
WESTON

"Bon appétit." I carry a platter with two medium-rare steaks and pan-fried potatoes into the living room, where Linnie has banned me for the past half hour.

"Wow, that smells great." Linnie lounges on a nest of blankets and pillows. She's moved the couch so it serves as a backrest, allowing us to sit on the blankets and lean on it. From someplace I've never noticed, she's produced several pillar candles and lit them all, casting a warm yellow glow over the room.

She's set the game table with more linens Jordan and Tim must have bought—French provincial place mats and napkins in reds and oranges with an olive design. Place settings for two and a votive candle burning in the middle.

The blankets and pillows are a mismatched assortment of red and blue plaids along with yellow flowered pillows from the bedroom and navy ones from the slippery couch. But somehow it all works.

"I never thought this place could look this . . . homey." I squint as soon as I say the words, because they're not exactly right. Do I want this cabin to look homey? I envisioned it as a getaway place to hang my hat when I'm done skiing for the day up at Lake Tahoe, or as a place to crash in the summer after waterskiing at the lake or hiking.

I never imagined it as a second home or any kind of a home, not in that sense.

Maybe it's the lingering memory from kissing Linnie earlier that has my brain feeling stupid things like wanting this place to feel like a home. My home.

The entire thought is ridiculous, because it doesn't fit in with my life—going on the road for games, dating a string of women with no attachment and no future, having a house that does not feel like a home. Because it can't. I can't.

So I swiftly correct course. "I mean, it looks comfortable. I like the pillows and everything. So much better than that Slip 'N Slide couch. We really ought to throw that out with the garbage."

Linnie hasn't said a word, and I realize she's staring at me. "That is one gorgeous piece of meat."

She's talking about the steak. Of course she is. And for once she doesn't seem aware of the possible double entendre.

Because it can't happen.

We agreed.

I should put the tray down on the table, and we should have dinner like normal people. "I finished it in the oven. It's my secret weapon. Of course, since you're the only one who knows, I'll have to have you disappeared. I think that's how it works."

"Steak with a spy, then I meet my end." She nods soberly. "If that's how it has to be, this is the way I'd like to go out. Can we at least sit by the fire first?"

She gestures to the fireplace, where she's arranged a half-dozen logs, all standing on end and meeting at a peak in the middle, ready to be lit. "Looks good." I choke on the words without meaning to.

The satisfaction in her face dims. "What are you not saying?"

"Nothing."

"Liar."

I shrug. "I just do it differently. Doesn't mean your way is wrong."

She practically pounces on me. It's a good thing I've already put down the tray, because she flies at me and drags me over to the fireplace. "Show me. How do you do it?" Her hair is still damp from her shower, and the smell of vanilla cookies collides with my senses, making everything else unimportant.

Kneeling, I take apart her arrangement and stack them, two facing one way, two on top facing the other way, with one diagonally across the middle. She rolls her eyes. "Well, that's basically the same thing."

"It's completely different."

She tosses her hair over her shoulder, and I pause to watch the waves dust her shoulders on their way down. Some kind of perfection, and she doesn't even know it. "Why are we arguing about this?"

I have to laugh. "Maybe because you're stubborn and I like to be right?"

"Sounds like an awful combination."

And yet it feels like the perfect combination. "I think we're doing okay," I say quietly. She tips her head against my shoulder, and the skin heats along my neck.

Shaking myself off the road my body keeps wanting to go down, I tell her we can try the fire her way.

"Nope, no need. It worked great last night. I don't need to prove anything. I'll watch and learn." An unreadable mask under furrowed eyebrows meets my gaze. She hunkers down and gets eye level with the logs, like she's judging a baking contest and peering in to see if my fondant is spread evenly.

Yes, I watch *The Great British Bake Off.*

"Hey, no ogling my wood."

Her mask gives way to a smirk. "I wasn't ogling."

"Whatever you were doing, cut it out."

"I was simply observing." She tips her head from side to side as though considering a better description. "And wondering how you got so experienced at laying hands on your wood."

She's doing it on purpose. She must be. Refusing to cave, I simply nod. "Told you, honey, camping. My hands are large, and they're used to a nice, firm piece of wood."

Her eyes narrow, but not before I catch her swallowing hard. I love it. "I was talking about building fires. Not sure what the size of your hands—or the firmness of your wood—has to do with it."

"So was I. Been building fires in the woods for years with my big brother. I grew up in Colorado, remember?"

As stubborn as they come, she squares her shoulders and smiles, victorious. I'm not sure why until her next question. "You have a brother? I love this, Weston—actual information instead of just vague references. See, I knew we were . . ." She points two fingers between her eyes and mine to show kinship. "How much older? Is he a footballer too?"

I have a split second to shut down the conversation or divert it back to wood arrangements. It's what I *should* do. I never answer questions about my family or upbringing. Hell, I never bring up my past, and now this is the second time in two days I've spilled something to her that no one else knows.

And yet something about Linnie and the way she seems to lay herself bare without hesitation or self-consciousness makes me want to be honest with her. It's a first for me, and it makes me uneasy as much as it feels oddly liberating.

"Not an actual brother, at least not by birth." My voice sounds hollow and rough, like a rusty lawn mower that someone revved to life after a decade. "Big Brothers. It's an organization that sets up foster kids with mentors, and they do activities together—bowling, gardening, whatnot. Mine was into camping. Still is." I shrug, explaining as though the words haven't been lodged behind my vocal cords for most of my life. As though it's nothing that I told her this.

When really, it's everything.

She turns her entire body to face me, eyes sparkling, begging for more. "Did you say foster kids? You grew up in foster care?"

I could say that the words slipped out, but if I was going to talk about having a Big Brother, I was going to tell her all of it. I stand in front of her, willing her wide eyes not to glisten with interest and sympathy. I don't want her to feel sorry for me.

"It's not what you're probably thinking. It was a group home for boys. Stable, not like being bounced around from family to family."

Outside, the snow is still coming down with steady persistence, and a light breeze sends the flurries sideways, so the flakes stick to the window. But it's the warmth in her eyes that threatens to melt every bit of snow from the landscape. I knew it when I first saw them—they speak without needing words.

"How was it, then?" She tips her chin up, challenging me not to give her a pat, polished response, but her tone is gentle. My neck heats when her eyes trace my features. She's memorizing them. Learning me.

"I—" Shaking my head, I know I should stop talking. This story has done just fine locked up in a box. No use airing it now.

She puts a hand over mine, encouraging and gentle, with enough pressure to let me know I'm supported, somehow. "You can talk to me. I'm just an ordinary girl who likes motor grease. I won't hurt you."

There's so much I want to ask about that statement, but I

can't do it all at once, especially when I'm on the cusp of telling her something I've never put into words.

I'm sitting in front of her like a kid trying to convince his fifth-grade teacher not to give him detention for copying someone else's paper. "It wasn't great. I'm not saying that. Of course I'd have preferred to live with a family."

My own family.

"There were fifteen of us in sort of a dorm situation with chaperones. Kind of like being at camp full time when I wasn't at school."

"Seems like you're putting a positive spin on a shitty situation." Even through her gentle smile, the words come like carving knives, slicing through my bullshit.

"Everyone has challenges. My life . . . is good. Nothing to complain about." The words finish their downward cascade and I take a breath. Linnie's eyes haven't left mine, and I search them for the pity or discomfort I always expected to see if I finally told someone the truth.

Instead, she sits with her face turned up, interested, open. Like she'd sit in this room or out in the fucking snow for ten hours if I felt like talking.

The idea of that instantly overwhelms me, and I turn back to the woodpile to stack up a few more scraps of kindling. The heat on the back of my neck is now a sheen of sweat. "I want a little more of the small stuff as kindling. That doesn't offend your fire sensibility, does it?"

Her lips settle into a line, but it's the only indication she doesn't like my change of topic. She doesn't try to pry out more information or make me feel better. Her quiet acceptance is what I need, or I'll dart out of sight like a scared rabbit.

"It's okay." She studies me, letting me decide what happens next. And as much as it felt like a tiny burden was lifted by sharing a shred of myself, I feel drained. I don't want to talk anymore.

As if she knows, she moves closer, turning so she's pressed up next to me. I wrap an arm around her shoulder and pull her in. I feel some of the tension seep away from my body, almost as though she's absorbing it with hers. Making my burdens lighter.

When I feel her shivering under my arm, I realize I've forgotten all about lighting the fire. It's freezing in here. "Sometimes when I talk to you, I forget about what I ought to be doing. Fires to be built, meals to cook—I forget about all of it." My voice is quiet near her ear, and I feel her shudder again, but this time I don't think it's from the cold.

"I get it," she says softly. "Sometimes I'd rather listen to you talk than do the logical things."

"I'm not usually like this." Another admission. They're flying freely from me now, and I don't care. "What are you doing to me, Linnie Cheltenham?"

Her quiet laugh sounds like a melody. "No earthly idea. I talk a lot, and sometimes I lose the forest for the trees."

"See, and you say you're not a mountain woman."

I light a long match, and the kindling ignites nicely, yielding some snapping sparks and casting a pretty orange glow across Linnie's skin. It takes a few minutes of patiently fanning the tiny flames, but then the bigger logs catch. Linnie holds her hands out toward the fire to warm them. "I'd say it's a damn good fire," she says, nodding.

She leans her head against my shoulder, and I'm smart enough to know to shut up. Smart enough to know when I've got it good.

CHAPTER 17
LINNIE

The steaks tasted amazing, the potatoes were godly, and the whiskey went down smooth.

The fire still looks great, but unfortunately, as soon as we finished dinner and I asked what Weston felt like doing, he looked like he'd seen a ghost. He's been scurrying around the cabin for the past hour as though he's in search of a vital dice game we both know doesn't exist.

"Oh. I haven't looked in here," Weston calls from the bathroom, where the dice certainly are not.

"We don't need to play dice. How about chess?" I ask for the third time.

"I forgot how to play chess. I'm sure I can find the dice."

"You didn't forget how to play chess, and there are no dice in the loo."

He's been in and out of every room in the house fifty times, and I doubt even David Blaine could produce a dice game by now.

As he passes by again, I hold out a glass of red wine. He takes it, kisses my temple, and keeps going. I'm already halfway through my second glass, so my boundaries are getting fuzzy.

147

I've had twelve talks with myself about not giving in to lust, if that's what this is.

Grabbing one of the dusty volumes from the bookshelf, I study its faded brown spine, where gold letters are barely visible. Flipping the book open, I see it's a first edition of *Alice in Wonderland.*

Taking it over to the pile of blankets and pillows in front of the couch, I read the first few pages, wondering if I'm the one who fell down a rabbit hole. I know Weston is freaking out, and I suspect it has something to do with his earlier confessions, but I can't figure out much.

I'm tempted to text Tim and ask him for advice, but something tells me he might not know this side of Weston. Guys don't always talk, and the last thing I want to do is betray a confidence.

Finally Weston comes padding back into the room, shoulders sunken in defeat. "I don't think there are any dice." He stands next to where I'm sitting with the book in my lap, and I notice that he's finished most of his glass of wine. I reach for his hand and pull him down onto the blankets.

"No," I agree, patting him on the hand.

He lets himself be guided down and stretches his legs out toward the fire. I stand and get the bottle of wine from the table and refill each of our glasses. Holding mine up for a toast, I say, "To fire builders."

"May you forever have wood, as much as you desire," he adds.

"Aw, he's back. I missed the inappropriate Weston."

"Sorry about that. I guess I needed some space."

I elbow him gently. "It's a small cabin. Anyone would be going batty, especially when dealing with a talkative, stubborn one like me."

"Stop. You're lovely."

He may just be being nice, but it makes me smile. "Thank you for sharing your space with me for the past few days."

Staring into the fire, he nods and lets out a long sigh. "It's been a pleasure, Linnie. Really."

The fire crackles and pops, and I inhale the woodsy scent of burning logs. Sitting side by side with our backs against the couch, we're quiet, mesmerized by the flames.

Sometimes I wish I was the kind of person who could leave an issue alone. Weston hasn't scurried around for the past hour for kicks. He's been avoiding me, maybe afraid I'll bring up his foster-care upbringing. And now he's finally settling down. I should let him be.

I would. Honestly, I would, if I thought it was what he wanted. But my instinct says he might be the kind of person who benefits from a pesterer like me. He might need someone to draw him out.

Turning to look at his profile, I'm struck again by the strong line of his jaw and angular slant of his nose. It's a regal profile, the kind that belongs on a coin. If he wasn't a professional footballer, he could do whatever he wanted, I have no doubt. It's not just his face, which is admittedly gorgeous. His stoic nature is the type that makes people pay attention when he finally does speak.

It's no surprise he's the center midfielder, a pivotal position that demands the highest level of fitness and the greatest flexibility. He's a defender and a striker and a strategist all at once. And yet he told me three sentences about his upbringing and needed two hours to recover.

"Hey," I nudge him again. He turns to me, and the guardedness I saw earlier is gone.

"Hey."

"You okay?"

He quirks an eyebrow and gives me a rueful smile. "You

mean, am I done chasing a phantom game of dice to avoid talking to you?"

"Bingo."

"Yeah. No. I don't know."

"That about covers it."

He gives me a partial smile that might as well be a grimace for all its success at convincing me he's happy. It's like he's working to repair a hairline fissure in his strong facade while at the same time willing it to crack open and let me in.

My heart aches to reach him somehow.

"Confessor's remorse?"

"No." He rakes a hand through his hair, pushing it back from his forehead and giving me a clearer view of the deep, vulnerable brown of his eyes. "Yeah. Maybe." He forces a feeble laugh.

"We don't have to talk about foster care. Or parents. Or the debutantes at Queen Charlotte's Ball."

"Debutantes? What if I want to talk about those?"

"Then we talk."

He inhales a deep breath and lets it out slowly. "Okay."

But is it? Okay?

"I'll tell you anything you want to know about cotillions and balls and debutante parties, but then you must do me a solid and tell me some things. I won't specify what those things need to be, but they must be equally juicy." (Side note: I know nothing of debutante balls, having grown up in a small, working-class town, so it will all be based on what I've read in Regency romance novels.)

I extend my hand to shake, and the river of chills nearly knocks me sideways. I never want to let go of him.

Leaning my back against the couch, I extend my legs out like his. He bends his knees and pulls his in so our feet are next to each other, both clad in warm socks—his blue, mine pink and white. His leg grazes mine and I almost sigh.

The thrumming drumbeat of my pulse is nearly audible. The electricity between us penetrates down to my bones.

His voice is quiet but steady. "I never knew my dad. My mom raised me alone, and I remember my life with her, mostly kindergarten, first and second grade. I went to a public school in our neighborhood. Longmont, Colorado, north of Denver."

It feels like I'm watching a butterfly that's just alighted on a branch. I want to get closer and inspect its wings, but I don't want to scare it away. So I sit perfectly still.

Weston rubs both hands over his face, and for a moment I fear he's finished talking. But then he continues, staring again at the fire. "It was just the two of us, and we were close. She picked me up from school every day, had me in the after-school program until she could be there. I also got to school super early, whatever time the early drop-off started. And I remember loving that. Time on the playground with the other early kids. Time with my mom in the afternoons. Baking cookies, making noodles for dinner."

"Sounds nice."

"It was great." He smiles, remembering. "Sometime when I was around eight, she got sick. Which made no sense to me because she worked in a doctor's office. She was a phle-botomist, drew blood from patients."

"That's a big word for an eight-year-old."

He swallows. "I learned it later. Anyhow, apparently she got stuck by a hollow needle, which they use for certain kinds of blood draws. The problem is that the patient's blood gets inside the hollow center, and this particular patient was sick with HIV. Back then, contracting it was pretty much a death sentence."

My eyes go wide as I start writing the rest of the story in my head. And I think about eight-year-old Weston, an only child who loved his mom more than life.

I want to reach for him, support him somehow. But I'm so bad at this. I don't know what he wants, so I drop my hand over his.

"Oh, wow. I'm sorry. That's . . . a lot." I think about my own father, who isn't getting any healthier, and swallow down a sudden welling of tears. This isn't the time. It's not about me. "I'm sorry you had to go through that."

He shakes his head. "I didn't really go through anything. She gave me up to foster care before she died—before she even really got sick. I didn't understand why she was leaving me there. She just told me they were nice people who'd take care of me and it was for the best." He inhales a jagged breath. "I figured she left me there because she didn't love me."

"Why would it mean she didn't love you?"

His hand pulls back as though I've become contagious. If a hazmat suit was in reach, he'd be putting it on and sealing himself away. "I don't think that question needs an answer."

"I disagree."

His face contorts into a grimace, mouth pulling down at the corners, eyes flashing with stern defiance. "Then I guess we disagree."

Turning away, he goes back to rearranging logs in the fireplace, but there are only so many ways you can move logs around before it becomes redundant. He surpasses that point but continues anyway. The flame starts to dim because he's spread the logs out too far, so he moves them closer together again. The flame kicks up a notch.

"Weston."

"I'm not doing this with you right now."

"Okay, then when?" I reach for his shoulder to pull him back gently from his log-arranging activity. His muscles are taut, shoulders pulled up toward his ears. "Weston, look at me."

Dropping the fire poker, he stares at the flames for a full minute, saying nothing. Then, grudgingly, he turns so I can see his face. He looks more exhausted than angry. "Linnie."

"Yes?"

"She left me. That's my legacy. Being left behind."

"It's one instance. Hardly a legacy."

He doesn't answer initially, and I foolishly think maybe he agrees with me.

His next words are so quiet I almost don't hear them. "It wasn't just one instance."

The fire chooses that moment to pop, startling me so much I jump. When I look at Weston, his mouth is pulled into a grim line.

"What do you mean?" He wouldn't have said it if he didn't want to talk about it, right?

His expression remains unchanged, his voice quiet. "I had one serious relationship a few years back . . ."

I can't explain the way my stomach drops. I shouldn't feel a tinny hollow taste in my throat at the mention of a relationship. Of course he'd have relationships. One look at him and most women would follow him wherever he wanted to go. And I certainly have no claim on him, no reason to feel what I feel. But it's jealousy, plain and simple.

"Okay . . ." I can't knock the rust from my voice.

"I loved her, or, at least, I thought so. But eventually I found out she was cheating on me, so . . ." He rubs a hand over his face and closes his eyes for a long beat. When he opens them, his features look composed. He's good at that, at shaking things off. Maybe it's a sports thing. "Two times was enough to teach me not to gamble on feeling too much."

"The past doesn't necessarily dictate the future. Maybe the

third time will be the charm." I say it knowing full well that I can't be the third time for him. Even if it's not for the same reasons, I'll be leaving too.

He shrugs off my statement like it's irrelevant. Or untrue.

"It's formative. My mom didn't love me enough to stick around. She left me with strangers and never contacted me again. Yesterday was the anniversary of when she left. It always hits me hard for a week or so."

I feel my lungs deflate. It hurts to know that he's been carrying this burden the entire time I've been here and hasn't said anything. I tentatively reach for his hand, turning it over and interlacing his fingers with mine, As I absorb the warmth of his skin, I can feel his racing pulse.

I ache to comfort him, but I have no idea how to do that when I don't understand how she could walk away.

"Maybe she thought she was giving you the best life she could," I posit. "Later, once you found out the reason, did you feel at least a little bit better?"

"If anything, I felt worse because she never gave me a chance to try and save her."

The words break me. The idea of this grown-up little boy believing there was something he could have done to change things. "Oh no, love. You couldn't have saved her. Not if she was that sick."

Weston swallows down the rest of his wine and rises to his knees. He leans forward and pokes the logs in the fireplace. A burst of sparks erupts while he continues to stare. "When people ask about my family, I just say I grew up in Colorado and that's that. They assume it was a typical suburban childhood with snow and mountains, and I'm fine with that."

"You could tell people. No one would judge you for not having a storybook narrative."

"Some would."

"Fuck them. It's a beautiful story, Weston, and you shouldn't be embarrassed by it. You should tell the world that story—get it off your chest and maybe it will set you free. If anyone judges you for being who you are, fuck 'em."

He startles, turning to face me. "You don't give a shit what other people think. I love that."

He doesn't know. Has no idea how much I care about what one specific person thinks. It's just easier to sit where I'm sitting and see his life clearly.

"I don't have it all together, trust me," I say quietly.

He stares at the fire, and I watch the orange light of the flames lick the sides of his face, making him look like he's watching a beautiful sunset.

It's all I can do not to touch his cheek, run a finger over his lips, offer him some tenderness and comfort. He's so beautiful, I can't take my eyes off him. When he looks at me, I swear he can see every emotion laid bare.

"What do you want, Linnie?"

The words feel caught in barbed wire. "I-I told you. I want to get my life together. Stop snogging men for meaningless reasons."

His eyes fix on mine. Intense, daring. I should look away, but I can't escape their pull. I feel my resistance to him dissolving into dust. "Tell me what you want right now."

It's like he's hypnotized me.

"I want you." The words leave me before I have time to censor them. It's the worst possible thing I could say to him. Worse than admitting it to myself, which I've tried my hardest not to do.

I can't face him, and the ensuing silence between us affirms that I've said the worst possible thing.

You can undo it. Take it back. Say something else.

"What I meant was—" I don't even have a plan for how to

finish the sentence, which is a good thing because Weston's hand is cupping my jaw, his lips brushing carefully over mine.

It's not a tentative question. It's an answer.

A promise.

Turning, I face him more squarely and dare a look at his face. Eyes dilated, jaw slack. Still, there's that tic in his cheek muscle that I've come to understand means he's holding something back. His pupils are so dark they nearly blot out the color of his eyes.

He wants this, and not just because I said it first.

"I can't hook up with you. I can't keep doing that to myself. I deserve better."

He shakes his head, a quiet laugh warming me to my bones. "That's not what this is. Not how I see it."

I can't help it. A cackle erupts from me at the ridiculousness of the situation. "It's exactly what this is. You and I having sex after knowing each other for exactly three days is the very definition of a hookup."

"No."

"No?"

"You're wrong."

He kisses me, and for a moment I forget about how wrong he is—how wrong all of it is. I want to block it out. It would be easy. I've done it so many times.

"It's my pattern," I say. "And I don't want to do it anymore."

"I don't want you to."

"So . . . ?"

"Maybe this time it's different."

He's not making sense. It can't be different. I'm just feeling all the lust and physical chemistry that leads to one memorable night of orgasms and a momentary chance to forget the rest of life swirling around me. Then it's over. Then I walk away.

He runs a finger along my temple, and my skin melts from

my bones. "So, your turn. Tell me about waltzes and parties with the Queen of England."

"Weston . . ."

"What?"

"Can I ask you one question, then I promise I'll tell you about the Queen?"

"Sure."

"You said everyone calls you Weston. Why? And do you have a first name?"

His lips fight a smile. "That's two questions."

"I'm bad with maths."

"Danny. It's Danny. And no one has called me that in a really long time."

The confession makes him look unburdened. He's told me a lot, even in his choices not to say more.

"So . . . full disclosure, I was never a debutante, but I've always been fascinated by the dresses," I begin.

He leans away, and I can tell he's watching me, but I continue facing the fire. "That's not what I'd expect. You don't seem to need frilly things."

"Even mechanics like to get dressed up," I say quietly.

"Hey." He reaches two fingers for my chin, the delicious burn on my flesh causing me to blink a beat longer than necessary. He turns my face toward his, and my jaw goes slack at the proximity. "That's not what I meant. You're not just an ordinary girl covered in motor grease."

My words sound different coming out of his mouth and I can't avoid a smile.

"There's nothing ordinary about you. And you don't need ball gowns to be beautiful. If anything, they'd just camouflage all the ways you're stunning on your own. That's all I meant."

His fingers release my chin, but I stay frozen in place,

staring at him. "No one has ever said that to me before." The words are out before I can edit them.

His Adam's apple works as he swallows, but his eyes don't leave mine. "Well, then," he says, nodding, "no one has ever told you the truth."

Our faces are inches apart, and it would be so easy to close the gap. It's second nature for someone like me, who's made a study of the fastest way to go from flirting to kissing. But I don't dare move.

Neither does he.

Unrequited feelings hang in the balance as we size each other up. And I slowly back away, turning and crisscrossing my legs so I'm looking at him more squarely. "I do love a frilly dress," I continue as though we weren't just interrupted by all *that*. "I suppose it's the fantasy element, imagining walking down the stairs in a fancy ballroom or twirling with a parasol in a garden." I hear myself and immediately clam up. It's silly when I say it out loud.

Weston picks up my hand and rubs his damn thumb over the back of it. I don't dare look down in case he's incinerated it, and I'll now have to go through life without a hand. Besides, it's much more pleasant to look at his jutting cheekbones and three days' worth of beard that makes him look like a hot mountain man.

"I don't think there's a man alive who could resist you in a dress like that. I know I'm having trouble and you're here in sweatpants."

"Weston."

"Sorry."

"Please *actually* be sorry. You can't say things like that when I've told you there will be no snogging."

He laughs.

"Stop. It's not funny."

"I know. I'm sorry. I really, really am." But he's laughing harder, and I have no idea why. Now it's no longer a quiet titter but a full roar of a laugh. His body begins shaking, and tears stream from his eyes.

"Stop it." I elbow him in the ribs. It makes him laugh only harder.

He tries to apologize, but he only ends up mouthing the word *sorry* because words are impossible. He's so bewildering.

"What is happening?"

Shaking his head, Weston continues laughing. He opens his mouth to speak, but nothing comes out. Finally, a few words: "I have no idea."

The laughter is contagious. I can't watch him shaking, a nasal wheeze replacing peals of laughter, without it taking its toll on me too. I start to giggle.

Before long, we're both wiping our eyes, lost in hysterics for no apparent reason, but it feels too good to make an effort to stop.

Weston starts to settle himself, only to start shaking again with silent laughter before putting his head on his knees in defeat. "I can't stop," he whines. I don't answer because I'm not capable of it.

Finally, after a few false starts, the giggles begin to abate. I pick up the wine bottle to top off our glasses, but only a few ounces remain. I pour a bit into each glass, and we use it to swallow down the rest of our laughter.

The giggles taper off, leaving us looking at each other. No, staring. I can't look away from his eyes, even if I wanted to. And I don't.

He's so beautiful, his lips parted, eyes glassy. I reach for his jaw and let my fingers trail along the sharp ridge of his chin.

His hand pushes into my hair, and he tips my head up a few degrees, bringing our mouths together. We pause, an inch apart, so close I can feel his breath rake my skin, and it sends chills down to my toes.

"I know I can't have you, but I'm not going to pretend I don't want you. It's fucking impossible." The deep gravel in his voice sears my skin. His exhale carries the remaining shreds of my resistance off on a breeze.

"You can have me." The words tumble out before I can stop them.

"Linnie . . . ," he whispers.

"Yes," I tell him, hoping he understands that I mean yes to everything.

His lips meet mine in a deep, hot kiss that tells me he absolutely understands.

It's not like I've made a conscious decision that this is the right moment to throw my principles to the wind, but my body has made the decision for me, and Weston is on exactly the same page.

There's no stopping us either. I'm depleted of thought, exhausted from holding myself back from what I've been wanting for days.

His mouth feels so good against mine. His lips taste like red wine; his skin smells like pine trees and maple syrup.

And I don't ever want to stop.

"What do you want, Linnie?" His voice is a gruff whisper against my ear, sending chills down my neck. I feel an intense pang of wanting between my thighs.

"More," is the only possible response.

"You can have more. You can have it all," he says, his hand running along the hem of my shirt and hiking it up until I feel the room's cool air hit my skin. His hand warms it instantly, working over my waist, his thumb rubbing slow circles.

"I—" With no idea how to respond, I trail off, the words meddlesome when we could be kissing instead.

Even if this should be familiar territory, it feels foreign. Partly it's the slow, intentional pace of each stroke of Weston's fingers against my skin, each sweep of his tongue against mine. He's not in a rush to the finish line.

Maybe there is no finish line.

Maybe this is what it feels like to tiptoe around the perimeter of love, dipping a foot inside briefly, knowing there's a whole pool to explore. I shouldn't even let that word into my consciousness, but it's found its way there anyway.

Get rid of it.

I free myself of errant thoughts with a sudden ramp-up of intensity. Instead of staying on my side, facing Weston and giving him access to slowly drive me mad, I sit up and position myself over his legs, forcing him to roll to his back.

"Here. This is better, isn't it?" I ask, my voice husky as I roll my hips over his erection. I feel his body respond, an uncontrolled twitch beneath me as I move, circling slowly. A groan leaves his lips, and his eyes drift shut.

I slide a hand between us and pull the string of his joggers, loosening them so I can slip my hand inside. His hard length feels good in my hand, and his jagged exhale lets me know how good it feels to him.

Then he reaches for me and tugs my hand away. "Linnie," he says, his eyes opening to swallow me in their depth. He shakes his head slowly.

"Why not?" If this is a game, I'll play the game. His body is telling me he wants this, so maybe he wants me to beg for it a little more. "Weston, I want you."

"Not like this."

"Then how?" I ask quietly, my voice sultry and teasing.

He sits up and lifts me off his lap, sliding me onto the blanket next to him. Swiveling around to face me, he searches my face, his eyes suddenly distant. "Linnie, what are we doing?"

I cock my head and squint. "Well, I thought we were going to have a proper shag, but now it seems like we're having a roundtable on foreign policy."

He shakes his head. "No. What just happened? Why did you suddenly flip a switch and shut off your emotions?"

"I didn't do that." I look away from him, caught.

"You did. Why?"

It would be easy to lie or pretend I don't know what he's talking about. This is my game, and I know how to play it, how to stay emotionally detached, have my fun, and walk away.

So do it.

I want to, but I can't. Weston has broken my autopilot somehow, so I bring my eyes up to meet his. "Do we have to talk about this?" I whine.

The tension in his face starts to dissolve, eyes softening. "We do. Talk to me, Linnie."

I open my mouth but no sound comes out. So I close it and try to will away the gremlin that's taken over my brain. Trying again leaves me gaping like a dying fish. "I don't know what to say."

He takes my hand and pulls it between us, resting it against his chest. I can feel the steady beat of his heart, feel his chest rise and fall with each breath. Placing his other hand against my lower back, he scoots me closer to him so we're sitting cross-legged, facing each other, knees touching.

"I guess . . ." I inhale as a stall tactic, but I can't hold the air in forever. When I let it out, some of my resistance goes with it. "I'm afraid to want you this much."

"Is wanting me necessarily a bad thing? Because I want you . . ."

"I feel ill equipped to let myself feel what I feel. In case I'm wrong about where this is going. I'm usually wrong."

"The past doesn't necessarily dictate the future. Someone pretty brilliant said that to me."

His hand moves from my back, up my rib cage and over my collarbone, where his fingers trace the shape of the bone before moving up the column of my throat. He guides my chin upward, never taking his eyes from mine. Their melted chocolate pools drown me, and I forget what conversation we were having.

Bringing his lips gently to mine, he barely skims my mouth.

The light touch makes me want to demand more—more contact, more pressure, more intensity—but he holds me where he wants me, only allowing the tiniest taste of what he plans to give.

Not allowing me to have anything if it doesn't feel like everything.

By holding me back, he breaks down my resistance.

The next kiss is deeper, more demanding. He takes my bottom lip into his mouth, sucking it lightly before letting it go. His tongue sweeps across the seam of my lips, and I open for him, ready for more, but he shakes his head and pulls back.

"We're going to do this differently. It means something to me."

Without realizing I'm doing it, I'm nodding. It *does* mean something. I'm just not sure I want it to.

And then I stop thinking and give in. My hands come to Weston's face, cupping his jaw so I can look at him. My eyes trace his face, the angle of his cheekbones, the beginnings of a beard, the eyes that swallow me whole, the lips I can't resist.

When I lean in to kiss him, he doesn't try to hold me back. I dissolve into his lips, allowing myself to feel what it does to every nerve ending when our mouths connect. Sighing with relief, I kiss him more deeply, and he nips at my bottom lip. It's honey drizzled over ripe berries. Perfection on a warm summer day.

His hand moves to the nape of my neck, tangling in my hair, twisting it into a knot that he uses to hold me at the angle he wants.

Now it's both of us meeting in the middle, our mouths finding each other, tongues swirling and tasting. We're both losing the grip on our restraint until it feels effortless. It's a kiss worthy of movie reels and long goodbyes.

I moan against his lips as they plunder mine, dragged out to sea and begging to stay adrift. This feels nothing like the purposeful snogs after a night at a pub. They were means to an end. This *is* the end, the most vital and beautiful thing I can imagine in the world, and we haven't even left the dock.

It scares me for what comes next, but I want all of it. If this is what it means to want someone for more than a one-night-stand, I'm powerless to push it away. Why would anyone stop after just one night?

My heart pounds in my ears, panic replaced by the sweet drumbeat of giving in to actual feelings.

It's all completely new. Like I've been seeing the world in shades of gray and someone pulled open the blinds, and the sunlight dressed everything in brilliant color.

Weston's hand slips under my shirt, roaming up my waist and palming one breast, massaging it, rolling my nipple through the silky fabric of my bra. I moan at the exquisite plea-sure that's almost too much. And yet not anywhere near enough.

I push up the layers he's wearing, shoving them higher until he helps me take them off. And then I take a moment and stare, appreciating every muscular contour of his chest and abs. Skin golden and tight over every ripple.

I'm about to say something silly about God's handiwork, but Weston's mouth claims mine in a searing kiss, and my commentary flees.

It feels so good that I want to give over to the feeling and soak him in like I'm a dry sponge. I feel myself losing the will to walk away and feel nothing. I love it and hate it equally. Giving up that last bit of control sticks in my throat like a jagged chicken bone.

And then I let it go. It flies off into the night like the millions of snowflakes that have blown past me since I've been here, light and carefree.

"Okay," I say, leaning back just enough to see Weston's eyes.

"Okay?"

I nod. "I'm not afraid of making the same mistake again."

"What changed?" he asks, quietly wary.

I think about how to put it into words, and it takes so long that Weston moves a little farther away, watching me. My eyes flit around as I think, wanting to say precisely what I mean, which is hard when I don't know what that is.

"With you, it doesn't feel like a mistake."

The amber within the brown of his eyes lights up like I've just flipped a switch. He says nothing, but his look tells me everything. The words he wants to hear, even if neither one of us knows what to do with them.

I lift my hand again to caress his cheek and notice that it's shaking. He grasps it and holds it to his skin for a moment before bringing it to his lips and kissing my palm. When he lowers it, I know he can still feel the quiver, and I wish I could stop my nervous twitching.

"Sorry. I don't know why I'm shivering."

"No need to apologize. You're nervous, that's why."

"I shouldn't be."

"It isn't a *should* or *shouldn't* sort of thing."

"It's silly. There's no reason for a case of nerves."

His eyes close for a long beat. "We're not going to do this tonight."

"We're not?" Now I'm confused, because I thought the whole point was for me to get my priorities straight, and now I have.

"We're going to stay right here, doing just this for another very long while. And you're going to sleep on it and make sure it's really what you want."

I start to protest, but his lips on mine make it impossible. They also seal the deal.

CHAPTER 18
WESTON

I wake up in the middle of the night after what feels like the sleep of the dead.

Checking my watch, I see I've been out for a solid two hours, but now my brain whirs and my heart races like I'm getting ready for the league championship.

My mind goes instantly to Linnie. I can't believe I let her talk me into sleeping in the bed and leaving her on the pile of blankets in the living room, like a puppy. Once the image of her invades my consciousness, there's no way I'm falling back asleep.

Now I'm not thinking about her curled up on blankets. I'm thinking about her curled around me. I'm. So. Fucked.

Throwing an arm over my eyes as though it will block everything else out, I dive into my thoughts. Strangely, the earlier feeling of panic over telling her things no one else knows has dissipated completely. Instead of feeling robbed of closely held secrets that protected me from the world, I feel oddly free.

She'll be leaving town in a few days, and everything I've told her will go with her, safely locked away at a distance of thousands of miles.

Do you want that?

Does it matter?

Now I'm thinking about how her lips look when she speaks —soft, kissable. And how they feel and taste when I take what I want from her. There's no retreating from that thought.

It's four in the morning, but it might as well be noon for as tired as I feel. Throwing the covers off, I decide to creep into the living room to make sure it's warm enough out there. I grab an extra blanket from the chair at the foot of the bed, just in case.

Linnie. She's curled up in the armchair next to the desk, one arm thrown over the back of the chair, the other wrapped around her knees. Having curled herself into a tiny ball, she fits within the confines of the chair, but it can't possibly be comfortable to have her knees bent in half like that. Yet she sleeps.

The peaceful curve of her lips, her eyelashes fanning over the tops of her cheeks—she continues to be a puzzle to me, this gentle beauty who goes at the world with guns drawn when she's awake.

The fire has died down to a quiet crackle, and the room has cooled considerably. I tuck the blanket around Linnie, but it looks bulky, and she shifts awkwardly in the chair, still asleep.

Fuck it.

Before I can talk myself out of it, I scoop her up, half expecting her to scream and thrash in my arms for fear of being carried off by a moose. Instead, the moment I lift her, she snuggles against my chest like it's where she's meant to be.

I carry her to the bedroom and place her carefully on one side of the bed. When I cover her with the sheets and blankets, a quiet sigh escapes her, but she doesn't wake.

Climbing into my side of the bed, I'm careful to give her enough space so it won't feel like I've kidnapped her and carried her to my lair.

Still feeling wired, I lie in the dark, intensely aware of Linnie's even breathing. It's soothing in a way I've never experienced with any woman I've briefly dated, maybe because I don't let most of them spend the night. And the ones who do . . . well, I've never paid much attention, because I'm not interested. They know and I know that it's temporary.

Just like this.

Linnie is only in town for a few more days, but now that the storm is tapering off, we'll be headed down the mountain soon enough, and she'll try to salvage the rest of her San Francisco vacation, and I'll go back to my life.

But for now I want her in this bed with me, even if it's just to sleep.

Of course the last thing I can do is sleep with her curled up mere inches away from me. My arms still pulse from where they touched her when I carried her to the bed. Almost like they're begging me to pull her close again.

That's what makes it all the harder when she sighs quietly next to me and her hand reaches out and drops onto my chest. I should move it away. Better yet, I should erect a wall of pillows between us.

After slipping from the bed, I go back to the living room, warmer by ten degrees thanks to the smoking embers from the fire. Something we'll need to deal with when we finish the renovations of this place—central heat. People who lived in mountain cabins back in the day must have had thicker blood than me. Or a lot more blankets.

I should sleep out here again. Now that Linnie is tucked into the bed, I feel better. But not as good as I felt a moment ago when I was there next to her.

I bring in an armful of pillows and line them near the center of the mattress, which seems to have gotten smaller in the three minutes since I was here. Or maybe it's that Linnie has stretched out her small frame and moved toward the middle of the bed. It only makes me glad I pulled her out of the cramped chair.

The golden strands of hair stripe the white pillowcase, and her round cheeks and rosebud lips make her look angelic in the dull light.

There's no room for me once the pillows are there. I'd be clinging to the edge of the bed all night, trying not to end up on the floor. So I have a choice—either go back and sleep on the living room floor and risk sitting out this weekend's game if my back spasms again, or I can get rid of the pillows and stay on my side of the bed.

I choose the latter, mainly because it's what I want. Sliding in next to Linnie, I feel the urge to gather her up close to me, but I vow to keep my hands to myself.

I say this over and over again in my mind, and eventually the monotony must drive me to sleep.

CHAPTER 19
LINNIE

The sun wakes me, and I have the instant sensation that something's different. Not unusual for me to be woken by the sun—it's how I wake up at home in the summer without setting an alarm. But it's not summer, I tell myself, slowly shucking off the veil of sleep. And I'm not at home.

Right. I'm at the cabin, where I don't recall drifting to sleep last night after drinking several glasses of wine and kissing Weston for hours, while he insisted I retain my boundaries until I was certain of what I wanted.

I'm grateful for that because I still don't know what I want. I'm leaving in three days. I shouldn't keep kissing Weston, no matter how much I like it. This relationship doesn't have a future.

It takes me a few minutes to come to full consciousness and realize where I am—in the cabin's bedroom, which I'm pretty certain isn't where I fell asleep last night.

The next thing I realize is that my face is smooshed up against Weston's shoulder, my arm draped across his chest.

Holy shit. Did I sleepwalk in here?

The thought strikes me as ridiculous because, as far as I know, I've never sleepwalked anywhere, let alone in a cabin that belongs to someone else.

I recoil and pull my arm back, which causes him to stir. It's only then I realize my legs are intertwined with his, and that suddenly makes me crave a soft pretzel with mustard. Also ridiculous.

And as much as I know I need to unwind my legs from his before he realizes I'm here, my body somehow takes charge over my sensibilities and tucks in a little tighter to him. Like a baby sloth curled up in a tree. It's utter madness, especially now that Weston is starting to wake. In another second he'll find me here, and I'll have to explain myself.

His eyes open lazily and catch sight of my own. Mine are certainly round with terror, which is what I expect to see from him in another second after he realizes I've taken over his bed. And his body.

Instead, a slow smile glides across his lips, and he reaches for the hand I just removed from his chest. He returns it to where it was, a fingertip stroking the back of my hand.

He must be sleeping. Dreaming—of someone else. There's no way he realizes it's really me here in his bed, or he'd be freaking out like I am. Instead, eyes still closed, he exhales, "Good morning."

I jerk my hand back again and try to jump out of the bed, but our legs are still tangled, a situation he does nothing to help. "I'm so sorry," I groan.

His heavy eyes work their way open, instantly sharp. "What? Why are you sorry?"

"I didn't mean to sleepwalk in here. It's never happened before."

Why do you insist that's true? You live alone and wouldn't really know.

"Oh shit. Maybe I do it all the time."

His eyes drift closed again, and again, I wonder if he's in the middle of a dream starring Pippa Middleton. "Do what?"

"Sleepwalk from room to room. Again, so sorry."

He shakes his head slowly against the pillow. "I brought you in here," he says, voice thick with sleep.

"You . . . what?"

"You were shoved into that tiny chair, and I didn't want you to wake up with your body in knots, so I carried you to the bed."

"But why?!"

"I just told you why." He clears his throat, and I watch him blink himself awake, confirming that he's fully aware that I'm here. In fact, it's because of him that I'm here.

"But—"

He silences me with a finger over my lips. "Relax, Linnie. It's okay."

"Is it? I don't see how it's okay that we've just slept together."

"We didn't have sex."

"Still. It feels like we did."

"I promise you, we didn't." He's trying not to laugh at me. Trying and failing. The crinkles around his eyes that I normally find charming now feel like the enemy. He points at the window, where a wide slit between the curtains lets in a bright ray of light. "Look at that. Sun's out."

I knew something was different. "Well, look at that. I almost forgot what the sun looked like."

I kick our legs apart and spring from the bed, looking down to make sure I'm actually fully dressed, and cross my arms over my chest anyway. And without my glasses or contacts, Weston is blurry again. I should find it a relief, but I don't.

"Why are you squinting at me like that? You were doing that the other day when you burned the cheese to the frying pan? Can you not see me, Linnie?"

"Oh, hell, this is when you decide to be bloody Sherlock Holmes? No, okay? I can't see you without my contact lenses. I don't sleep in them, and I wasn't expecting to have to face you first thing in the morning."

Weston taps a finger against his lip, and I do wish I could see him better, because I swear he's smirking at me.

Or studying me.

Or . . . "What?" I blurt finally.

"Why weren't you wearing your lenses yesterday while you were cooking?"

So. Caught.

"Um, I forgot?"

"Is that a question? Because I think the answer is *bullshit*."

He sweeps the covers off, and my eyes go directly to his blurry body, because if he's half-naked, I want to see it. But all I see is a blurry chest and six-pack and blurry gray sweatpants. Slowly, he comes around the bed to where I'm standing and tips my chin up to look at him. Hair perfectly rumpled, eyes dreamy, lips plump and crooked to one side like he's fighting a smile. Damn, if he doesn't wake up in the morning looking like dessert.

"Why weren't you wearing your contact lenses when you were trying to cook?"

"I wasn't trying. I was cooking."

"Linnie . . ."

"Because that way I could claim blindness if the meal turned out badly?" I feel like I've gotten caught lying by my teacher—and, sadly, I'm no better at coming up with excuses than I was at age twelve.

"I might have actually believed that if you didn't sound like you were asking a question."

"My voice is just scratchy in the mornings."

"Linnie."

"Fine. It was so I wouldn't have to look at you. In sharp focus."

At this close distance, there's no mistaking the smirk spreading across his face. He presses his lips together to stem its movement, but that only makes me want to take an even bigger bite out of him. To hell with *eyes up here,* I make a point of letting them wander down to his granite-carved chest and the generous ripple of each abdominal muscle beneath it. I feel my salivary glands preparing for breakfast.

"I feel like I should be insulted by that." But he's smiling.

"You should. I find you very unattractive and difficult to look at. Please back away so I'm relieved of the harsh glow of all those abs."

Now he's laughing. "You are adorable."

I cross my arms. "I'm not. Don't say that."

"Why not? It's absolutely true." The words come out with some sort of accent that might be a mocking British tone if it wasn't so plainly bad.

I hold up a finger. "One, save your acting for flopping on the soccer pitch. You don't need to go to the ground *every* time you get slide tackled. And two, I am strong and self-sufficient but hardly adorable."

He gets in my face, and I can barely handle the proximity without obviously inhaling him. "One. Thought you never watched a game." He waits while I gulp air and wish my words back into my dumb head. "And two. You can be all three. And you are. Deal with it."

Smug smile still plastered on his face, he sweeps past me

and goes into the bathroom. As the door closes behind him, I grumble and resist the urge to stomp my foot against the mattress. Then I do it anyway.

From inside the bathroom, Weston's voice growls, "Adorable."

CHAPTER 20

LINNIE

After several days here, it's become a given that Weston will do the cooking and I will observe from afar. I gratefully do all the dishes, and since I do, in fact, work at a pub, I've put myself in charge of making sure we have sufficient beverages at all times.

That includes right now, when I'm mixing instant cocoa into mugs with hot water while Weston is bumping around in the next room in preparation for some activity he hasn't yet specified. I think he even left for a bit while I was in the bathroom and went over to June's house.

Three days ago, the idea of agreeing to an activity without knowing all the details would have been a no-go. But I've come to trust Weston enough that I don't think he'll send me out into the woods to be devoured, so I'm trying to go with the flow.

"Mmm, that smells good," Weston says, coming into the kitchen in yet a different collection of Strikers gear. This time he's wearing a blue hoodie under a black jacket with the Strikers logo on the back. Black sweatpants emphasize his footballer thighs and narrow hips. "I think there are some to-go cups we can put it in."

"To go where?"

"We're going for a walk, and I'm going to introduce you to the mountain creatures that live here. None of which are moose."

"In the light of day, I wouldn't mind seeing a moose."

"They don't live here. Or anywhere close to here. You understand that, right?"

"It doesn't much matter. The point is that if I did see a moose, it wouldn't scare me during the day. I'd know how to deal with it."

"That's right. You'd put your arms in the air. Pretend to be a bear. I really hope we do see a moose, because I'm dying to find out how this all works out for you."

"And if it doesn't?"

"What?"

"What if I don't scare off the moose?"

He extracts a tiny cannister from his pocket and holds it out for me to read the label: BEAR SPRAY. "Do you feel confident it works on moose?"

"I feel pretty good. But if not, I guess you'd make a pretty tasty dinner for all of its friends."

"And you'd just stand back and watch with the satisfaction of being right?"

He nods. "I might also laugh."

"That's not very nice."

"When did I say I was nice?" He winks. "Besides, there's no chance a moose would win."

I turn away so he won't see my smile, pretending to be busy opening cabinets and looking for to-go cups. I find them in the second cupboard, and by the time I've transferred the cocoa and screwed on the lids, Weston has laid out several tennis rackets on the kitchen island.

"We're playing snow tennis?"

He glances at me questioningly, follows my eyes to the rackets, and tilts his head to the side like I'm adorable. "These are snowshoes. You wear them on your feet so you don't sink into the snow."

"Seriously?" I grab one of the contraptions and investigate it further. Sure enough, there are straps that look like they could attach to something, and if I'm honest, I'm quite relieved we aren't going to play tennis. "Okay, then. Let's go pet some moose."

AN HOUR LATER, I've discovered two things. One, there are no moose in the California mountains, at least none willing to come out and play. And two, snowshoeing is exhausting.

It's basically mountain climbing on a vertical slope in freezing temperatures with irritating tennis rackets flapping underneath one's shoes.

Weston has taken the lead, given that he presumably knows where we're going, and I'm trailing several yards behind him, trying not to chew off my own hand so I can throw it at him.

I've put on every article of warm clothing in my suitcase, plus the parka from the cabin, a pair of mittens Weston keeps in his training satchel for cold nights, and a red beanie with a pom-pom on top, courtesy of June.

Every so often, Weston points to some barely visible thing in the distance and calls out, "See those? Ground squirrel prints," or "Deer scat." I pretend to know what he's talking about and grunt appreciatively, but I stopped caring about seeing animals about four minutes into the trip.

I stay focused on the snowy mountain under my feet so I don't trip and fall into a snowbank. Weston plods along like a jolly snowman who's just discovered he has legs.

Sipping hot cocoa while also hiking lasted about five minutes before I realized I couldn't multitask, so I capped the to-go cup. Weston slipped it into a side pocket on his backpack and put his on the other side.

"I know this is probably child's play for you, what with how you train for football every bloody minute, but can we take a little breather?" I gasp. We've tromped uphill for what feels like a century, and I've barely noticed the scenery because I'm concentrating on not expiring.

"Just a little farther. Then, I promise, we'll take a break." He slows his pace slightly, which helps, but the man has been focused on some imperceptible thing, and he's hiking toward it like it's the Holy Grail.

Meanwhile, I gasp and wheeze like I've never seen the inside of a gym. Or taken a walk.

I can barely see Weston in front of the large backpack he's wearing. I mean, it's really quite large, spanning wider than him and extending down past his bum. I can't imagine what he has in there, but I've begun to hope it's a tiny plane to get us out of here. It feels like my only hope.

"Weston?"

"Yes?" His voice is blocked by the ridiculous backpack.

"Weston!"

"Linnie!"

Oh great, he thinks this is a game.

Sucking in all the air I can, I make peace with the idea that these may be my last words on earth, so I make them loud. "I'm not a snowshoer. Did I forget to mention?" The words come out between gulps of air. "And the altitude . . . I'm a bit knackered . . ."

He stops and turns. "Geez, Linnie, you're white as a sheet. Sorry. Why didn't you say something earlier?"

Shaking my head is the best I can do. I double over, put my hands on my knees, and breathe.

He rubs circles on my back, which I can barely feel through the thick parka, but I like it anyway.

"Just breathe," he says.

I do as told, but somehow now I'm breathing properly. Sucking in air with wheezing gasps, only to exhale and suck in more. I sound like a dying goose.

"Are you hyperventilating?"

OMG, why is he asking me questions I can't answer?

I glare at him and continue my weird breathing, unable to steady it. "You're hyperventilating." He wheels around as though a medic might appear from between snow-covered tree branches. Finding nothing, he puts one knee on the ground and guides me to sit on his other knee, which he holds up like a small chair.

I sit. I breathe. I focus on not freaking out that there isn't enough air in this forest to sustain me. He continues rubbing my back, his arms wrapped tightly around me, holding me close.

Between the warmth of his body, the break from mountain climbing, and the apparent availability of air in the forest, my breathing starts to return to normal.

We're in the middle of a billion tall pines with no obvious trail. I have no idea how Weston knows where to go, other than defaulting to hiking straight up.

"I exercise. I swear," I say, feeling taxed again just getting those words out, so there's no bloody way I'm admitting that the exercise of which I speak consists of yoga, not cardio. Never cardio.

"You don't need to defend yourself. It's the altitude. It's not you."

I look at him, fresh as a daisy, breathing and speaking

normally. The only indication of exertion is that his beanie is slightly—slightly—askew, like he may have wiped a single bead of sweat from his forehead and displaced it.

"Uh-huh."

"Sorry. I get going on a pace and I forget what I'm doing." His eyes trace over my face, ascertaining whether I'm okay, and land on my lips, which are probably bright pink from the cold. The warm chocolate brown of his eyes reminds me why I've agreed to come on this snow hike—I really like Weston. And if he wants to drag me up a mountain to some destination, I think I'll like it too.

"It's just," I say, carefully calibrating my breaths, "I left my oxygen tank back in England. Really wish I'd packed it."

He gives me a small smile, even though I feel I've earned more with all the hiking.

"Color's back in your face. Feeling better?"

I nod, and Weston adjusts my hat, straightening it and arranging my hair over the front of my jacket. "Can you go a bit farther? I think you'll be happy when we get there."

I nod again. "Though I'd love it if you told me where 'there' is."

"Soon. All will be revealed soon."

A light wind starts to blow snow flurries across the landscape, spinning the flakes so they look like tiny children dancing across the white floor. Above us, the sky is cloudy white, but the wind swirls the clouds so no two seconds of sky-gazing are alike.

We start moving again, Weston practically jogging up the snow hill while I trudge along, focusing on breathing all the air.

My chest aches as the cold air hits the bottom of each lung, but I no longer feel a sense of imminent death.

Weston doesn't try to engage me in conversation, which helps the breathing situation, but every so often he looks behind to make sure I'm still chugging along, and I give him a little salute. Or my middle finger.

"Okay, this is it," he calls, and my head jerks up at those life-affirming words. It takes me a few more paces to catch up to where he is and another moment to free my snowshoe from where it gets stuck in a hole, and even the hole is against me, seeming to rub its evil hands together, ready to pull me to the center of the earth.

Weston catches me just before I topple over and helps free my foot from the stubborn snowshoe before I can kick him with it. Then he unstraps my other one and puts his arm around me. We walk over to a patch of perfectly placed boulders with a flat-enough surface for us to sit on.

"Have a look." Weston gestures to the winter wonderland beneath our feet and leans over to unzip his giant backpack, which he's placed on a rock behind us.

For the moment I'm just relieved we've stopped moving. Then, once the risk of acute suffocation passes, I start to notice things.

We've reached the peak of a mountain, and there's nothing else higher than where we are. Behind us is the pine forest Weston somehow navigated without a compass or a GPS, at least nothing I saw. In front of us . . . wow.

I don't sit yet. There's too much around us and beneath us in the distance to see. The snow has stopped falling, and with the newfound visibility, I see mountains looming ahead, adding to the sense of wonderment at how vast and snowy this place is. And blissfully devoid of people.

A small frozen lake glistens under a few brave rays of sunlight. The clouds have blown toward a neighboring mountain ridge, yielding a jagged crevasse of blue sky and enough sun to light up the snow to nearly blinding brightness.

Snow hangs on every tree bough, and other than the tracks

left by our snowshoes, the blanket on the ground is pristine. "This is amazing." I don't say more, not because I can't draw enough breath, but because I can't find the right words to do justice to the beauty all around. The lake. Trees looming toward the sky. White piles of snow everywhere.

"This," Weston says, gesturing around us, "is why I bought the cabin with your brother. This hike, which, admittedly, I've only done in the summer. Straight from our back door to the peak of the mountain, and it's not an official trail, so it's basically unknown to anyone who doesn't live here."

Leaning back on his elbows, he takes in the view, which has shifted again as the clouds return to hide the sun. The lake below looks more gray than white.

I lean back next to him on the flat rock, my feet grateful for the break from walking. Weston rummages in his backpack and pulls out a dark-red blanket from the house, wrapping it around us, but I'm barely cold.

"How did you know how to get here without a trail?" I ask, snuggling against him.

He maneuvers me between his legs, pulling me toward his chest and wrapping his arms around me. I've given up trying to resist these bits of affection, partly because my body begs for more whenever he touches me, so it's no bloody use at pushing him away. It feels natural to be with him this way. He points to a tree to our left. "Do you see the markings on that tree? The red and the blue stripes?"

They're small and very high up the tree trunk, but I nod.

"Those are trail markers for cross-country skiers. I followed the blue markings to get us here."

He doesn't release his hold on me, so I settle into the comfort of his shoulder. I'm starting to think it was worth the near-death experience of getting here, especially when I feel his lips against my temple.

"Thank you for coming up here with me. You're a good sport."

I'm tempted to say something sassy in reply, but I decide to take the compliment. "You make it easy to say yes to things."

I hear him inhale and I half expect a confession of some kind. I've started to understand that's how he prepares himself. But all he says is, "I'm glad."

Sitting atop our perch, we gaze at the world below us, absent of humans, everything dusted in white. "You grew up in a place like this?" I ask, awestruck and hoping the question doesn't sound intrusive. I tear my gaze from the beautiful view to look over my shoulder at Weston.

He doesn't turn to face me, and his brow furrows. "Not exactly like this. I mean, it was a town. There were sixty thousand people in it. So views like this . . ." He spreads his arms wide. "We had to work for them, same as today. But always worth it."

"You and your Big Brother?"

From behind me, I feel him inhale sharply. I put up a hand. "I'm not trying to make you talk about it. I was just curious about your life."

His expression relaxes, and he picks up my hand, which I kept warm on the way up by shoving it in my pocket. But now it's cold. He rubs it between his, which are equally cold, but the friction helps us both.

"Mostly with him. He was more like an uncle than a brother, easily twenty years older than me. And he liked to hike and camp, so that's what we did together."

His voice is so quiet I almost mistake it for the breeze until he points at something a few feet away. "Look."

I follow his finger but see nothing. "I'm looking. Not seeing. Unless you're pointing at snow. I see that."

He pulls me tighter and leans us to the left so I have the

same vantage point, then points again. "There, next to the cluster of saplings. Do you see it?"

I don't. "Um, maybe? Yeah, I think I do."

His low chuckle tells me he doesn't buy it for a second. "Give her a second and she'll probably move."

"Her?" I half expect to see June on a snowmobile, since she's the only person I've seen for days.

Just then I see a flash of brown amid the white, and a quartet of long, graceful legs leads a large doe in our direction. Tiny spots of white dapple her brown coat, her eyes glistening black. She's only a few yards away. "How did I not see her?" I whisper.

We both sit motionless, watching her pick among the low branches of the saplings. "They camouflage. That's why I wanted to sit here. Best chance we'll have of seeing animals. If we're moving around and making noise, they'll hide."

A ripple of panic hits me when the deer turns abruptly to stare at us. She must have heard Weston's voice. "Is she going to attack?" I ask, my whisper too loud for her not to notice us, if she hasn't already. The deer continues to stare.

"No. Not unless you eat her babies."

"I would never," I say way too loudly, and the deer turns and bolts. Four quick jumps and she's invisible among the brown tree trunks, her white tail the last thing I see. "Sorry," I say quietly.

"Now she whispers," Weston mocks, so calm and comfortable out here.

"Sorry." I tuck into myself, embarrassed for being so scared when he makes it seem like there's no reason to be afraid. Of wild animals.

He brushes a tendril of hair from my cheek and shakes his head. "You don't need to apologize. Is that the first time you've seen an animal up close?"

"You know what animals I'm used to? Dogs. And sheep. I can milk a cow like nobody's business. But this . . ." I spread my arms wide. "This beautiful wild nature thing is a little bit intimidating."

"I promise you, we're so much more of a threat to these animals than they are to us."

"I guess when you put it that way, it's kind of awesome to be out here in their world."

He shrugs. "It's how I see it."

Weston pulls our to-go cups from his backpack, and we sip our respective hot drinks on top of the world. It really is spectacular to have this view to ourselves.

I've come to love my unexpected mountain vacation, and I idly wonder how the city of San Francisco could possibly be better than this.

This. Pulled snug against Weston with his gravelly voice warming me from the inside out—I could get used to this. And now that I've proven that I don't need to fall into bed with a man, that it's not my identity or my destiny, it makes me want to fall into bed with this man. Because it feels different.

And maybe . . .

"Hey." His voice slips into my reverie. "You hear that?"

I strain to listen through the quiet air for some hint of what he means. Then I do hear it. A motor.

"That's the snowplow hard at work. We're getting off this mountain, Linnie. Probably by the end of the day."

"Well, thank heaven for that," I say. But I don't mean it. Not at all.

Weston leans close again and whispers, "Maybe we should head back down to the cabin. What do you think?"

Stretching out my legs and tipping my head against Weston's shoulder, I feel too content to move. "I think that given the choice between being airlifted off this mountain so I don't have to walk and spending more time in the freezing cold right here like this, I know what I'd choose."

"What would you choose?" His whisper in my ear thrills my senses.

"I'd choose this."

I'd choose you.

"I'd choose this too." His gentle smile widens just as the sun peeks through the clouds again, showering him in gold dust that does the impossible—makes the chocolate lakes of his eyes deepen, makes him look even more beautiful.

"Can we stay up here a bit longer?"

"We can stay as long as you want."

We stay for at least an hour. And no, even with the sun dipping in and out of the clouds, the weather doesn't get any warmer. But it feels warm because I'm wrapped in his arms.

"I think you'll like part two of this adventure. It accomplishes both of your objectives—getting down quickly and doing it with my arms around you to keep you warm."

"You're driving the airlift?"

"Ha. Not exactly, but . . ." He leans back to where he's shucked off the giant backpack and pulls it over. After unzipping it, he frees a large blue plastic thing that looks like a . . . oh, because it is a . . .

"You carried a sled?" I ask, disbelieving. I can't tell if it's heavy, but the sheer size of it proves how unwieldy the backpack must have been.

"Fastest way down the hill." His gaze sneaks to me, gauging whether I'm game for this level of adventuring. "Hope you're not too disappointed I didn't bring two sleds. I know how you love a competition."

"Nope, no way I'd be disappointed with this."

Weston carries the sled over to a spot at the side of the boulders. When I follow him and look down the mountain, I see a tiny postage-stamp roof visible through the trees. "Is that the cabin?"

"I don't think that's ours, but it might be June's. Ours is hidden a bit by her hill."

Ours.

He doesn't stop to correct himself, and then I realize he doesn't mean ours like his and mine. He means the cabin he owns with my brother. But the small twinge of joy I felt for a brief moment, thinking about the cabin being ours, still has its hold on me. My skin is kissed by electric eels. Tingly. Feverish.

When he puts the sled on the snow and holds a hand out to help me onto it, I let myself pretend we're the only two people who exist. Caught in a snow globe. And I feel happy.

Once I'm seated, Weston lowers himself behind me, putting one leg on either side of me and reaching one hand for a hardy sapling to anchor us so we don't slip down the hill prematurely.

Except then we do . . .

Weston lets go of the branch in order to put the backpack on, and that millisecond is enough for the sled to gain purchase on the slippery snow beneath us.

"Whoa!" I hear from behind me as our combined weight launches us forward at rapid speed. We are flying! The sled only picks up speed as the friction underneath melts the snow and makes it slick and fast.

"Shit. Shiiiit!" Weston yells, trying to arrest our speed by sticking his foot out. That only serves to spin us around so now we're racing down the slope backward. I cling to his knees because they're the only part of him I can grasp.

"Stop, you're going to fly off!" I yell, not wanting to ricochet off with him.

Weston digs his heel in once more, and we pivot around again, this time facing mostly forward and hitting every contour in the snow, bouncing hard on the landing and grunting with every awkward bump.

"Sorry!" he yells as we careen down the mountain, picking up speed and carving through fresh snow, which sprays up into our faces. I can barely see, which is probably a good thing, because there are trees and who knows what else in our path, but Weston manages to guide us by leaning so hard from one side to the other that we manage to turn.

"Don't be sorry!" All I can do is hang on to him and hope I don't fly off the sled.

I hear myself screaming, but it's not out of fear. This is the most exhilarating ride I've had for as long as I can remember. I scream the whole way down the mountain like I'm on the best roller-coaster ride of my life.

I shrug up my shoulder to wipe the snow from one eye and see that we're down in a thick stand of trees, carving a narrow path on the one straightaway of snow between them. I have no idea how we haven't slammed into a tree trunk, but we're still flying at high speed.

"Woo-hoo!" I yell as the top of Weston's street comes into view. I can see at least one house looming large, and I'm about to ask Weston how he plans to stop this runaway train when we hit a giant divot in the snow. It's more like a cavern. Or a crevasse.

For some reason my brain is stuck in synonym overload as we fly through the air, Weston gripping me so tightly I think I'll have bruises.

After we land, we don't stop. The sled swerves to the side and spins around until it dead-ends when the hill finally flattens, stopping so abruptly in a two-foot snowbank that we both fly backward off the thing.

I have a sense of being airborne, but only for two seconds before I'm dumped down into deep snow on my back. Weston, still holding on to my arm, splats in the snow next to me. And partly on top of me.

Snow is most definitely crammed down my knickers, instantly freezing my bum, and an equal amount shoved up my back. A shower of icy flakes rains down on all the parts of me that aren't covered by Weston, whose face is tucked into my neck.

I'm more exhilarated than I've ever been, possibly injured, definitely cold, and certain of one impossible truth—I am falling in love with Weston.

It's inconvenient and bound to leave me sad and disappointed in a few days, when I leave America for my real life back in Saltney. But for now I decide not to think about that.

CHAPTER 21

WESTON

We're wet, we're snowy, and we're lying in a heap at the bottom of the slope. I feel Linnie shaking beneath me, and I worry I've hurt her. Maybe she's in shock from the landing or shivering from the cold.

"Linnie! Are you okay?"

Between the wild ride and the even wilder crash at the bottom, I must have pummeled her. She's wearing lots of layers, so maybe that protected her from getting crushed. Still, I have her pinned beneath me in the snow.

Then I hear the now-familiar wheeze of her silent giggles, and I push up onto my hands so I can see her. She's half-covered in snow, gobs of flakes coating her lashes, a dusting of ice crystals over her face. Her eyes are closed and she's convulsing with laughter. It's the most beautiful sound. Uninhibited, authentic.

When she opens her eyes and looks at me, the spasms of laughter begin anew, this time more audibly. Tears squeeze from the corners of her eyes, and the unbridled joy makes me a different kind of happy than I've ever experienced.

I'm sure I look like a human snowman, since I landed facedown. I don't even attempt to wipe the snow away and can barely feel my face anyhow.

Ice clings to my eyebrows and cakes the scruff I have after several days without shaving. It's a struggle to work my jaw in the cold, so I can't get a word out. But Linnie's laughter is contagious, and before long I feel it racking my body. Rolling off to the side, I lie next to her in the snow and join her.

Most people I know who play sports for a living have moments—the lucky few have lots of moments—when everything lines up and a ball comes off a foot or a bat or a racket and yields perfection. Sometimes game-winning perfection. I've had more than my share of those moments, more than any kid from a small town could hope for. I've felt the adrenaline rush when the roaring crowd elevates my one-on-one performance into a stadium-worthy event. There's nothing like that feeling. It's a drug, the success, the victory, the adulation.

Then it ends.

Then normal life resumes and we begin the climb again. I've grown so used to that feeling that I don't question it. And I never wondered whether there's a different version of joy.

This, listening to Linnie laugh and feeling the warmth of her body next to me, despite the chill in the air and the snow coating everything, this is joy. And I don't want to lose it. Not yet.

"Linnie," I say when the laughter subsides enough that I can breathe. "Are you okay? Did I crush you?"

She shakes her head, which causes some of the ice caked in her hair to fling in my direction. "That was so much fun. I might even hike up that hill again to do it once more."

"Really?" I roll to my side to look at her.

She nods but gives me a definitive, "No. No more hiking. But I loved the ride."

We gather ourselves up and survey the damage. We're snowy, but the layers of clothes protected us from bruises.

Holding on to each other for balance in the piles of snow, we amble back to the cabin, where I deposit the snowshoes and sled by the front door and get a fire going. Linnie doesn't bother to notice which method I use.

She appears with a note she found taped to the front door. "It's from June. She says the roads are mostly cleared. That's good news . . . right?" She doesn't sound convinced.

"Yes, great news." My tone is brighter than it needs to be, because I know she wants to be in San Francisco, and I don't want her to feel bad about wanting it.

"I should let my brother know we'll be back later." She frees her phone from the pocket of her jacket and pulls up Tim's number. But she doesn't type anything. "So . . . we don't have to rush down the mountain. Maybe we can stop for dinner? Once more for the road? I should be taking advantage of the time in San Francisco, but . . ."

Her finger stays frozen over the screen, so I chance a look at her face. Her expression reflects what I feel—obligation to get back to San Francisco, but no desire. So I take a gamble.

"Actually . . . ," I say, reaching for her phone. She watches while I start typing a message to her brother, my best friend.

Linnie: *Road won't be clear until morning. Have to stay one more night.*

An utter and complete lie. Her eyes shoot from the phone screen to my face. Then her hand moves over the phone and she presses send.

"One more night," she confirms.

"Just to be clear," I tell her, my eyes boring into the depths of her green, letting her gaze swallow me up. "Neither one of us is sleeping on the fucking floor."

There's no way I'm leaving this cabin without showing

Linnie exactly how I feel about her. I have no idea what her plans will entail when she gets back to the city and spends the rest of the week with her brother. I have no idea if I'll even see her.

So I have tonight.

CHAPTER 22

LINNIE

After the text message whooshes away, Weston pulls me close, his arm circling around my waist and tugging my hips against his. The other hand slowly unzips my jacket. With each chug of the zipper links, I feel my body saying yes to him.

Yes, I want you to keep going until I'm stripped of every article of clothing.

Yes, my skin is humming with the need to be touched, licked, stroked until I melt.

Yes, I'll take my time and feel every delicious moment because I can't bear *not* to feel a single one.

When my zipper hits bottom, Weston lifts the jacket off my shoulders and turns my back against the cabin door, pulling our hips flush. I can feel him hard against me, lighting me up from the inside and dousing my skin with heat. His mouth claims mine. No more hesitation, no questions asked about whether I'm ready. I am, and he knows it.

His kiss is hot, wet, controlling. Holding my face like it's a delicate thing, he ravishes my mouth like it's the opposite—

there to meet him halfway, tongues sliding against each other. A perfect fit.

"Not letting you out of my sight tonight, so get used to it," he growls against my ear. I nod, my body slack in his arms. I have no fight left in me—I want him, even if I have to recover from it later.

"Not going anywhere," I pant as we toe off our snowy shoes.

Weston plants tiny kisses along my jaw, down my neck. He kisses the hollow of my throat before swiping the skin with his tongue. A tiny sigh escapes me, and he swallows it in another long, commanding kiss.

While our mouths fuse and our tongues tangle and explore, Weston unbuttons his own jacket and slips it off his arms. It lands on the floor on top of mine.

His hands roam down over my waist and hips until they're planted firmly under my ass, which he squeezes in generous handfuls. "Been wanting to get my hands on this luscious ass for days," he rasps against my lips.

I melt against his chest, shivering at how he makes my skin feel like a live wire.

"Come." Weston beckons with one finger, leading me through the living room. "You're freezing."

Shaking my head, I try to form the words to tell him he's wrong. He's lit a fuse that can end only in an explosion. I'm melting. I'm burning up.

But I can't speak, not when his lips find mine again, and this time I allow myself to have what I've been wanting since I drove up the mountain and saw him for the first time.

His kiss is tender, cherishing. As if there's no rush now that we've crossed this divide. No race to get each other's clothes off, have a proper hookup, and part ways before either of us has a chance to like it too much.

It's so much better this way, slow and languid. So good it's almost painful.

"I-I don't know how to do this," I admit. He might as well know the lot of it. "I'm more of a cut-to-the-chase kind of woman."

His smile spreads slowly, like a fire catching on kindling and lighting me up with it.

"I think you do. And if not, I'll teach you." I feel something so foreign I have to check myself—is it trust?

He takes my hand and leads me to the bedroom. Even though I woke up in this bed with him, now it feels so different. Intentional. Exhilarating.

I'm also scared to death because I've left the dock fully aware that I can't swim, and I'm here without a life jacket. I have to trust him or I'll drown.

Danger. Go back to shore!

But when his lips brush mine, I feel the thoughts slipping away. He is the life preserver I need, and my body responds to him like he's unlocking parts of me, bit by bit, setting me free.

I feel like a virgin, only not the fumbling kind in the back of some bloke's car. I feel stripped clean of the mistakes in my past and freed of my own judgment.

My skin hums when Weston runs his hand under my shirt, pushing it up and baring my stomach. I shiver from the flash of cold, but he immediately warms me with his mouth, kissing a line up my flesh and pushing my shirt higher still.

Habit has me wanting to shove it over my head and get naked as soon as possible, but he quells the instinct as his lips sear my flesh and his tongue sweeps higher, teasing the under-sides of my breasts through the fabric of my bra. "I want to see you," he rasps, and I nod, letting him set the pace. Because it's perfection.

Slowly he works my shirt up over my shoulders, lifting my

back off the bed to unhook my bra before slipping it over my head. He lays me back down gingerly, like I'm a jewel he doesn't want to lose in the rumpled sheets. I look up at him, watching him just as carefully as he's taking me in.

The chocolate of his eyes melts into his pupils, dilated and simultaneously focused, rolling over every curve of my body and causing a breath to well in his chest. Exhaling, he shakes his head. "Fuck. You can't be this beautiful. It's almost immoral."

I'm certain I could say the same about him, only he's still wearing all his clothes, something I'm desperate to remedy. But I quell that instinct in favor of being in the current moment, letting his words sink in until an unbridled smile lifts the corners of my lips. "You are a charmer, Danny Weston."

At the use of his first name, he sucks in a breath. I worry for a second that I've overstepped. He locks eyes with me and I wait, frozen.

His only movement is a single finger tracing the line of my jaw, following the curve of my cheek, and pushing a few stray tendrils of hair away from my face. He looks at me reverently, but he's still unreadable. It's part of what I've grown to like so much about him—the complications in his thoughts that manifest in his expressions.

A shot of boldness urges me to double down. "Danny," I whisper and watch his eyes dilate, black pupils nearly indistinguishable from the molten brown.

Then his lips crash to mine, giving as much as they're taking, guiding me into a rapturous kiss that lasts for minutes ... an hour ... I don't know.

I pull him down hard against my body, needing the weight of him. We're untethered, following instinct instead of reason. Lifting me higher than my imagination dares to take me.

Sighing against his mouth, I let my hands roam beneath his

layers of shirts, running my nails over the skin at the small of his back. His hand moves from where he's cupping the side of my face to the hem of his shirt, helping me push it higher.

We stop kissing only long enough to get it over his head, and then we're lost again, skin flush against skin, the rush of sensations too overwhelming to sort out—the warmth of his body, the glorious feel of his skin flush against mine, the intensity of a kiss that goes on and on.

In a fluid motion, Weston rolls us to the side and pulls me so that I'm straddling his lap. Looking down at the taut skin carved over muscle beneath me, I actually start to salivate, which makes me giggle.

His quizzical expression dissolves when I tell him, "You should burn all of your shirts. All of your clothing, really." I lower my mouth to his chest and run my tongue over every ripple, tasting his skin and groaning despite my attempt to show restraint.

I rock against him, relishing the feeling of him hard against my center, exactly where I need him. But it's not enough. I'm not sure anything would be enough to satisfy the carnal craving I have for this man.

And because he's Weston—star athlete with abs of steel— he has no trouble flipping us entirely over before I even realize he's done it. Now he's straddling me and leaning down to clamp down on my nipple with his teeth. The delicious pain rips through me and I gasp.

He soothes it with his tongue, drawing circles around the peak before nipping the tender skin once more. He cups my other breast and lavishes attention there, nipping and licking until I'm writhing under him and moaning his name.

"Danny..."

He continues kissing down my abdomen until his face hovers above my unsexy knickers. They're beige boy shorts, but the way his eyes roam over me makes me feel like they're the most gorgeous French lingerie in the world.

"I need this pussy. Now," he whispers, sliding the stretchy fabric down in one fluid motion. Once he gets them over my feet, he runs a hand from my foot all the way up my inner thigh until I'm trembling beneath his touch.

He follows the same path with his tongue, slowly licking up one leg while his hand traces the sensitive flesh of the other.

When he reaches the apex of my thighs, he sighs. The light breath on my most sensitive parts makes me quiver and moan. I'm completely his. My body is an instrument, responding to his touch but having no use on its own.

My hands tangle in Weston's hair, and I lean up to watch him as his tongue traces my flesh, lightly teasing my clit before licking straight up my center. "So fucking wet, Linnie. So goddamn beautiful."

I want to believe him. Men have told me things for years, all designed to get into my knickers, but I always knew it was all talk. I barely heard them when they spoke. But now—this—I'm soaking up every word and tucking them away like nuggets of gold.

His eyes flash to mine and I feel myself slipping away.

"God, Danny . . ."

He slides a finger inside me and continues circling my clit with his tongue until I'm flying. Higher than the sled took us earlier. Higher than the stars.

Then I'm coming apart, moaning his name and begging him not to stop. He quickens his pace, adding a second finger and curling it around my G-spot.

And that's it. I'm launched out of my skin and into a place of pure bliss. So high that it takes me several minutes to regain my senses and return to earth.

When my eyes blink open, Weston's face fills my frame of

vision, and I can't help the lazy smile that drifts over my features.

"I think I've effectively ruined my hookup streak." I'm trying to lighten the mood, but it's impossible to deny the intensity of what just took place, and Weston doesn't buy into it for a second.

"This was never going to be just a hookup," he says, stating empirical fact like a tenured professor. He shakes his head. "That's not what this is. I wish it could be so simple, believe me, because it would make my life so much easier, but . . ." He shakes his head, regret for what we're both losing evident in his face—control over our emotions that would be so much more convenient than this. Feelings.

I reach for him, and he moves up the bed so our bodies are connected at every juncture. Wrapping my hand around his hard length, I stroke him until he groans against my neck. He feels so good in my palm, thick and pulsating as I run my thumb over the head, circling until I feel moisture at the tip.

He places a condom in my palm, and I roll it on, anticipating the languid, aching pace that will build me up again. He does not disappoint. After sliding inside me, he moves so slowly that I feel every nerve ending fire as he goes. And with a final thrust, he fills me.

He's a flame and I'm a bone-dry pile of kindling.

We move together because we're meant to be exactly like this, eyes locked on each other, emotions that are returned but unsaid. Taking each other higher, sighing through kisses and moaning through bliss. And shouting expletives when there's nothing left to say.

"Danny . . ."

All restraint over my emotions . . . gone.

CHAPTER 23
WESTON

Never was there a sexier sound in the world than my own name from Linnie's lips.

"Danny..."

That's all it takes for me to tumble over the edge with her into something that scares the hell out of me for how much I love it. I'm instantly addicted. She's every temptation in a gorgeous, curvy body, and I'm wrapped around every curve.

The only sound in the room is her breathing, and I listen to it slowly return to normal, tracking my own.

Nothing needs to be said. Words can't do justice to what I just felt, and even if they could, there's beauty in the simplicity of silence.

After a while Linnie shifts beneath me and I roll to the side, an idea occurring to me. There are still a few unused items in June's stash from her basement, and we haven't eaten anything in hours. Not that I'm planning on cooking.

"Don't move," I instruct, sliding away from Linnie and feeling an emotional gut punch for it. I pull on a pair of sweatpants because it's still damn cold in the cabin, and I kiss her temple. Then her lips.

I'm coming right back, I tell the ache in my chest, trying to push down my reaction to her, now that I've let my heart off its leash.

"Mm-hmm." Her dreamy expression reflects how I feel.

In the kitchen I scrounge through the last remaining bag and prepare a few things before returning to the bedroom with a plate and two beers.

Linnie sits cross-legged on the bed in a T-shirt. "Why are you wearing clothes?" My words tumble out, accusatory.

"I figured we were moving on to another activity." She points to her lower half, still bare. "But just in case, I split the difference."

"Good thinking." My voice is worn sandpaper, filed down to uselessness. "Brought us some snacks. Not Maltesers, but maybe a fair second."

She squints, confused, after I point to the assortment of chocolate on the plate. I took a chance that our neighbor, who seems prepared for every eventuality, might have a candy stash. It would've been a bit too convenient if she actually had malted milk balls, but the Junior Mints, See's toffees, assorted truffles, and chocolate-covered raisins would have to do. Linnie's closed-mouth smile rounds her cheeks and makes her dimple pop. She looks angelic.

"Sex *and* candy? Weston, you must want me never to leave."
You don't know the half of it.

"Purely self-serving. I want to keep your energy up for another round. Or ten."

Linnie gingerly reaches for one of the toffees as though it's inside the open mouth of an alligator that might bite off her hand. When she pops it in her mouth, her eyes drift closed, and for a second I feel a pang of jealousy.

"Oh my god, this is so good. You must have one." She

nudges the plate toward me, and I pop a couple of chocolate-covered raisins in my mouth, washing them down with beer.

We sit on the bed, sampling the different candy, and I feel newly gratified each time Linnie is delighted by another type of sweet.

"It's like a little surprise party for my mouth," she says, savoring a raspberry truffle. I've stopped reacting to all the suggestive things she says. And she's stopped getting embarrassed.

"God, I hate surprise parties," I grumble at the mere suggestion.

Linnie looks at me like I've just told her I hate bunnies, especially the lop-eared ones who gobble down carrots in Instagram videos. "How? Why?"

"One, they're never a surprise. Leading to two, I have to try and convince everyone all night long that, yes, they really did trick me and, no, I really didn't see it coming."

"Wow, you're bleak."

"Not bleak, just practical. If I want to have a party, I'll have a party. I'm not antisocial. I'm very capable of throwing a party when the situation merits it."

"*When the situation merits it?* Who are you and what have you done with Fun Weston?"

"I wasn't aware there was a *Fun Weston*."

"Yeah, I had my doubts, too, but put a soldering iron in your hand and it turns out you're a party." She thinks about it and revises her findings. "Okay, maybe not a party. More like a few notches up from a funeral."

"Yeah, I don't do funerals either."

She waves her hands like a referee. Then she makes a T with one hand on top of the other. "Time-out, hang on. What? How does a person *do* or *not do* funerals?"

I don't know why I've started down this path of confession. Something about her makes me want to admit everything, flaws and all. I stand up and pace in a circle. "I just mean I don't go to them."

Her voice pitches up to a near shriek. "But what if someone dies? You have to go." We're at moose-level screeching.

Trying to drown the conversation in a swig of beer, I shake my head. "I don't have to do anything, and if I need to say goodbye to a loved one, I can do it in my own way."

She watches me for so long I start to wonder if she's okay. In the time I've known her, she's never been this quiet for this long. Her eyes dart around and finally land on my face. "I guess that's reasonable, but I'm still not sold on the surprise-party thing. What do you mean they're never a surprise?"

Relieved she doesn't want to belabor the other topic, I gratefully riff on my aversion to surprises. "Oh, you know. Someone always spills the beans. Even if they don't mean to, they say something, and I figure it out. It's just . . . I'd rather plan my own party. Okay? No big deal."

She stares at me, and I prepare for an onslaught of arguments. Instead, she nods. "Yeah, I get that. I'm impossible to surprise."

"See, now, *that* surprises me."

"Why?"

"Because you take delight in everything. I feel like even if you knew about a party, you'd still find something surprising in the execution of it."

"Nope. It's impossible. My overly suspicious mind prevents it."

I can't help it. I laugh. "I'm going to find a way to surprise you."

"No offense, but you won't. Not that I discourage the attempt. Just don't feel bad when it doesn't work out."

"Oh, it will work out, I assure you." Now it's game on. I have no idea what kind of surprise it will be, but I'm one determined son of a bitch, and you can bet I'll come up with something good.

"Okay."

"Okay?" I side-eye her suspiciously. There's an argument coming, I just know it. She doesn't agree this easily about anything.

Delicately, she lifts her own beer to her lips and takes a slow sip, wiping her lips afterward. It all has the effect of making me want to lick them clean, and I realize she's manipulating me.

Wagging a finger, I shake my head. "Nope, not falling for that, honey. Not going to distract me with your sexy lips."

She crosses her arms, pushing her cleavage up and emphasizing the swell of her breasts under the flimsy shirt.

"Nope, I can resist those ripe, full breasts. Watch me." My voice sounds like I'm gargling gravel.

"Weston, can you give me a hand? I can't seem to unhook my bra." She turns and lifts the back of her shirt, revealing the milky white skin that nips in at her waist. There's no bra, just her perfect skin, begging me to put my hands on it.

Swallowing hard, I take a giant step backward. That's how good I feel about my chances of resisting her. Laughing, she turns and advances one step, then two. She traces a line from my elbow, down my forearm, ending at my hand. She brings my fingers to her mouth and slips each one between her lips. One. At. A. Fucking. Time.

"Fine," I pant. "For you, I'd go to a funeral. But not a surprise party, never a surprise party." I'm desperate for her, almost willing to give up my last request.

"Done. Enough talking." She drops to her knees in front of me and pulls at the string on my sweatpants. When she raises her eyes to mine, I'm caught in their storm. She nods, slips my pants down my legs, and licks her lips. I'm seeing stars, and she hasn't even touched me yet.

This woman . . . she'll be the end of me . . . and the beginning of everything I've ever wanted.

CHAPTER 24

LINNIE

Driving down the mountain, I have a strange feeling of emptiness. It's the same exact drive I took in the opposite direction several days earlier, but everything is different.

Weston.

I've become so used to being around him twenty-four seven that I feel like I'm missing a limb simply by having him a couple of yards behind me in a separate car.

A part of my heart aches to have him closer, and I'm not familiar with that part of myself. Where was it before? Did it exist? Did I exist in the way I want to before I met him?

Get a grip on yourself, Lin.

Is this what happens to people when they snog the same person for hours upon hours and let their emotions get involved? Their brains turn to pea soup.

I check my rearview mirror for the four-hundredth time since we started down the mountain about a minute ago. Yes, he's still there. Yes, I'm fairly certain I can see his abs. Well, clearly not. But I remember them in full bas-relief after last night, and that image will sustain me for days.

We agreed to stop halfway to *The City*, as Weston insists on calling it. It makes me think of the Emerald City in *The Wizard of Oz*, and I wonder if it will feel as magical. Something tells me there's no way for it to feel as magical as the past few days we've spent together.

My phone buzzes, and I assume it's Weston, calling to give me a hard time about my driving on the right side of the road. "I think I'm doing quite well. I've only run into the curb a few times," I chirp after hitting the button.

"You've done what?"

"Oh. I thought you were someone else," I tell Tim, who is going to be in for quite a surprise when he sees his car. I figure there's no need for him to fret about it any longer than he has to, which is why I still haven't told him all the details about the busted headlight or the fact that I let Weston solder his oil pan.

"One of your lads from back home, then?" he teases. Normally his ribbing about my dating life would lead to several minutes of banter, but I'm not in the mood.

"Something like that."

"Just wanted to tell you Jordan has planned a fun night out for us, so I hope you got some rest at the cabin. Weston wasn't too distracting, I hope, with all his exercising and indoor-fitness rubbish."

I'm glad this isn't a FaceTime call, because at the word *distracting*, I feel my cheeks heat. As confirmed by a glance in the rearview mirror.

"He was fine." I cough like a chain-smoker, but Tim doesn't seem to notice.

"I love that bloke, but he's certifiable. I'd have gladly taken the excuse to have a few days off from training, but Coach said Weston let him know he was working out."

"Yes, there were some push-ups. Sounds like he's trying to keep his job."

"Oh. He told you about that, then?" Tim sounds surprised, and I realize I may have betrayed myself by letting Tim know I penetrated Weston's stoic exterior.

"We had to pass the time somehow, you know. Came down to talking."

"Right, sure. Okay, well, drive safely and get ready to see the city."

"Will do."

Spending a night out in San Francisco doesn't feel like it will be nearly as fun as a night *in* with Weston. But somehow I don't think I'll be able to convince Tim and Jordan that I really don't need their tour of the city after I've made such a big deal about wanting to see everything.

Glancing once more in the rearview mirror, I wonder if it's the last I'll see of Weston, for good.

"THAT OUTFIT IS SO CUTE!" Jordan says when I come out of their spare bedroom in a short blue T-shirt dress, black biker jacket (left behind by an actual biker who snogged me good about a year ago), and black booties.

"Thanks. Not too much?" My legs feel bare, and for the first time in my life I'm struck by a sense of not wanting to look too sexy.

"No, it's great."

I take in her outfit—a tan sweater and brown boots tucked conservatively under the rolled hem of her boyfriend jeans. I look like I'm trying way too hard in my outfit, but that was sort of the point when I packed it. I wanted to make a splash in the big city. Now I'm not feeling it.

"So . . . where are we headed?" It takes effort to keep the pep in my voice when all I can think about is Weston and the hole in my chest I've been feeling since we parted.

"A bar on Union, then dinner, then . . . who knows?"

"Perfect. Sounds fun."

Does it?

I try to shake myself out of my attitude slump. I'm only here for another two days, and I haven't spent any time with Tim and Jordan. I need to rally and stop thinking about Weston.

All I can do is think about Weston.

An hour later, we're standing in a crowded spot with lighted bottles of top-shelf liquor on shelves above a long wood bar where people hover three deep and try to catch the attention of an attractive bartender with a shaved head and a diamond stud in his eyebrow.

Tim pushes through the crowd and hands Jordan and me chocolate martinis that are supposedly the best in town. He hangs an arm around his girlfriend and smiles. "Belated happy birthday to you, Lin. I'm glad you're here." We clink glasses. "And I just want to apologize again for getting you stuck in the mountains. I'm sorry you didn't get the trip in the city you wanted."

"Oh, that's okay. Different kind of adventure." I feel guilty because I loved my time in the mountains with Weston, and I haven't told Tim how well we got on.

I don't keep a lot of secrets from my brother, but Weston is his teammate and best friend. It would be horrible if I dropped a bomb on him that led to tension between them when I'm leaving town anyway and likely won't see Weston again.

"I'd planned to invite him to join us, but after you've been stuck with him for days, I figured you might need a break," he says.

"Oh, right. It has been a lot of together time," I say, trying to find a way to suggest it's just fine if Weston joins us without attracting suspicion. "I mean, I don't want to be the one to spoil his good time. If you want to invite him, invite him. I'm sure this bar is big enough for the both of us."

Half my words get lost in the loud buzz from the crowd, and Tim doesn't respond, so I'm not sure he heard me.

The idea of seeing Weston tonight sends a thrill through my chest, so I excuse myself and walk to the loo to text him.

Linnie: *Hey. How's it going?*

His response comes so quickly I suspect he must have already had his phone in hand.

City Boy: *Hey. Lonely. Where'd Tim take you?*

Linnie: *A bar called Pacific Cocktail Haven. It's crowded and loud. Apparently we're going to the Roaming Goat next.*

City Boy: *He likes that place.*

Linnie: *Want to come meet us?*

He doesn't respond right away. I wait for the telltale three dots to indicate that he's typing, but I get only radio silence.

Because our mountain tryst is over. Of course it is. I'm just too naive to acknowledge it. One more man in Loose Linnie's string of unimportant hookups. I even told him about my past. Why would he see me any differently?

I put my phone on the counter and press my fists into my eyes. Stupid, stupid. My resolution didn't even last through the first half of my trip to California.

My phone buzzes.

City Boy: *No.*

I roll my eyes. Like I really needed to see his response.

But the dots are bouncing. Apparently he isn't finished telling me just how disinterested he is in seeing me again. When it buzzes once more, I tell myself to ignore it.

Then I look anyway. Like Pavlov's bitch.

City Boy: *I don't want to stand in a bar with Tim where I have to keep my hands off you. Sounds like utter torture. Can you get away from them and come here?*

I don't need the poorly lit oval mirror over the sink to confirm what I can feel. Yes, I want to come to wherever Weston is. And yes, my smile is so wide I'm in danger of breaking my face.

"Hey, thank you so much for this fun night out," I tell Tim and Jordan. Their twin smiles are so cute, I hate that I'm about to lie to them and race out the door. But I do it anyway.

They completely understand how exhausted I must be. Jet lag and poor sleep at the cabin, blah, blah. They'll leave quietly for work in the morning and let me sleep in. We'll reconvene tomorrow for lunch.

Fifteen minutes later, I'm knocking on Weston's front door.

CHAPTER 25

LINNIE

"I wouldn't have thought this was something you'd be keen to do, Lin," Tim says to me for the third time since I suggested our evening plans.

"I'm starting to think maybe it's something you're not keen to do since you keep mentioning it." I poke his head from the back seat while Jordan laughs at the two of us.

"You guys, I love this. I rarely see my brother because he travels so much. Siblings for the win," Jordan says, turning around and giving me a wink.

Part of the reason I'm excited about tonight's plan is that I don't have to dress up. After being in the mountains for the first half of the week, I've gotten quite comfortable in jeans and hoodies, and after one night in high-heeled boots, I'm over it. So I've brought about half the items from my suitcase with me in a plastic bag, hoping I can find some takers for them tonight.

Jordan checks the GPS on her phone and directs Tim to the women's shelter in the Mission, where Weston told us to meet him at five.

He's waiting on the sidewalk in front and ushers Jordan and me out of the car before sending Tim to find street parking somewhere down the block. And he's wearing the chambray apron from his YouTube videos. Giving the ladies at the shelter the good stuff.

"Did you have trouble finding it?" he asks Jordan, kissing her on the cheek.

"Not at all." Jordan shifts from one foot to the other, wobbling in two-inch pumps she's probably had on all day. I wonder if one day I'll have a job where I need to wear heels. I kind of hope not.

Weston studies Jordan and pats her on the shoulder. "Thanks for doing this. With you all helping, I'm going to make something special tonight."

"Oh, I'm excited. Count me in whenever you need a hand."

Tim saunters up, apparently having found a parking spot not too far away, and Weston points him inside, followed by Jordan. Before I go in, he pulls me back for a fast, hot kiss, and my brains spin a bit as I walk through the door.

We spend the next hour in an industrial kitchen on the ground floor of the women's shelter. I help Weston make boeuf bourguignon in a very large pot, and I marvel at how comfortable he is in the kitchen. Even though I watched him make us food at the cabin, this feels different. More official.

And more important. He's making a really good meal for women who might otherwise be on the streets. I feel touched and grateful to be able to come here this once so I can see why he does it every week.

Tim and Jordan are tasked with salad dressing for a simple green salad and flourless chocolate cakes for dessert.

Once or twice I catch Tim glance my way. He seems to be enjoying himself, and I smile back at him, feeling his gaze linger on me—and maybe Weston—a bit longer than usual. He says nothing, but I wonder if we look like two people who've developed an easy rapport from being stuck in the mountains—or two people who can barely keep their hands off each other.

And I'm not planning to ask.

We all take our turns using the mixers and stirring the pots, but there's no mistaking the fact that Weston is mostly making this meal himself and giving us a cooking lesson at the same time.

Every so often our hands brush while stirring the sauce or putting the food on platters, and I feel the unmistakable flare of fireworks that I'm going to miss so much when I go back to England. But I won't think about that now. It will just make me sad.

Weston leans close and says, "I'm a goner for you, Linnie. I tried to talk myself out of it, but it was no use." My heart twists in my chest and I debate running away from all my responsibilities, quitting my business plans for a guy, doing exactly what my father wants because he doesn't think I'm good for anything else.

Which is why I need to get on that plane and finish what I started back home—my degree, standing up to my father, asking for what I want.

Even if what I want is standing in front of me. Even if I'm falling in love with him.

When it comes time to serve the meal, we bring out the platters to a round of applause from the women seated at the long tables in the dining room. Weston walks around chatting with a few of the women he knows who've lived at the shelter for a while, and they all pat him on the shoulder and grin up at him in the way a proud mother would look at her son.

I hope Weston feels the love.

CHAPTER 26
WESTON

The sun practically bangs down my windows, bright and warm in the early hours of the morning. Somehow, in the six years I've lived in the same small house in the Pacific Heights neighborhood of San Francisco, I've never managed to purchase window shades. This morning, when the warm rays dance across Linnie's face and turn her hair into a golden halo, I congratulate myself for being a lazy homeowner.

We've both been awake for over an hour, and we haven't moved from the bed. Left to me, we'd stay here all day, but I can't miss another day of practice. I want to ask her to meet me this afternoon when we're finished, but I know Tim has plans for spending her last evening together.

Yet I can't say the words, "Goodbye, Linnie." Horrible words.

Tim and Jordan have been extremely understanding of Linnie's purported exhaustion, but since tonight is her last night here, there's no way she can make up yet another excuse for why she needs to leave early. She needs to stay for the entire dinner they have planned at Zuni Café and for whatever shenanigans they think she'll enjoy afterward.

"Having a reputation as a party girl really takes its toll," she quips after explaining the plan for tonight. I've come to terms with the idea that I may not see her after this morning.

When I think about her leaving my bed, it hurts in a deep part of my chest I'd left for dead. I don't want her to go. Not just this morning. I don't want her to go at all.

"Yes, must be very draining," I say, twirling a strand of her hair around my finger. "So . . . ," I begin, ready to rip the Band-Aid off the inevitable goodbye.

"So," she says, waggling her eyebrows and rolling on top of me.

"That wasn't exactly what I meant . . . though I'm not opposed."

Dropping her lips to mine, she kisses me, and I kiss her back, and our kisses become one continuous thing that has to be bigger and better than normal kisses between normal people. We've elevated kissing to an otherworldly level. We are the Greek gods of kissing. Invincible. Powerful.

"So I guess this is it," I tell her, launching into the cheesiest goodbye possible. I don't want to let her go, not ever. But she's given me so much more than she planned this week. It's only right that I let her have some bit of her vacation without me.

"You're invited, silly." She tilts her head to the side, confused. "Did you really think we weren't going to see each other after this morning?"

"I . . ." The words die in my throat because they're horrible words. Strung together in horrible sentences about how I've enjoyed our time together, and I wish her well, and we should keep in touch. Maybe connect via the occasional FaceTime.

No. Off with the heads of those sentences. Exile for those words.

"Weston . . ." She shakes her head. "No, sorry. You can't get rid of me that easily. Let's meet up before dinner, have a little time for just us, okay?"

And there it is again. Hope.

It has no business taking up residence here. There's nothing to hope for, at least nothing with a snowball's chance of happening. But it's there. Feathers and all, ready to take flight. Like a beating organ left behind by its body, ever hopeful of continuing on without the benefit of the vessel that supports it.

My stupid heart.

CHAPTER 27

WESTON

As our Ferris wheel car peeks over the top and begins making its way downward, I point out as many sights as I can around us. Riding the SkyStar Wheel by the Academy of Sciences in Golden Gate Park felt like a good way for Linnie to see as much of the city as possible in the shortest amount of time.

She grips my hand and points with the other. "Transamerica building, right? I think I've mastered the city."

"Practically a local." I love her enthusiasm and wouldn't dare point out that the Transamerica Pyramid is the only triangular building around.

She snuggles into my side and tips her head against my shoulder, every soft curve of her finding an equal and opposite space to meld with mine. Another bittersweet moment that won't last nearly long enough.

Kissing her temple, I allow myself to fantasize about what it would feel like if we didn't face a ticking clock, if today could be the first of an infinite string of days. Morning training, lazy afternoons spent exploring the city, long nights tangled up in each other, making time stand still.

The verdant park unfolds beneath us as we get closer to the bottom, and I can't help feeling like every inhale and exhale is the exact opposite of the infinite time with her I seek. There are only so many breaths left before she leaves, and it hurts me in a place I didn't think existed.

Maybe for other people, but not for me. That part of me was smashed and broken, and I learned to live with the shards that made up enough of a heart to function.

Now I feel what's left of it facing a crossroads—becoming whole or shattering beyond repair.

I don't see another option. The status quo doesn't exist anymore.

A light breeze passes over us, warm and playful and so different from the icy winds from just a few days earlier in the mountains. It's comical to think back now on the two of us out there in a blizzard, trying to duct-tape a gushing pipe.

"Why are you smiling?" Linnie asks without moving to look at me. After only a few days together, she knows when I'm smiling.

Maybe it's for that reason, or maybe it's for so many other ones that I can't name, but I know I can't let her slip away.

"People smile when they're happy."

She chuckles. "I'm not asking about people. I'm asking about you."

"I'm smiling because I'm happy."

She says nothing, and there's no other sound or shift in her body, but I know she's smiling too.

Maybe that's what love is—the knowledge, beyond a doubt, that your heartbeat is her heartbeat, her happiness yours, two smiles speaking without saying a word.

When the ride operator opens our car to let us out, Linnie sinks into my side, and my arm comes over her shoulders like we've done it a thousand times. Effortless. Right.

"You should stay." I could say the words slipped out, but it wouldn't be true. Not when they've been repeating on a loop in my brain for the past three days.

"I know, right? I wish I could. Just a few more days, we'd have so much fun." Her voice flits through the air like autumn leaves, so casual. I realize she's not on the same page. This was a vacation romance, even if it feels like more than a fling to me.

I stop walking, forcing her to do the same.

"No. I mean . . . stay." My stubborn, insistent desire.

She lifts her face and our eyes lock. I'm struck, just as I am every time I look at those green irises, by how damn beautiful they are. But now I know the person hiding behind them is the real beauty. She could be wearing a mask and I'd know it like I know my own name.

"I-I can't stay. I still need to make things right with him like you said. And figure out my life. I can't just run away from it all."

Her forehead creases, and her lips pull down into a frown that would pain me if I didn't hope it means she's at least considering it.

"You wouldn't be running. You'd be giving yourself a fresh start. You could work here, live here. You're so talented and smart you'd have people begging to give you jobs." She gives me an unconvincing smile. I know what I'm asking of her, and I know it probably sounds nuts since we haven't talked about anything beyond her vacation.

"I have to go." She says it slowly, nodding as though that will make me agree. "But Danny . . . I'm not like them. We'll keep in touch. Please don't feel like I'm abandoning you."

It's exactly how I feel, even though I know it's not fair to ask her to fix me. I run a finger over the crest of her cheek. It feels better when I'm touching her. "I know I have to figure my shit out. I do. You're the first one who's made it feel worthwhile."

I look into her eyes to make sure she understands. "The only one."

She exhales and looks at the sky, and I can see the conflict in the quiver of her lips. I'm pushing too hard. I don't know how to do this the right way.

"Maybe at least think about coming back to visit?"

That makes much more sense. I should have proposed it first. Another trip, more time together.

A guarantee.

Proof.

Knowledge that I'm enough and that she wants to stick around.

"I mean . . . I can try." She gives me a partial, unconvincing smile. "It's a long flight and I'm trying to save money to finish my degree, but . . ."

I'm asking too much. Maybe I could convince her to let me buy the ticket once or even twice, but it's not realistic to expect her to jet-set halfway across the globe to see me, and my schedule is unforgiving during the league season, which starts in a couple weeks.

There's no obvious workable plan. "No, I get it. It's impossible."

"Maybe not impossible, just . . . hard."

I look up at the foggy sky as though the answer is written up there someplace. I see only runaway white, wispy clouds. "I don't want it to be hard. We're brand new. It's too soon for it to be hard."

She nods. We agree. Relationships are challenging enough without starting at a deficit. And if we're going to give this beautiful fledgling thing a fighting chance, we can't do it from across an ocean.

At least that's how it feels to me.

"But I'll see you tonight," she says brightly, squeezing my

hand. It feels like a consolation prize, and I don't want to be consoled. I don't want one more night that will make it even more painful when she walks away.

"I . . . don't think I'm going to come." Steeling myself against the shock on her face, I say more words and hope they're convincing. "I've monopolized you since you've been here. You really should spend your last night with Tim and Jordan."

"I want you to join us. I told you that," she says quietly.

I shake my head. Maybe it's my own shortcomings, but it feels like a bad idea for me to fall in love with her more than I already am. More than a bad idea—it feels fatal.

"I don't think it's a good idea. We should say our goodbyes now, and maybe we'll find a way to see each other again."

"Of course we will, and we'll keep in touch. I'll text whenever I can and try to call."

She'll text. She'll try to call.

None of this sounds like she's thinking about me the way I am her. Because this is a vacation relationship. She may be finished with meaningless hookups, but all we are is a meaningful one. A baby step forward for her.

A mammoth one backward for me. I tried to be what she needed, but I can't save people. I can't make them stay. I knew that.

I know that.

I flinch when her fingers graze my temple and she leans in to kiss me. It feels like a goodbye kiss. It has to be.

"Linnie." A sudden lump in my throat locks up the remaining words and phrases. They won't make sense. I can't explain my logic, but I know the best thing is for me to walk away.

Turning her head up toward mine, she shows me every bit of proof that I'm making the right decision—her soft parted lips, pink round cheeks, hair spilling like a golden fountain across her shoulders, eyes deep green and soulful. I can't have her across an ocean and *have* her the way I want.

"Weston," she deadpans, winking. "Come out tonight."

Every part of me wants to say yes. I always want to say yes to her. But I need to preserve what's left of me.

"I can't." I want to tell her I'm fucking in love with her, but I can't do that either.

The unfettered exuberance dims. I have to own the fact that I caused it, and it breaks me deep within.

"Can't?" Her words are careful, slow, assessing. "Or won't?"

I shrug. "Does it matter? We've reached the end either way."

"I don't want that." Her voice breaks on the last word, and I pray she doesn't cry. I don't want to do that to her. And I don't think I'll be able to take it.

"I don't want it either," I say, but then I shake my head. I already asked her to stay. I'm out of ideas if she can't work with me here.

Nodding solemnly, she doesn't argue. "I have to go back to England. My dad isn't well. It's impossible for me to stay," she stammers, hitting me with all her ammo.

"I know. I'm not trying to make it harder." Tiny dots of moisture gather in the corners of her eyes, and it pains me that I'm making her upset.

"It's hard because I care about you, and I wish I could stay. I do. I just . . . can't." A single tear rolls down her cheek. I wipe it away with my thumb, but a second one follows.

I feel exactly the same way—bereft, unmoored, heartbroken.

"If I see you later, I'm going to love you even more than I already do, and that'll just make it harder." I sound like the air is being choked from my lungs. Maybe it is. I'm drowning.

I see her eyes widen when I say I love her, and I don't even care if she doesn't say it back. What's the fucking point if it's over?

She nods, her voice quiet. "No, sure. I get it."

I'm not sure she does. I'm not sure I do.

So even though I'm invited to join them tonight, I decline. It feels too hard to wait until later to say goodbye. Right now, it's hard enough.

But that's what's handy when you don't get too used to people sticking around. It gets a bit easier each time they go.

CHAPTER 28

LINNIE

England is gray. Gray and cold and lonely and devoid of anything that can warm me.

Was it always like this?

I've spent my entire life here without complaint. True, I haven't traveled much, so I couldn't make many comparisons, but still. My life has been rooted in Saltney forever, and I've never dared presume it could exist anywhere else.

And yet . . . it did.

"You're going to take the finish right off," Mary chastises after finding me polishing one particular spot on the bar for over a minute. I hadn't noticed her hovering near me, twin tendrils of dark hair curling around her ears, longer pieces pulled into a ponytail. She peers at me through round wire-framed glasses and gives her red lip gloss a rub between her lips.

Startled, I pull my hand back. Then I give the bar one more sweep with the rag as though I meant to spend so much time working the two-hundred-year-old hunk of wood to a sheen.

"Can't a person take pride in her work?"

Mary chokes out a disbelieving laugh. "That wasn't pride. It was daydreaming."

Moving to the far end of the bar, I find another spot to polish, hoping she won't follow me there. But that's like hoping to stay dry when a fat water balloon falls on your head. If I'm stubborn, she's the entire pack of mules.

"You have to stop moping around. The bar can't take it. There isn't enough varnish to withstand your mood. Why don't you take a break outside for a couple minutes, try to clear your head?"

"My head is fine."

I move away from the bar and start pulling glasses from the crate where they've dried overnight. I stack them on the shelves behind the bar, working too quickly, forcing normalcy on myself when I feel anything but. Shouldn't be surprising when a glass slips from my hands, shattering on the floor at my feet.

Meeting Mary's eyes, I prepare for the tongue-lashing I'm about to receive. Her boyfriend owns the place, and she does all the bookkeeping. I don't need her to tell me that she knows how every quid is spent around here.

"You can take it out of my salary," I say through gritted teeth.

Wordlessly, Mary walks to the supply closet and comes back with a broom and mop. I hold my hand out for the supplies so I can clean up, but she doesn't look at me. After sweeping the shards into a pile, Mary bends down and scoops the mess onto a laminated menu before throwing the lot into the rubbish bin.

"I'll mop," I offer, but I already know she won't let me. Having to stand here and watch her do it is my punishment for ignoring her advice.

"Go outside," she orders, dousing the floor with a slop of water and pushing it around with the gray strings of the mop.

"I'm sorry. I just . . . I miss him so much." It hurts to say the words out loud, so I've kept them tucked tight inside, even though I don't have to say them to feel them. Or to know they're true.

"I know you do. Take. A. Moment."

I do as instructed, annoyed as soon as the cool air hits my face, because it actually feels pretty good. Wandering a few doors down the street, I notice that the sky's typical gray has none of the magic of the California gray sky. Unlikely to produce snowflakes or crack open to reveal the sun, the sky here is just what it is—cold and unsurprising.

It's midmorning, so most of the businesses on this stretch of road have begun opening for business, even if it's just a single employee inside turning on lights and running a rag over surfaces, cleaning off dust.

I cross the street and sit on the grass next to Chester Cathedral, which is where I take my breaks during the day. Something about the soaring grandiosity of the old stone church makes me feel relaxed in its shadow. I assume this is what Mary was getting on about, so here I sit.

For my entire life, I've been cursed with having a sister two years younger and a hundred years wiser. She's the yin to my yang, but only because the yang has always been inexperienced and clueless and lets the yin boss her around.

Irritated that Mary knows what I need better than I do, I'm also grateful she forced me out here. I'm a mess, and the worst part is that it's not my usual, familiar kind of mess. It's not a temporary hangover or a bit of regret over a hookup. It's not me feeling frustrated with my dad for never seeing me the way I wanted to be seen.

This is a new mess. It's an I'm-in-love-and-have-no-bloody-idea-what-to-do-about-it mess. I have no coping skills for it. So I'm not coping.

Since I've been back, I've cried more than I ever do. And to be clear, I've never before shed a tear over a man.

I've taken extra shifts at work, mainly so I'm too busy to think about Weston. Then I think about him during every hour of every shift, no matter that the pub patrons don't look like him or speak like him—somehow they all remind me of him. Or, really, they remind me that he's not here.

Sucking in a cleansing breath of air does little to raise my spirits. I've been a surly, exhausted mess for the past two weeks, and the time difference has made it all but impossible to connect with Weston, other than to read his texts after the fact or listen to the occasional voice mail.

They're all versions of the same thing.

City Boy: *I miss you.*

Linnie: *I really miss you too.*

City Boy: *Just wanted you to know.*

Linnie: *I do. I hope practice went well.*

On a game day, I substitute "game" for "practice," but otherwise we don't have much to say to each other that hasn't already been said.

I don't tell him I love him because that's ridiculous. Can I love him after only knowing him for a week?

Yes. I can. And I do.

The door opens across the street, and Mary marches out of the pub, straight over to where I'm sitting. She holds two cups of coffee, and she gives one to me before sitting next to me on the grass.

"You could yell at me just fine at the pub. Didn't need to come out here for it," I say. The coffee is hot and prepared exactly the way I like it. "Thank you for the cuppa."

"I'm not here to yell at you. Maybe talk some sense into you, but I hardly think yelling is what you need."

"Good, then."

Mary drinks a couple of sips of her coffee before gathering herself up off the grass in a hurry. "It's sopping wet out here."

"Yes."

"Isn't your bum getting wet, then?"

I shrug. Sure, my pants are soaked through, but I've stopped caring about most things, so a little water is hardly worth a discussion.

"Get up."

"You just told me to come out here."

"I said to get some air, not this." She points to where I'm collapsed in a heap, arms wrapped around my knees, head flopped on top of those. "Come back inside."

"Quit ordering me around. I'm having a crisis," I tell her.

"I know. I get it."

It's the first time she's ever said that. She's always been so capable and driven, which made it a little hard for her to empathize with my choices. I wonder if something's changed or if she's just trying harder.

"It's so easy for you. You've always known exactly what you wanted to do and gone after it. Whether it was a guy or a job . . . you always know. I'm not like that."

"You're exactly like that. You're the one who decided you weren't happy with your dating life, so you changed it. You're making decisions for yourself, not to spite Dad. And you're planning your future. That all takes an enormous amount of guts."

"Thanks, Mare. Good to have you as a role model."

She gets a faraway look in her eyes. Her upper lip twitches, which has always been a sign she's lying.

"Mary?"

"You're sweet." But she shakes her head. "Guess I'm having a bit of a crisis too."

"What?"

I can't have heard her right, but she nods.

I've been so wrapped up in my own drama—for years—and it's been easy to assume Mary's life is perfect. Or maybe it gave me a safe harbor to think so. I peer up at her. "Talk to me, Mare."

She blinks, steeling herself. "Harry's been cheating on me for over a year. Nearly two." Mary chews on her lip as though she's calculating the exact number of days.

Meanwhile, I practically shout, "What?"

"You heard me."

"I heard you, but what the fuck, Mary? Guys don't cheat on you. Maybe on other people, but not you."

She shrugs. "Guess he didn't get the memo."

I feel an uncontrollable need to punch something. Preferably Harry's stupid face, but he's not here.

"Are you kidding me with this?"

"Sadly, no." She's so calm. That's the difference between her and hotheaded Linnie. I'd be out with a can of spray paint looking for new places to tag "wanker," and she looks like she might reapply her lipstick and go for a walk.

Mary works her neck like she can rid herself of all the kinks associated with her no-good ex. At least I assume he's her ex . . .

"Hold on, you've broken up with him, right? This isn't some bullshit where he says he fucked up and you forgive him."

I don't know what I'll do if she tells me she wants to stay with him. I don't know how I'll hold her on the pedestal where I've insisted she live for most of our lives. I'm able to stand up for myself only because I have her as a model.

"I suppose you know what Dad thinks I should do."

"He thinks you're lucky to have a man who's willing to marry you." I can hear our father's voice saying the words. Doesn't matter that Mary runs circles around Harry when it comes to business smarts and works twice as hard as he does to keep his pub afloat. Dad still thinks a cheating man is better than no man at all.

She nods.

"Well, fuck that. You don't need Harry."

"I don't need Harry. Or his stupid fucking pub."

"Right." It dawns on me that if Mary tells Harry off, we'll both be out of a job. "Okay, then. You tell Harry to go fuck himself, and I'll tell Dad I'm taking over the garage. New start for us both. Cheltenham women don't take shit from anyone."

Mary smiles despite herself. "No, we don't."

It's funny when the thing you've been meaning to do happens slightly before you're ready. I always planned to quit working at the pub, but I figured I had time to decide when and how to do it. But now, it's done. No turning back.

CHAPTER 29

LINNIE

I can't tell if it's my imagination, but I feel like my dad's aging faster these days.

"Heard you went on holiday." My dad's voice rumbles from his throat because he's too lazy to sit up straight. He blames his job for his poor posture, but I've always suspected that he wore his hunch proudly. A sign of a life devoted to his job. The hallmark of a journeyman mechanic who spent his life bent over an engine.

"You heard?" I cock my head to the side. "I told you I was in California visiting Tim. You heard it from me, remember?"

"I suppose I did." He's sitting on a folding chair in the corner of the garage, where he's perched himself for the past year and a half, starting when his doctors told him he was too sick to keep hunching over car engines. Or sliding under them.

Now he comes to the garage every day and watches, occasionally—or regularly—telling one of his employees they're doing something wrong and making them bring parts over to him so he can inspect them and tinker a bit.

Tim bought the land the garage sits on outright last year, so there's no danger of the garage ever losing its lease. It can live on as Cheltenham Auto as long as there's someone to run it.

Because I'm a masochist, I say one more time, "I'd be happy to take it on, keep it in the family."

I don't know what I was expecting him to say, but he manages to surprise me with something I never fathomed. "I sold it."

"What?!"

If anything, I assume he's put pressure on Mary to have Harry take over the business after the two of them get married. She already runs Harry's pub. I honestly don't know how he fills every day when she does everything required to keep the doors open and the ledgers profitable. He's the natural choice to run the garage. No one ever says as much, but it's the last-ditch excuse I manufactured for why my dad refuses to let me take over the business.

It has to be that. The reasons I told myself for years—that I'm not smart enough, skilled enough, worthy of carrying on the Cheltenham Auto family name—no longer hold up. I know that now.

But this . . . "Sold it to who?"

My dad's forehead creases, and his mouth twitches as though, once again, his uneducated, incapable daughter is asking the wrong question. "Someone who offered a fair price."

"So that's it? No discussion?"

He bends his head as though something in his lap has suddenly drawn his attention. When he speaks, he's addressing the worn fabric of his work trousers. "It's the right decision. I'm too old to do the work, and I'm paying blokes who don't know anything about cars."

"But Tim owns the land. He worked it out so the garage can operate with Cheltenham Auto on the shingle even if you spend all your time playing chess with your mates."

"I don't play chess anymore."

"Why not?" I'm getting more and more riled up the more I feel like he's given up—on his legacy, his hobbies. Worst, he's given up on me. Or maybe that happened a long time ago, and I just clung to a shred of hope that I could convince him otherwise.

He shrugs. "None of my mates are any good."

"Excuses, Dad!"

"I don't need to justify my choices to my daughter."

"You do when she wants to carry on the family legacy. Why won't you even consider it?" I sound whiny, but I'm past caring.

He dismisses the thought with a wave of his hand. "Not what you should be doing with your life."

I know I should keep my mouth shut. I know he's not in any kind of mental or physical shape for a fight, but I've gotten myself so riled up since I've been back that I'm having a hard time keeping my words in my head, where they belong.

"I don't think you get to decide that. Maybe when I was little and I didn't know it was a bad idea to eat fruit without washing it; then you could tell me what to do. But I think I've done all right. Haven't I?"

His mouth works silently like he's chewing some invisible thing or trying to swallow his words before they have a chance to come out. He grimaces and coughs. "You've had me worried over the years, is what you've done. All the blokes, all the time you spend at that pub. None of that looks good on a proper lady. No man wants to marry that."

"I know," I say quietly. I've earned his dismissiveness with my antics, and maybe I've pushed too far. Maybe there's no going back now, no setting the record straight with a man who's always seen the worst in me.

So much so it became what I saw in myself.

"Dad, I want to do it. More than anything. Why won't you let me take it over?"

He starts to speak, which leads him to cough, which leads to an uncontrolled coughing fit that racks his body so hard I worry this might be it. He might die right here and now, and I'll live the rest of my life knowing I pushed him over the edge with my insistence that he let me run the business.

"Dad, I'm so sorry," I say, as his nurse appears from the office, reaches for a jar of mentholated rub, and applies some on his bare chest in the V of his shirt. *This is the extent of his medical care, a woman standing by with a jar of goo?* As soon as he can breathe again, he can bet we'll be talking about something a little more robust. No more salves and ointments when he needs a real treatment protocol.

When he's breathing normally, I bend and kiss him on the cheek. "I didn't mean to stress you. I'll come by later, okay?"

"Wait," his voice croaks. I turn and he's waving me back, his bony hand covered in crepe paper skin. "Is this really what you want? You want to run this place?"

"I've been saying it for years. Yes."

He nods. Then he shakes his head, his eyes red and heavy with puffy bags that look like they're doing the heavy lifting of keeping his face on straight. "Okay."

"Okay? Really?"

He nods again. "I'll call the bloke who's buying the place and ask him to give you a job. If you can clear away other people's dirty pint glasses, I suppose you can crawl under their engines. What's the difference?"

"Wait, are you saying I can run the business?" I'm confused because he said okay and then made it sound like I'll be working for someone else.

"I'm saying you can work there. Isn't that what you want?"

"Dad, no. I've been taking business classes. I've been saving up so I can finish my degree. I'm learning about marketing and return on investment. I want to build it into a bigger shop with several locations, even."

My dad's gray eyes look pale in his face. Tired. The wrinkles beneath them and the sag of his jowls drive home how hard he's worked his whole life to keep the garage going after taking it over from his father. And the best he can do now is tell me to crawl under some bloke's engine. Like he's fed up from talking about it.

"I'm offering you an opportunity. Take it or don't."

"I-I don't want that." I choke over the words because I can't believe I'm saying them. After so many years of wanting a job in the garage, anyone would think I'd be over the moon at the chance to work at the place. But not anymore. Not when it will belong to someone else and have his name on the shingle.

"I guess it's not what I want after all," I concede.

My dad nods, a small smile revealing his crooked bottom teeth, brown from tobacco stains. "Take the money from the sale, do something else with it. And promise me you won't work so hard that you forget to have a full life. You're the boss of you. Remember that."

I feel a lump swell in my throat, thinking about Weston saying the same words. I never thought I'd hear them from my dad. Maybe he's giving me a chance I never considered, always married to my stubborn insistence that he pass down the garage. And I never thought there would be a day when I missed Weston more than I already do.

"Love you, Dad," I say on my way out the door. He looks tired, and his nurse helps him up from his chair to take a nap.

He nods and grunts as he shuffles from the garage, but he doesn't say he loves me back. Even if he does.

∽

"To the sale of Cheltenham Auto and the new road ahead," Mary says, raising a glass high.

Tonight she's working at her new job in a new pub that hired her on the spot after she sent Harry packing, but I'm sitting opposite her across the bar with a pint in my hand. Even though I still intend to keep picking up extra shifts until I have all of my schooling paid for, she insisted I take tonight off to celebrate.

Not one to argue with my smart sister's logic, I agreed.

The pub is filled with regulars I don't know yet, but now that Mary has hired me full time I'll soon learn their names and their drink orders. And then I'll start working on a business plan. Maybe it will be an auto garage, maybe something else, but I don't intend to fritter away the proceeds from the sale. I intend to invest them.

I've barely touched my pint of ale, not because I don't feel like celebrating, but because I'm distracted. I've been waiting until it's late enough here to call Weston. He's the first one I wanted to talk to after I left my dad's, but according to Tim, they have a game this weekend and they're training all day.

Checking the time for the third time in as many minutes, I do the math once more—eight hours behind. I know he won't see it, but I send a text anyway.

Linnie: *Hey City Boy. Thinking about you. And I have some news.*

I wait for a moment on the chance the little dots will start bouncing. Nothing. I shouldn't be disappointed, especially since I'm the one who walked away.

Sure, we've texted and talked, but mostly it feels like we're dancing around the elephant in the room. And her girth gets larger by the day, the longer I go without coming up with a way to see Weston again. I feel him slipping away.

And yet, when I left the garage, he was the first phone call I wanted to make. That has to mean something. I just don't know if it's enough for him.

I pocket my phone just as I notice the pub has gone suddenly quiet. Searching for the reason, I find Mary standing in the center of the room, blinking back tears.

Jumping from my chair, I race to her and grab her shoulders. I don't know if I'm steadying her or myself, because the second I see her eyes, I know. Her expression looks nothing like it did when she told me about Harry. As shocked and upset as she was, I saw a fierceness in her that told me she already knew she'd be okay.

That's not how she looks now. "It's Dad. He—" Her voice cracks, and she drops her head to my shoulder.

"What happened?" I whisper.

"His nurse said he took a nap a few hours earlier, and when he didn't get up, she went to check on him. He passed away in his sleep."

"Went peacefully, then." I feel the tears well in my eyes, and I forget all about calling Weston. I forget about everything outside of this room, where my sister is now my only remaining family in Saltney. I put my arms around her and pull her close. She'll always be the high-functioning together one, but she'll always be my little sister.

"You know how much he loved you," I tell her. "You know, right?" She nods against my shoulder.

I tell myself he loved me too. I know he did.

CHAPTER 30
WESTON

It's another brutal day of training. Lately they're all brutal, mainly because I've been working myself harder than I should. In my position as center mid, I already run more than most of the players on the team, but over the past few weeks, I've been everywhere on the field at once—defending, dribbling to pass off to strikers, dropping back to the defensive line.

If it were during a match, Coach might appreciate my extra drive. But this is just training, and I'm more likely to get injured from overworking my muscles than improve my game. Try telling that to my brain.

No matter how much I run, I can't outrun the ache in my chest that makes it hard to breathe. I never thought it was possible to miss a person so much that it feels like I'm missing a part of myself. It makes no sense.

But there it is. I'm working with half a heart.

"You're killing yourself out there, and you're going to pay for it," Tim tells me as we're shoving our gear into our lockers after practice. I took a quick shower and intended to leave without talking to anyone, as has been my habit for the past month. "I don't want to see you on the injured list."

I roll my eyes. It's not really his problem.

"It's all of our problem if our starting center mid goes down. Come on, let's grab a beer. I'm buying."

The locker room is full of guys changing clothes, some packing up for the day, others taking their time, standing around in their sliding shorts and chatting. For the past month I've raced out of the training facility as quickly as possible, not wanting to make small talk, not wanting to explain my less-than-stellar mood.

A blanket of cold air hits my face when we leave the facility, and it feels frostier out here than a half hour earlier, when we finished practice. The dense fog hangs in front of us as we wait for the light to change.

The bar down the block from the training facility is as good as any, an Irish pub with one pool table in the back, two dartboards on a wood-paneled wall, and a curving central bar with iron-legged barstools and several TVs playing sports.

I've come here a lot over the years, but this is the first time I've been out with just Tim since Linnie left town, not that he's been pestering me to spend time together. He and Jordan are still in their newly engaged bubble, where they don't much notice what everyone else is doing.

Still, sitting at the bar next to him feels loaded, somehow, and I wonder if he brought me here for a last meal before facing the firing squad because Linnie told him about us before I had the chance to say something. If there even is an "us."

We each order a burger and a basket of fries, a rare splurge on a Friday night during the season, when we're normally eating lean chicken breasts and broccoli.

"Sure thing, boys." The red-haired bartender smiles through dark-red lipstick and adjusts the black apron around her waist.

She goes to the kitchen to put in our order, and Tim leans back on his stool, pressing his palms against the bar.

"I won't be here next week." It seems like he's speaking to the TV over our heads, his neck pitched upward, eyes focused on a college basketball game I know he doesn't care about.

I look at him for explanation because we're in the middle of our season and players don't just take a week off. He stays focused on the game.

"Everything okay?"

He waits until the green team finishes its drive to the basket and scores before responding. "My dad died two days ago."

"Oh, wow. I'm sorry."

He nods.

"You doing okay?" It's the wrong question but I have no experience at this. No idea what to say.

"We didn't see eye-to-eye about a lot of things. But it's hard to think of him gone. Guess I'm okay."

My thoughts immediately go to Linnie. Our communication has been patchy the past few weeks, partly because of the eight-hour time difference, partly because it's sometimes easier not to hear her voice and feel an even bigger void after we hang up the phone.

So we've mostly texted, and I've made a lot of excuses about long hours on the field and away games that consumed all my time and attention.

All lies.

The only thing that has consumed me is the incredible hole I've felt in my heart since she left. I've tried to set myself straight, because this should be familiar territory for me. I should know how to pick myself up off the ground after someone I love takes off, because I've done it before. Yet somehow I feel rusty, unable to shake it off the way I should.

Give it time. Eventually you'll forget her.

"Did Linnie have a chance to make things right with him before he passed? I know she wanted to talk to him about the garage."

Tim shakes his head soberly. "Dad found a buyer." My mind races. I know how much she wanted to run that business. I can't imagine how she feels knowing it's in someone else's hands.

My mind spins off, thinking about how easy it would have been for me to buy the place if I'd know it was an option. "Do you know who bought it?"

Tim's eyes cut to mine and he studies my face. Then he shakes his head. "No. And I know what you're thinking. She doesn't need one more man in her life trying to make decisions for her. You want to be with my sister, don't buy shit. Be with her for *her*."

"I-I would. I want to. She left."

"Because she had to stand on her feet, prove that to herself. She doesn't have a decade-long career to gamble with."

He turns back toward his glass and takes a long drink, but his words surge through me like lightning in my veins. I don't gamble. With anything. Years of protecting myself have left me unwilling, and that's my burden to bear.

Unless I do better. For myself. For her.

"You should be there. At the funeral. For Lin." It shakes me from my train of thought, and it's the last thing I'm expecting him to say.

Our burgers arrive, and we busy ourselves putting on ketchup and arranging toppings on our buns. It all feels like an elaborate dance designed to fill the conversational vacuum, when I should be filling it with a response.

"What?" I cup my hand around my ear as though I may not have heard him correctly. He shoves two fries in his mouth and chews a few times before answering, his eyes fixed on mine. They're not Linnie's surreal shade of green, but their intensity rivals hers when he stares me down. "You heard me."

How long has he known?

There's no point in lying to him. "She told you." Of course she did. She's a better person than me.

He shakes his head. "Didn't have to. Took me all of five minutes in the same room as you two to see it." He rubs a hand over his face, hiding his expression, so I'm not sure yet whether he plans to deck me. "Of course Jordan swears I'm an idiot because it only took her three."

The silence hangs between us like a blackout curtain.

"I'm sorry, man. I should've said something."

"You should have." He opens his mouth, then seems to reconsider saying more. He pops in another fry, but I know the onus is on me to explain.

"I kept my distance. But things just . . . happened." It sounds so lame and inadequate, both for the magnitude of what I feel for Linnie and for the delicate dance between us that ended with my heart twisted in knots.

"She's my sister." His voice goes up an octave, and I feel even worse about betraying his trust. I prepare myself for the rest of what I know is true—the litany of reasons why you don't fuck around with your friend's sister.

"I know, and—"

He holds up a hand to stop me. "What I mean is, she's incredible. I know my sister, and I know she's pretty fucking special. Couple days alone with her . . ." He shrugs. "I'm not surprised she has you wrapped around her finger."

For the first time since she flew home, I chuckle. "*Special* doesn't even begin to describe her."

"So what is it? Are you trying some long-distance thing?"

I'm about to take a bite of my burger, but I put it down. *She hasn't told him?* "No. We're . . . not really trying anything. She's there and I'm here."

"Well, that's the bloody stupidest thing I've ever heard. Surely you can do better."

I have no answer. Even if I want to do better—be better—I have no earthly idea how that's supposed to work. "I still have Coach breathing down my neck because he thinks I've become 'unhinged,' plus I'm not even sure how she feels. I asked her to stay and she didn't."

A cheer erupts in the bar when someone on one of the TVs scores, but I couldn't care less.

"And?" Tim prompts.

"And what?"

He exhales a frustrated breath, punctuated by knocking his fist into my shoulder. "You're a fucking footballer. You take a shot on goal and don't score, do you fold?"

"I don't need a lecture, especially about soccer."

"Kinda think you do, mate. If you don't ask her again—and again, if it's what you want—then the problem is you. Don't you put it on her because she didn't drop everything for you the second you asked. If you quit after asking once, you'll never get her to say yes."

Third time's the charm. Same thing Linnie said to me, just not in so many words. Figures she's smart enough to give me the exact advice I needed to figure out how to be with her. Figures I'm dumb enough not to take it.

Tim signals the bartender for two more beers, and I notice he's finished his while I haven't touched mine. I take a sip. It's warm and sour, but I force a little more down. Maybe it'll give me some clarity.

"Come to England for the funeral. Don't buy her a garage. Be there for her."

He doesn't understand what he's asking of me. The only funeral I ever wanted to go to was my mom's . . .

"I-I can't. Funerals and I don't really mix. But I promise to call her. I'll make things right with her."

"You do what you need. I'm not going to pressure you to fly to England. But, mate, for fuck's sake, do something."

I decide I can give him that. No idea what it means yet, but I'm going to figure it out.

Nodding, he zips his jacket. It's the only sound in the room I hear, and it feels final.

If I drop the ball now, it's on me.

CHAPTER 31

LINNIE

"I think she loved me and gave me the best life she could." I've rewound that part of the interview a half-dozen times, watching Weston's eyes each time he says the words. *My* words. He's looking straight into the camera, and I swear he's saying them to me.

At least that's what I tell myself. Seeing him own his story and tell it rather proudly makes my heart full. Even if we're not meant to be together, I'm glad he's starting to believe he's worthy of love. Maybe some other woman will be the beneficiary of that, someone who lives locally and adheres to a fitness program and cooks acceptable meals.

I still can't believe he went to *Sports Illustrated* and gave them an exclusive televised interview to talk about his upbringing, his years in foster care, and his struggles with trusting people. His words were touching and beautiful. "Those years made me who I am today. I didn't see it that way for a long time, but I see it now. She acted out of love."

He put everything out there. The interviewer teared up more than once. So did I.

Right up to the last part where his words left me reeling, "I realized recently that loving a person can mean letting go. But sometimes, it means giving chase. I was never brave enough to do that before, but things are different now."

"This sounds interesting. Care to be more specific?" the interviewer asked.

"Not yet. But when I have news, I'll share it with you."

Life is strange. On the day of my dad's funeral, a day when I'm getting closure in one area of my life, seeing Weston's interview opens up a river of questions in another area of my life.

It's hard to imagine he's not surreptitiously communicating something to me with his cryptic implications. Problem is, I'm someone who needs words, and I have no idea what he's trying to tell me. And maybe it has nothing to do with me—maybe he just feels ready for a change.

I hope it sets him free.

But I can't think about any of that right now because I have a funeral to get to. The church in town is tiny, so Mary and I have arranged to have all our friends and family come to the church across from our former job in Chester.

I dab the tears from the corners of my eyes, trying not to cry off the mascara I just finished applying. I've cried so many tears for my dad over the past few days, I didn't think I had any left.

I woke up this morning feeling numb. Maybe that's a good thing on the day of a funeral. Just get through it, save the feelings for all the days and months afterward.

My black dress is simple, tied at the waist, and I wear it over leggings and black boots. The weather is typical for March, rainy and cold, so I grab a coat and gloves.

A horn honks, but it doesn't sound like Mary's car. Still, she said she'd pick me up right around now, so I leave the house, locking the door behind me.

But it's not Mary's car. A red MINI Cooper sits on the right side of the drive, odd because no one ever parks on the right, and I don't recognize the car. One of my dad's friends must have misread the information and thinks he's meant to be at our house instead of the church.

Walking down the drive, I peer at the windshield but can't make out who's inside until the driver's door swings open and Weston unfolds himself from the car.

My heart squeezes, and I feel my pulse take off like a racehorse. For a second Weston looks nervous, uncertain, but when I take a step toward him, he takes one toward me, his face cracking open like the sun through a cloud. He wraps me in his arms, and I circle mine around him, closing my eyes against how good it feels and opening them instantly to make sure I didn't fabricate all of it. He's really here.

And after a couple of minutes of clinging to each other, it occurs to me that I have no idea why. He hasn't called, and the few texts he's sent expressing condolences have gotten mixed up with a string of others. Life has been chaos.

"How did you get here?" I manage finally, backing away slightly but not wanting to let go of him. I settle for putting my hand on his forearm, needing some connection to ensure I'm not imagining him.

He casts a sidelong glance like it's a trick question. "An airplane. And this." He points to the car. "Though I have to hand it to you, driving on the other side of the road is tricky. You are a ninja, among so many other things, Linnie Cheltenham."

I want him to tell me more, tell me everything. But there's no time right now, so I cling to his arm as though it's the only way I won't lose him again.

"I mean, I just saw your interview—which was beautiful. But it said you were in-studio in San Francisco."

Realization dawns and he nods. "Prerecorded. I did the interview yesterday."

"Oh." I stare at him, unsure about the appropriate thing to

do when you see the person your heart has been aching for when you're meant to race off to a funeral.

"Linnie." He reaches for my hand. My stomach flips.

"Danny." His eyes soften, and I take a step closer to him and squeeze his hand.

I decide that the appropriate thing to do is to kiss him. I don't care that loyal customers of Cheltenham Auto have driven from around the county to be here to honor my dad. Tipping my head up, I reach for his cheek and tilt his face down until our lips meet. I just need a moment of this. I need to breathe him in and feel his lips to know he's really here.

And once I do, I don't plan on letting him go.

SEVERAL HOURS LATER, we're back at the house, and most of the guests have had their fill of dark beer and snacks from the pub where Mary and I work. She's still not sure if she'll stay for the long term, but it's a job. I've been picking up extra shifts there, too, and saving even more money now, because this job pays better wages. Damn cheapskate, cheating Harry.

Weston and I sit side by side on folding chairs behind the house, each of us a little tipsy from the beer but mostly from the heady feeling of being near each other. I have my legs folded under me and my chair scooted as close to Weston as possible.

Tim puts his arm around me and kisses my cheek, sliding into the chair on my other side. "That was rough, but I think we did him proud." Jordan perches on his lap, and he wraps his other arm around her.

"He was a complicated guy, and he did things his way, but I know he loved us," Mary says, dragging a chair up to join us.

"He did," I say, mostly believing it. Families are tough.

From the ample pockets in her black dress, Mary produces cans of Guinness and hands them to all of us.

"To Dad," Tim says, popping the top on his. Before he can take a drink, Mary squeals, "Wait, do you still think you can finish that before me? Because I've been around pubs for years, so . . ."

"Oh yeah? That sounds like a challenge," Tim says, straightening up in his chair.

"This I've got to see," Jordan says, taking out her phone and getting ready to record the moment for posterity.

"Go!" I yell, having no interest in getting in on the action. They slug their dark beer down so fast that it takes mere seconds, but Mary finishes about a millisecond ahead. She raises her can in the air, victorious.

"To Dad!" she yells, likely tipsy already.

My siblings and Jordan chat among themselves, and I lean against Weston, marveling at how miserable I felt this morning and how much calmer I feel now. Like a ray of sun has found its way amid the clouds of grief. A sign that the storm will pass.

"My dad sold the garage," I tell him.

He doesn't answer right away, but I know he understands the implications. At least so far as they impact my dream to own the place. But now, maybe . . . maybe I have different dreams. Our hands dangle between us, and he lifts mine, examining our intertwined fingers while he speaks.

"Tim mentioned it. I'm sorry."

In the days since he told me, I've started to come to terms with his decision, even if I still can't relate to it. "He just couldn't handle the idea of a woman running an auto garage. One of the original dinosaurs. Guess he stayed consistent to the end."

Weston nods and brings my hand up to his lips. Kissing it,

he leans back in his chair, crossing his ankles. I appreciate that he says more by not talking than most people say with words.

I, however, still need to use words. I still need to figure out the world by talking it through. "I know he loved me. He probably did what he thought was best."

It's hard to repeat my own words in this other context, especially since I've fought against someone else making that decision for me for so long. But maybe that's what being part of a family means—it's being bound by blood to the decisions other people make in your supposed best interests, even if they ought to mind their own business. Being family gives them the right to meddle, and it's up to us to sort out the broken pieces and try to turn them into a new sort of whole.

Weston listens, supportive, and lets me hash it out.

"I know he thought he had my best interests at heart, but he never asked me. A long time ago, he decided what that life should be and didn't give me a choice in the matter."

"I know. It's what families do. They make choices for us, and sometimes they're the wrong ones." My words, spoken about his mom, sound different now when applied to my father. Our situations are so different, and yet . . . here we are, both damaged from the best of intentions.

"I always thought he was trying to control me. Maybe in the end he set me free. I have to find my way, even if owning this place is the only thing I ever wanted."

"Is it still?" His words surprise me, not because he's asking a question no one else has posed before, but because, for the first time, I realize the answer isn't obvious.

"I . . . it doesn't matter now. It can't happen."

"Not what I asked. Is it what you want?" This time the question feels like it encompasses more than just the auto garage. Do I want this, life in Saltney? Do I want to be a continent away from Weston and my brother? Do I want to be limited by the four corners that have become familiar enough to feel suffocating?

I shake my head, even if I can't say the words out loud.

"Maybe he denied you the thing you've spent your life chasing, but maybe he gave you something you never gave yourself —options and choices. Maybe you want to own a garage, maybe you don't. Maybe you want to stay in Saltney, maybe you want to relocate. Maybe your business degree will open your mind to—"

I put a finger over his lips, and he freezes. "Stop," I tell him, tracing the line of his bottom lip and dragging my finger along his chin. I watch his eyes go hazy.

He nods. "Okay."

Hearing him rattle off choices makes it even more clear to me that there's only one clear path forward. From the morass of options, a single, glowing certainty emerges like the sun cracking the storm clouds and falling on fresh snow.

"No." I say it definitively.

"No?"

I shake my head. "No. I don't want all that. I just want you."

I wait, a tiny bit afraid he'll retreat, unwilling to believe this third time might be the charm. Maybe he's been too damaged by the first two instances of opening his heart completely and having it turned away. I have no way of knowing what he's thought about in the month since we've been apart. I just know how I feel.

"The City Boy footballer who's a dunce with tools?" he echoes, lighting up like a giddy toddler told he could pick something from the prize bin.

"Precisely that. Precisely you."

When it's your life, you get to choose. And I choose you.

He bends to kiss me. It's been weeks, but I melt against his lips, like butter in a warm skillet. Like no time has passed. We fall into a rhythm as though it's been beating in the background while we each figured out how to be better versions of ourselves.

His hand cups my cheek. Mine slips around his neck. Our mouths move against each other in a dance I could do all night. I *have* done it all night. It was never close to enough.

The world around us disappears. Voices fade into a background soundtrack. I see nothing but images of us doing this in every possible location—atop mountains, under heavy down covers, on hot sandy beaches. I feel everything.

When Weston breaks the kiss, he backs away just enough so we can focus. His eyes stay locked on mine, searching. "What does that mean? We try long distance?"

I shake my head. "No. I can't do that."

A flicker of pain strikes his eyes. I know what he's thinking. *People don't stay for me.* So badly I want to be the salve for that wound, but I know it would only be a temporary fix if he still believes he's not worthy of someone sticking around.

Slowly, he nods. "Actually, I'd hate it." He raises his chin a fraction, jaw hard, a muscle ticking in his cheek.

"I'd hate it too. The past few weeks have been . . . hard."

"Awful," he says at the same time.

"That too."

"What do you want, Linnie? Ask for it, and I'll give it to you. I'll give you anything you want."

"I want you every day. All the time."

The corner of his mouth twitches, a smile starting there and blooming across his face. So bloody handsome. It dissolves my focus into filaments. "So . . . I move to Saltney, try to sweet-talk the Manchester coaches into giving me a shot at their teams? Make a life change?" His ease at proposing the scenario makes me realize he's thought this through already. This was what he meant about being brave.

Now I'm the one with the blooming smile. I love that he'd do that for me. I love that he flew all this way for the funeral of a man he didn't know. For me.

Taking his hand, I squeeze it and hold it to my chest, where my heart thunders like I'm standing just inside the penalty box, poised to take the game-winning shot. Just me against the keeper. "I want to try it another way. Sweet-talk the people in San Francisco into giving me a shot on *their* team."

His face relaxes and he exhales a long breath. "I want that for you." He leans close, his voice a whisper against my skin. "I also want it for me because I fucking love you. So, so much. And I've stopped doubting myself and asking whether I deserve someone like you. It's not about *whether* or *if* or *why*. It just is."

"It just is," I repeat. So simple, so perfect for what we've stumbled into together. "I love you, Danny Weston. It's the truth whether we're here or in San Francisco or any place else."

It's the one thing I know for sure. All the rest of it, I'll figure out.

CHAPTER 32
WESTON

ne Month Later

"Happy birthday, old man," my teammate Donovan says before I leave the locker room.

"Thanks, but if I'm old, you're geriatric." At thirty-six, Donovan is the oldest on the team and still one of our most talented strikers.

"Fair, fair. Enjoy your night or . . . whatever you end up doing."

Nodding, I slam my locker shut and loop my gym bag over my shoulder. Donovan makes three. Three teammates who've alluded to my plans tonight without asking outright what I'm doing. I have an easy answer prepared—dinner with Linnie—but it hasn't come up.

Each person just gives me a vague send-off, telling me to have fun, as though everyone already knows what I'll be doing. At first, Tim let it slip that he'd see me later, and then backtracked and told me to "never mind."

Then I saw Coach and a few of my teammates discussing something on the sideline, but they broke apart and looked at the ground when I walked over.

Plus, Linnie has made it clear she likes to celebrate big, and despite waking me up with a the only present I really want from her, she hasn't asked me what I'd like to do.

All telltale signs of a surprise party.

Sure, I told Linnie that I hate surprises—specifically, surprise parties—but as she often reminds me, she is the boss of her.

Unfortunately it's forced me to pull the plug on a certain plan I had in mind involving a ring I bought her in Chester the day after she agreed to move to San Francisco. I figured the one chance I'd have of surprising her was to present her with an engagement ring on my birthday.

But I'll have to come up with another way to surprise her.

Just to mess with Linnie a bit, which she deserves if she's doing this to me, I call and tell her I've been held up at the field and won't be home until later. Her voice goes up an octave as she asks if I'm sure there isn't some way to get home earlier.

"Well, if I skip the shower. Might smell like a zoo camel, but it'll get me there closer to six."

"Oh, okay. Come dirty, then. No one will care."

"Who's no one?" I almost feel bad about being so surreptitiously evil. But then I remember that I'm going to have to spend the entire evening feigning surprise and convincing people I had no idea they were hiding in my living room.

"Just, you know, me. I won't care a whit."

On my way home I stop and pick up a bouquet of flowers for Linnie—lavender tulips and some greenery. Since I've told her I'll be a bit late, I have enough time to wander into a wine shop and pick out a bottle of cabernet I think she'll like.

Bottom line, even if she's surprising me with a party I don't want, I still want to bring her flowers and wine. I still want every night with her to be about the two of us, even if we're in a room full of people. Even if I have to pretend to be surprised.

I thought love was being so connected that we feel like we share a heartbeat. But now I'm starting to believe it's something hardier and more complicated than a kind of intertwined oneness. Maybe it lies in all the places where we aren't one, where we differ but find ways to be connected and love each other anyway.

Driving to my house in Pacific Heights, I realize how much more it feels like home since Linnie moved in. She spent a couple of weeks tying up loose ends in Saltney, but with Mary staying behind, at least temporarily, Linnie felt free to pack her bags for good.

With the garage soon to be under new management, Linnie has been making plans for how she'll put her share of proceeds from the sale to use. First, she's looking into business programs here. To start, she'll get her bachelor's degree and, knowing her, will probably work full time as well.

Small surprise, she's planning to study entrepreneurship, with an eye toward opening her own business. I won't be at all surprised if it ends up being something that allows her to use tools.

Sliding into my parking spot under the Victorian house I bought a few years after signing with the Strikers, I glance up and down the block to see if I recognize any of the cars as belonging to teammates or other friends. I have to hand it to Linnie—she's been here for only two weeks and somehow she's managed to get ahold of my friends and plan a party. It's why I'm not in too bad of a mood despite myself.

It's a nice night, clear with no fog. That can always change in San Francisco, but for now it's looking like the kind of night when we'll be able to see a few stars out my windows, which face east over the bay.

With the wine under my arm and the flowers in my hand, I

make a lot of noise coming up the stairs from our front door, enough so Linnie can get people to hide or do whatever she has planned.

When I reach the top of the stairs, I see nothing. All seems quiet in the great room, which has sweeping views from the Golden Gate Bridge to the Berkeley Hills. Same with the kitchen. Empty.

"Lin?" I call, confused about why she's having a surprise party in our bedroom or the tiny second room that doubles as an office.

"In here." Her voice is muffled, coming from the other side of the bathroom door. Where I'm about to attend a birthday party full of . . . kink?

Her smile hits me first when I open the door, which is remarkable, given how obsessed I am with her eyes. But today it's the smile—wide, expressive, painted with pink lipstick. She looks as happy as I feel when I see her.

And she's wearing the same fucking outfit she had on in the kitchen of the cabin that first day—gaping tank top, booty shorts and those ridiculous fuzzy socks. And she's standing next to my giant claw-foot bathtub, which is filled up with sudsy bubbles. Candles everywhere. Soft music playing.

She's moved a side table next to the tub and placed two beers on it, the same kind we drank at the cabin. There's even a charcuterie platter, complete with pickles, sausage, and the hallmark bowl of corn kernels.

"I figured out what your cabin needs when you finish the renovations," she says, pointing at the bathtub.

Then she drops her shorts. The top comes off next, leaving her in only the socks, her curves and soft skin pale and pink in the flickering candlelight. Propping one foot on the ledge of the tub, she turns and looks at me over her shoulder.

I don't need a single additional instruction.

"Don't move," I tell her, kneeling on the floor and slipping her leg over one shoulder. "Hold on to the towel rack, honey, because I'm not in the mood to go slow."

She does as requested, and I run my hand up her inner thigh, feeling the goose bumps that erupt over her skin as they erupt across mine as well. Her skin feels velvet-soft under my hands like flower petals as I move slowly upward, tracing the curve of her legs to where they meet at her sweet pussy.

My mouth is on her in an instant, ravaging her wet folds, circling her clit with my tongue, licking and sucking every inch of her because I can't possibly stop until she's moaning my name. And even then I need more.

"You're shaking." I watch her walk on wobbly colt legs to her phone on the counter.

"Mm-hmm." Her eyes are glassy. I love reducing her to nonword answers.

She turns the music louder and slips into the bathtub, beck-oning me to join her. After I slide into the water and face her, she moves onto my lap, locking our hips together and gliding against my erection. My head drops back against the lip of the tub. I won't last long.

"There are so many ways I want you. This is only the begin-ning." I take her water-slicked breast into my mouth and suck hard, eliciting the quiet moan that launches me over the moon.

It doesn't take long before the rest of my body follows suit, slipping against hers in the water, urging both of us up, ever higher, cresting the top and falling into the abyss.

~

THE WATER HAS COOLED to lukewarm, and the bubbles have dissipated. We push ourselves out of the tub, and I wrap us both in one of the large bath sheets. "This has been an excellent birthday." I kiss her softly and tug her bottom lip between my teeth before dipping my forehead against hers.

"Do you want your gift?" she asks, a smile spreading across her face.

"Pretty sure I just received it." I *know* I did.

She shakes her head. "Nope. Not even close."

Indicating a pile of sweats on the bathroom counter, she insists we get dressed so she can present me with whatever gift she's bought, which she's left behind in the living room. I notice her send a text, but I can't be bothered to wonder what she's doing.

A couple minutes later, she opens the bathroom door, and I trail behind her, my eyes focused on her pert little ass in my gray sweatpants, which are rolled up at the bottom.

Which is why I don't notice that the room is darker than when I came home earlier. And why I don't see that we're not alone until the lights go on and two dozen people yell, "Surprise!"

Turning to her, I see her elation mixed with a glimmer of fear. She's worried I'm upset. "Do you hate it?"

I shake my head, and I'm being honest. "It's fucking awesome."

Yeah, I'm surprised. She pulled it off, threw off my suspicions, got my guard down, and then disarmed me some more. But that's not it.

Looking from face to face in the living room, I see the usual people I'd expect—teammates, a few neighborhood friends I've introduced to her, Tim and Jordan. But there are way too many people here. I don't have this many friends. Do I?

As I home in on specific faces, I recognize them, but not because they're teammates I didn't know I had. I see players from LAFC and the LA Galaxy. Players from Seattle. They flew here for a birthday party.

Judging from their faces, they seem happy to have done so.

I recognize Blake Fulton, a celebrity restaurant owner, and Isla Finley, a bread maker known for the best sourdough in the city. A few San Francisco celebrity chefs are standing in my living room, and one is dressed in kitchen whites and fussing over the catered food along one wall.

"Turns out all your YouTube followers aren't just thirsty females."

"You found these people from my YouTube channel?" I ask, barely able to form words or ask questions, but I need so many answers.

And yet I only really need one.

"Will you stay here in San Francisco after your trial run? I think we've given it long enough, and I think you belong here. With me."

I scarcely believe I deserve it now, except that the warm grasp of Linnie's hand around my forearm steadies me and gives me a platform to stand on when I take a leap of faith.

"H-how did you pull this off when you've only been here a couple weeks?" I manage to ask her, unable to come up with any other words.

"You were right about me. Despite my unfinished formal education, I know how to do things. So I did a bit of homework and it all came together."

The words still don't come, but I start to accept that they're unnecessary. She filled my living room with family. Maybe my mom isn't here, maybe I don't have a family by blood, but I do have the one I've created over the years.

And I'm lucky, so lucky, to have her.

Now that the shock of my surprise has worn off, chatter has taken over the room. I hear a cork pop on a bottle of champagne and dishes clattering as people load up their plates at a buffet station in the corner by the window.

"Let's get you a beer. Calm your nerves down a bit." Linnie leads me toward where Tim is serving as a bartender, gamely wearing a bow tie and a black apron over his jeans. Half the guests swarm around him in need of drinks. We slowly make our way in that direction.

I know we'll be up late tonight, and I know I will get into long conversations with everyone in this room, one by one.

Before we get lost in that, I pull Linnie aside. I keep my arm around her, feeling especially raw and in need of contact. Not to mention I just like having her next to me.

When I open my mouth to try to do justice to what she's pulled off for me tonight, my emotions are choked back by a hard lump in my throat. As I feel my eyes go wet with emotion, the only words I can manage are "thank you."

Her dimple punctuates her smile. "I hope you'll forgive me this once. I know you hate surprises." Interlacing our fingers, Linnie pulls our hands to her heart, looking as happy as I feel. "But on the flip side," she whispers, "life with me is never going to be boring, City Boy."

Pulling her into my arms, I press our lips together until I can't tell where I end and she begins.

Then I correct her misconception. And my own.

"I was wrong. I don't hate surprises. You surprise me every day, and I love every minute of it." This time, when I bend to kiss her, I forget we're in a room full of people until the hoots and hollers around us remind me we're not alone.

I walk us toward where Tim holds up two glasses of champagne, nodding at us. "I'm so fucking in love with you, Linnie Cheltenham."

"And I love you, Danny."

I take in the crowd in the room, still mostly in disbelief over how good I have it. "It's pretty fucking perfect."

"You know why, right?"

I nod because I do know.

She says it anyway, her smile taking over the room and stretching the boundaries of my heart beyond what I ever thought possible. "Third time's the charm."

EPILOGUE

LINNIE

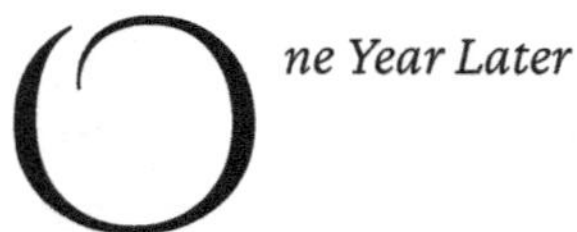 *ne Year Later*

"MORE FOG?" Mary whines, throwing open the window shades on the house I've shared with Weston since I moved here nearly a year ago. I've gotten used to the weather, so much that I've stopped commenting on it. Mostly.

Dressed in navy drawstring sweatpants and a fluffy white sherpa hoodie, she looks way too comfortable to go outside anyway. She tucks her dark hair behind her ears and scrolls on her phone. Holding the weather app up so I can see it, she points to the week ahead. "It says sun. Not this white curtain."

"It burns off every day. Then you'll get sun. You've seen it happen nearly every day." She's been here nearly two weeks, and it's the same refrain every morning.

"I'm keen to sleep through it, but I know you need my help shopping for later."

"Thank you for your sacrifice." I've asked for her help

figuring out the menu for the birthday dinner I plan to cook for Weston tonight. He told me his dream birthday evening consists of staying in with me.

If there is anything sweeter a man could say, I don't know what it is.

Mary peeks outside again, as if anything has changed in the past minute, and groans.

"Think of it like gray England skies, but with more...moisture," I tell her, secretly loving that she's the one complaining. She's always been so stoic about everything, and it's nice to see her drop her guard and fret a bit over a few annoyances since she arrived—a lost piece of luggage, a salad that included mushrooms when it wasn't supposed to, another foggy morning.

I've noticed more of the same from her over the past months, even at a distance. Like once she got out from under the dark cloud of her relationship, she uprooted old ideas about herself. For the first time in my life, I feel like the older sister with advice to give—and now that she's here, I intend to give it.

Mary reminds me of the life crossroads I'd arrived at before I met Weston.

It feels like ages ago that I felt so adrift, especially since things have fallen into place a little bit more every day since I moved to San Francisco. Tim's fiancée Jordan introduced me to her best friend, who started her own business, and she's been my fiercest ally in launching my startup baby.

Her business, Buckingham Pals, matches families with European nannies, and she grew it into a massive company from literally one client and an idea. She's the one who gave me the extra push I needed to launch Lightning Lin's Engineworks, a course for women to learn the basics of car repair. Turns out my peers in San Francisco are nuts about learning how to fix cars. Who knew?

Once I finish my business degree, I plan to expand my business, open a working garage, donate used cars to families who need them, find franchise opportunities...

I know, I know. Don't get ahead of yourself, Linnie.

Weston is a thousand percent supportive of my new direction and business dreams, but he often has to act as the voice of reason when I get my engines fired up a little too hot for my own good.

In the best possible way, I've met my match.

He and I have settled into such a perfect rhythm of the everyday that I almost can't imagine a time in my life when he wasn't intertwined in my every thought and decision. Every moment feels so right that it's hard to believe we've only been together a year. I understand now why people say that when you know, you know.

I don't belong with anyone else in the world. That, I know.

I also know that I want the same for Mary. She's a good person, if a bit cranky when she's tired and overworked, which is a lot of the time. And from everything I've gleaned from text messages and Facetime calls, things aren't going so well at home. Mary always smiles brightly amid her sarcastic gripes, but I can see through her attempt at levity. Strip away the smile, and she's putting up a good front for something else.

"I'm thinking of it like fog, which is what it is."

"Wow, someone needs coffee before her coffee." I walk over to where she's curled up in an overstuffed hot pink chair I bought on sale and convinced Weston we had to have. If I need any more proof that he loves me, it's this chair, which he called needlessly pink before straddling my lap while I sat in it and kissing me senseless.

Handing Mary a cuppa, I settle into a corner of the couch with my coffee.

This is her first visit since she came out for Weston's

birthday last year, even though Tim has placed a standing order with his travel agent to fly her out whenever she wants. Like me, she doesn't want to take advantage of his generosity, and she's been working hard at the pub that hired her after she left Harry.

But come to think of it, she's been here for quite a while, and I realize that's quite a lot of time off from a relatively new job. "How's the pub?"

"Can you be more specific? There are a lot of pubs in town, you know."

"Funny. Your job. The pub where you work."

"Oh, that."

She takes an overly long sip of her coffee and looks out the window again as though the weather might have changed. For once, I'm glad to see the same fog. She can't weasel out of an interesting conversation by talking about the weather.

"Yeah. What's up, Mary?"

She shrugs. "Nothing. It's a job, that's all. You know what it's like. Same as the last place, only I don't do much on the business side, so maybe a bit less exciting. At least they're liberal with the time off. I'm not an essential employee, so they barely notice if I'm gone."

Casting a side-eye in her direction, I try to decide if there's something she's not telling me. I get that her job is old hat, and maybe it's wishful thinking on my part, but...

"Would you ever consider moving here?"

"Moving? Permanently?' Mary's eyes widen behind her coffee cup, mid-sip.

"Yes, that's what moving is. Leaving one place for another." Looking around the living room, I can't imagine living anywhere else. The views of San Francisco Bay greet me every day outside the bay windows, and I can walk downstairs and outside to bars and restaurants within blocks of where we live.

A part of me—a big part—wants Mary to have this too. This city life. Even though I know she's a country girl—way more than I am.

"I won't lie and say I haven't thought about it, now that Dad's gone. But that's about all I've done. A lot of middle of the night thinking."

"I could talk to some people, help find you a place to live, a job?"

"Oh my god, one minute you move to the city, the next you have 'people'?"

"I don't *have* them. But I've met some nice ones who could be helpful. Like "

"Just promise me you'll think about it."

She looks skeptical. Or, at least, she tries to look skeptical. Problem is she can't keep the smile from edging up the corners of her lips, and I know I've planted a seed. Which is all that matters.

AFTER MANY HOURS and several trips to different grocery stores, I'm sweating in front of three lit burners and a hot oven. I've dispatched Mary to Tim and Jordan's house for the evening so Weston and I can have the place to ourselves.

I'm still no better at cooking than when Weston and I met, but I try more often.

I'm less afraid of failing at it, but fail I do. All the time. Maybe it's because I refuse to use recipes. They slow me down. And it's easier to accept it when I flub a recipe that isn't really a recipe.

As I stand here in a stretchy back dress that hugs my curves, along with a pair of high-heeled booties and a striped apron, I maneuver away from the stove so as not to splatter myself with bacon grease. The bacon isn't even part of a recipe. I'm only cooking it in an attempt to cover up several other worse smells in here. Plus, who can object to bacon?

My hair is piled on top of my head, secured with one pin that will let it loose when I'm done cooking. But I can't have it in my eyes right now.

Fully focused on the sizzling bacon, I don't hear the front door open and close.

"Mmm, smells good." The deep rumble of Weston's voice still curls my toes, especially when he comes up behind me, puts his hands on my shoulders, and kisses the side of my neck.

I know my stir-fried brussels sprouts smell like a nasty fart, and I overheated the oil to roast the potatoes, so a burnt smell lingers in the kitchen.

"Mmm, you smell good," I tell him, touching his lips with mine, though I'm almost smiling too much to kiss him.

He laughs. "I'm sweaty from six hours of training. I know I don't smell good."

We're ridiculous. So smitten, besotted, head-over-heels in love.

I don't care if he's sweaty, and I love that he'll overlook all my cooking foibles even though he's been conscientiously teaching me to cook, and I've been conscientiously not learning. I mean, why would I? He's excellent at it, and I want him to keep doing it, so I don't ever intend to get too skilled at cooking.

But tonight, it's his birthday. I've sourced recipes from all over the Web. If ever there's an occasion that warrants getting elbow-deep in ingredients, this is it.

Taking a peek in one of the pots, Weston tilts his head toward me. I look at what he sees—water. Just...water.

"Yeah, I was thinking pasta?"

He nods, which evolves into shaking his head. "Nope. And

not because I think it won't be delicious. I just don't want you to have to work."

"I'm not letting you cook on your own birthday?"

"Who said anything about cooking?" His voice is deep and gravelly. Sexy. His hair is all mussed from practice, slicked back with sweat. His dark eyes sparkle playfully. "I just want a little snack."

Leaning in, he kisses me again, deeper this time, and I forget all about the burned potatoes. I forget about everything. Dropping the spatula I was holding on the floor, I encircle his neck with my arms and let the kiss wipe the thoughts from my brain.

It's always like this—time stopping while we lose ourselves in each other, every one of my senses firing at his touch and scent and taste. It's a wonder either of us ever leaves the house and goes to work. Really. A wonder.

When we break the kiss, Weston tips his forehead against mine and smiles. "I missed you today. Felt like a lost dog."

I laugh. "It's only been a few hours since you've seen me, love." I'm teasing, but I felt exactly the same way today. "You're in an awfully good mood after six hours of practice."

"Because I'm kissing my favorite person in the world. What more is there?"

I point to the stove. "Spaghetti with…" I check the recipe to be sure. "Mushroom Bolognese."

He points to a brown handle bag on the floor behind him. I read the lettering on the side and see he went to one of our favorite North Beach restaurants.

"But it's your birthday. I wanted to do something nice for you."

"Oh, if I get my way, you will." His eyebrows bounce, and he flashes a wicked grin. I nod like a groupie in a trance.

I step closer and run a hand down his chest, letting my nails trail over his abs. He shudders and his eyes drift shut, but no one can ever convince me I'm not getting the better end of the deal when I touch him. "I'll do whatever you desire, and that can start right now if you want me on my knees."

His head drops to his chest and he groans. "Linnie..."

"Yeah?" I kiss the column of his throat, loving the scrape of his scruff against my lips. Dipping my tongue into the hollow of his throat, I taste his salty skin and sigh. I'm the lucky one here. "I'm yours in any way you want. Be absolutely sure of that, City Boy."

The smell of burning bacon pulls me back to reality. I turn off the burners and the oven and start to untie the red and white striped apron, but Weston holds up a hand.

"Wait. Keep the apron. I like it on you. This is exactly the picture I want in my mind when I remember this."

My mind returns to the blow job I just offered to give him and tries to mesh that with the fantasy he apparently has of me in an apron.

Which is why I'm not expecting what happens next—why I'm confused by what Weston is doing, kneeling in front of me, one foot on the ground. "I thought I was the one getting on my knees."

He shakes his head. "Not this time."

"You look like a footman," I say, my knowledge of royal employees mostly learned from books and TV shows. I'm not understanding what he's doing, and his expression has gone serious.

Instead of buffing my stilettos or cracking a smile at my joke, Weston looks up at me, his smile strained with unease. No...nervousness. Because he's not here to help me off or on with footwear. He's reaching into his pocket, just as I'm starting to understand things are going a very different way.

"Linnie, you are the best part of my life, dawn to dusk, every hour, every day of the year. You're it for me."

My hand goes to my chest. I don't know what I expect it to do—keep my heart from falling onto the floor? Because it's beating so wildly that it feels like it has its own plans to go rogue. "Weston…"

I don't even have more words to follow that one. I can tell I'm staring at him. My eyes must be the size of dinner plates. For a second, he looks worried, but then his eyes soften, and he reaches for my hand, which feels clammy and limp in his strong, warm hand.

And his touch brings me back to life. I swallow and take a breath. "Danny," I begin again, "you're it for me too."

He nods, a smile spreading over his features, lighting up his face, and if I didn't already find him so damn gorgeous, I'd be swooning all over again. As it is, I'm falling in love with him even more by the minute.

"I think you already do." My voice breaks on the last word. Just over a year ago, I could never have expected to hear these words from any man, let alone the best man I know.

He holds up a square velvet-covered box, but I shake my head. "You can't give me that. I should be giving you a gift. It's your birthday."

"I want you for life, Linnie Cheltenham. What better birthday gift could you give me than marrying me? Say yes."

He opens the ring box in his hand, stunning me with the sparkling emerald-cut diamond mounted on a simple band. "Can I please give you this now?"

I slump in defeat, loving the ring but feeling…so much. I can't begin to put it into words. Yes, I want to marry Weston. But somehow I'm still confused about why he's doing this now on his birthday. Of all days. "Today isn't supposed to be about me."

Smiling as though he's holding on to a secret, Weston watches me. His eyes flash, challenging me, and I can tell he wants me to understand some latent aspect of his meaning. "Why not?"

I'm stuck stating the obvious. "Um, because it's your birthday? A day for you, not me."

He doesn't move. "Don't you get it? I already have what I want. I want all my days to be about you." It's only because his words melt me into the floor that I don't immediately register the reason for the huge grin on his face. I haven't said yes, so I'm unsure why he's smiling.

My brain trundles through maple syrup, trying to make sense of the scene before me, and I know I'm missing something.

Finally, Weston can't stand it any longer. "Surprise," he says softly with a gentle finger against my cheek, which has gone hot with the uncomfortable feeling of not being in charge of the situation.

"What?"

What?

"You said you're impossible to surprise, that you always figure it out. Well..." He points between us, and I watch his satisfied smile take up residence. It's beautiful. The crinkles at the corners of his eyes, his straight teeth that no one sees unless he's truly happy, the boyish grin on this hot, chiseled man. "I had to find a way to do it."

Of course.

Only Weston would think to surprise me on his birthday, when I'm focused on him.

"Surprise." I nod in agreement, a little dumbfounded that he pulled this off. And so grateful that he did. "I could not be more in love with you."

His smile fades almost imperceptibly, a corner of his mouth tipping down. "Say yes, and I'll spend the rest of my life proving that isn't true. Let me give you a thousand reasons to love me even more."

"Of course I say yes. Even if I already know that loving you more is impossible." I watch as he takes the ring from the box and lifts my trembling hand. Sliding the ring onto my finger, he locks eyes with me. In their depths, I see everything I could possibly want.

He bends to brush a kiss against my lips. Soft, gentle. Not in a rush. Always knowing what I need, even before I know it myself.

It's all part of his charm.

BONUS EPILOGUE
LINNIE

T wo Years Later

THE KNOCK at my hotel room door startles me because I'm not expecting anyone for at least two hours. Mary is due then to sit and smile at me while I have my hair and makeup done. Which is why I'm standing here now in a towel and wet hair, wondering if I've overslept and didn't realize it.

No, that's impossible. Not when I set three different alarms to ensure I'd be awake and ready on my wedding day. Kind of important. Not the sort of thing I wanted to risk messing up.

Another knock jars me from my thoughts about clocks and watches, the second of which I now own, thanks to Weston. More than once, he came home after practice, and I'd yet to start prepping dinner. I claimed it was because I'd lost track of time, when in reality, I just prefer his cooking to mine.

His solution was to buy me a watch. It's a lovely tank watch with a brown leather band, and I do love it. But I still prefer his cooking, something I was forced to admit when I no longer had the excuse of time.

So I know I haven't overslept.

"Oh, bloody hell," I mutter, stalking over to the door. I fling it open to find Weston standing in the hallway holding a small bunch of yellow daisies. He's dressed in black workout shorts and a moisture-wicking shirt, his standard when he goes out for a run. Hair slicked back with sweat and legs pumped from hill running, he couldn't possibly look sexier.

Then there's his smile—as wide as his face, just for me.

"I was going to leave these on the doorstep so you'd find them later, but then I couldn't walk away without seeing you."

He pushes the flowers toward me, and I wrap my hand around his so we're both holding the daisies. His other hand lifts to caress my cheek, which he does every day, always looking at me and treating me like a precious gift.

"You're not meant to see me on our wedding day. It's bad luck." I don't realize I've creased up my forehead until Weston reaches over and smooths the lines with his index finger. His hand lingers on my cheek. He always seems to want to be touching me. I feel the same way.

"I'm pretty sure that's after you're wearing your dress. Why I made sure to come early." He presses the flowers into my hand, and I can tell from the haphazard assembly of the little bouquet that they've just been picked.

"Always thinking. That's what I love about you, Danny Weston." I've taken to calling him Danny nearly all the time. I don't care that everyone else calls him Weston. I like that I have my own name for him that no one else uses. "Well, just one of many things."

As long as he's already seen me and we may or may not be cursed by wedding rules no one consulted me on, I might as well kiss him.

I have vows written on notecards to reveal to him later, but one thing I can say for sure is that I'll never get tired of kissing him. When I tip my head up, his lips drop to mine. Gentle, careful. Confirming how we both feel rather than desperately searching for proof. He already knows how I feel about him. Or maybe he doesn't want to leave me with swollen lips on our wedding day.

"I hated being away from you last night. I thought about you all night long." His voice is a low rumble against my lips.

"I know. I missed you. It's a horrible tradition, spending the night apart," I breathe, wanting to make up for the lost time.

Our kiss grows deeper, and the towel I have wrapped around me starts to loosen. But I pull it tight and take a step back. "Danny...I love you, but I'm sending you home." At his puppy dog eyes that almost make me give in, I shoot him a warning glance, "Tonight. Give ourselves something to look forward to."

He groans like a toddler being told to put away a toy. "Yeah. I know. I just wanted to see you and give you something to put in that album you're making." He's been making fun of how I've saved every keepsake and ticket stub from our adventures over the past two years and put them in a scrapbook.

I draw them to my chest. "I will absolutely put these in the book. Thank you."

He turns to go, jogging in place and giving me a little salute. "I'll see you at the altar, soon-to-be-Mrs. Weston."

My smile stretches my cheeks, and my eyes go moist. How did I get so lucky?

He jogs down the hotel hallway, and my eyes linger on his tight, sexy ass as he goes. View never gets old.

∿

Seven Hours Later

"...to share joys and sorrows, to love and to laugh, from this day forward."

Our vows echo in my mind as Weston pulls me into his arms for a dance. "We did it," he says for about the tenth time since we said "I do" under an arch of climbing grape vines decorated with white daisies and yellow roses.

I think he's trying to convince himself, not me. I was fully present during the ceremony, but I caught glimpses of Weston's disbelieving expression each time his eyes roamed over me in my off-white silk dress that rustled in the light summer wind.

No one else is dancing. Partly that's because Mary hired a three-piece band for our cocktail hour, and they've been playing nothing but barely-recognizable British Invasion rock hits.

Weston is either oblivious to the strange music, or he doesn't care. I've learned a lot about him over the past two years, and despite being with him almost daily, he never ceases to surprise me.

"How did I not know you're such a good dancer?" I ask as he extends a hand and spins me away before pulling me close and dipping me down and up.

His eyebrows bounce. "Have to keep some mystery alive."

That's one of the best things about Weston—the fact that he's always learning about himself and never afraid of what he'll find out.

He spins me again. We're in our own little corner of the reception, but after a moment, I start to notice a lot of eyes on us.

Then some glasses clink, and more eyes fall on us. Then we're joined by Tim and Jordan, Mary and Jordan's best friend,

Sofia. Their dancing is far less polished than Weston's, and now it's a free for all of goofiness.

Mary hands me a glass of champagne and offers a toast. "May you fall asleep on the same pillow and dream of each other."

"Aw, Mare. That's so sweet."

Tim holds up a hand. "Wait." He feigns listening intently. "I think the band is playing "Back in the USSR." Always a wedding favorite," he deadpans. Jordan gives him a playful swat.

"Stop," Mary protests. "We like this band. They've got character, right Lin?"

"That they do."

We couldn't have picked a more perfect location—Cobblestone Vineyards in Napa Valley has the laid-back feeling we wanted, while being intensely photogenic. Rows of wine grapes stretch into the distance under an azure sky interrupted only by an occasional whisp of cloud.

A quiet cowbell chimes in the distance, and my siblings peel off toward where the dinner reception will be held. "Remember, you need to make an entrance, you two. Don't get so caught up in each other you forget to come to your own wedding dinner," Mary chides. I'd object to her accusation if it didn't sound halfway plausible.

"We'll be there," I assure her.

Guests start to clear out of the cocktail reception area, but Weston makes no move to follow them. Before long, we're the only ones left swaying in the middle of the vineyard as the day turns to dusk. I lift my head from where it's been tipped against Weston's chest.

"Hey, Mr. Cheltenham," I whisper.

I feel the rumble of his laugh when his arm holds me against him. "Is that how it's gonna be?"

I shrug. "Just trying it on for size. I like Mrs. Weston an awful lot too."

"I love Mrs. Weston. So very much." His gravelly voice sends ripples of goosebumps along my skin. I hope that never changes.

"She loves you back. And she hopes you'll still want to dance with her like this when we have twin babies crawling underfoot."

"Ha." Weston tips his forehead against mine. "Even more so then. We'll just have to look down every so often, so we don't step on them." His soft kiss feels like a punctuation mark on the sentence.

I fix my gaze on him until his eyes stop roaming over my face and focus. His expression goes serious. "What? I promise not to step on our future kids. Or even joke about stepping on our future kids."

I say nothing, pressing my lips together. His eyes go wide. "Hang on, is that your way of telling me we're having twins?"

"Oh. No, at least not yet." I wrap my arms around his neck and glance toward the reception. "Though, to be honest, I wouldn't mind getting started on trying."

He, too, looks over at the wine cave where a hundred people are waiting for us. "You mean...skip the reception?"

I shrug. "Or maybe just come really, really late."

His smile is all the answer I need. Kicking off my lavender sandals, I grab his hand. He bends to pick up my shoes in his other hand and turns us in the direction of the bungalows where we'll spend our first night together as husband and wife.

We take off at a run and don't look back.

ACKNOWLEDGMENTS

Readers, thank you. I would not be an author without you, plain and simple. I'm grateful for every word you read, every kind review, every thoughtful click and like and comment. I don't take a second of it for granted. Love you all.

Jesse and Oliver: You are my favorite humans and you make me so proud every day. And no, I still won't let you read these books

To my beta readers, editors, proofers, givers of feedback, and supporters—this was a group effort and I'm so grateful to have you in my corner. Amy D., Bethany B., Leah A., James G. —thank you.

Hang Le, your artwork and cover design is beyond measure— thank you for two gorgeous versions.

Thank you Valentine and the VPR team for your patience, advice, and other superpowers.

Bloggers and bookstagrammers—thank you for reading, creating incredible graphics, and partnering with me in getting the word out about my books. I value you more than you know.

And to my fellow authors: as always, I am honored to type among you.

ABOUT THE AUTHOR

Stacy Travis writes sexy, charming romance about bookish, sassy women and the hot alphas who fall for them. Writing contemporary romance makes her infinitely happy, but that might be the coffee talking.

When she's not on a deadline, she's in running shoes complaining that all roads seem to go uphill. Or on the couch with a margarita. Or fangirling at a soccer game. She's never met a dog she didn't want to hug. And if you have no plans for Thanksgiving, she'll probably invite you to dinner. Stacy lives in Los Angeles with her husband, two sons, and a poorly-trained rescue dog who hoards socks.

Facebook reader group: Stacy's Saucy Sisters

Super fun newsletter: https://geni.us/travisNL

Tiktok: https://www.tiktok.com/@stacytravisauthor

Website: https://www.www.stacytravis.com

Email: stacytraviswrites@gmail.com - tell me what you're reading!

f facebook.com/stacytravisromance

instagram.com/stacytravisauthor

BB bookbub.com/authors/stacy-travis

g goodreads.com/stacytravis

ALSO BY STACY TRAVIS

The Summer Heat Duet

1. The Summer of Him: A Mistaken Identity Celebrity Romance

2. Forever with Him: An Opposites Attract Contemporary Romance

The Berkeley Hills Series - all standalone novels

1. In Trouble with Him: A Forbidden Love Contemporary Romance (Finn and Annie's story)

2. Second Chance at Us: A Second Chance Romance (Becca and Blake)

3. Falling for You: A Friends to Lovers Romance (Isla and Owen)

4. The Spark Between Us: A Grumpy-Sunshine, Brother's Best Friend Romance (Sarah and Braden)

5. Playing for You: A Sports Romance (Tatum and Donovan)

6. No Match for Her - an Opposites-Attract Friends-to-Lovers Romance (Cherry and Charlie)

San Francisco Strikers Series - standalone novels

1. He's a Keeper: A Grumpy-Sunshine Sports Romance (Molly and Holden)

2. He's a Player: A Second Chance Sports Romance (Jordan and Tim)

3. He's a Charmer: A Brother's Best Friend Sports Romance (Linnie and Weston)

Standalone Novels - Adult Contemporary Romance

French Kiss: A Friends to Lovers Romance

Bad News: An Enemies to Lovers Romance